the simpleton

... An Alien Encounter

Written By

Mark Wayne McGinnis

 This book is a work of fiction. Names, characters, places, and incidents either are products of the author's imagination or are used fictitiously. Any resemblance to actual persons, living or dead, events, or locales is entirely coincidental.

Cover design by:
MWM

Edited by:
Lura Lee Genz
Mia Manns

Published by:
Avenstar Productions

Paperback Book ISBN: **978-0-9974514-7-4**

To join Mark's mailing list, jump to
http://eepurl.com/bs7M9r

Visit Mark Wayne McGinnis at:
http://www.markwaynemcginnis.com

Prologue

Cuddy Perkins stopped suddenly in his tracks and stared blankly at the tall line of trees before him. He tried to recall how he'd gotten there, but knew his forgetfulness was not out of the ordinary—nothing to be concerned about. He continued on, reveling in the enveloping coolness of the forest. He'd entered his favorite place in the whole world. A magical place. It made sense now—that he'd be here. He continued forward, allowing his hands to slide across the rough bark on two opposing stout tree trunks. Trees he neither knew the names of, nor particularly cared to know.

Though he knew deep down he'd walked there many times before, still, something strange was going on. He turned his attention to his feet. As he stepped—first with his left foot, then with his right—he carefully watched his size 13 Keds. *Yup* … they felt funny. He made a face—tightened his lips while squeezing his eyelids tightly shut. It was his *I'm so stupid* face. Bending over, Cuddy used his thumb to rub off some caked-on mud to expose the section of rubber where his toes were. He rubbed some more but the arrow still wasn't there. Then, using the same thumb, he wiped the other shoe and, sure enough, there it was! The arrow Momma had drawn with a Sharpie. He'd put his shoes on the wrong feet again. Weighing the hassle of taking them off then putting them on the right foot it would be *way too much trouble.*

Cuddy continued on, walking ever deeper into the woods, still feeling somewhat out of sorts. He briefly wondered if he were dreaming. His dreams, so vivid, often seemed more real than when he was wide awake. *And where is Rufus*? Glancing back, he already knew he wouldn't see his dog there. "Rufus!" he called out anyway into the shadows behind him.

The sound of trickling water helped orient him to his present whereabouts. Hurrying up his pace, Cuddy caught the glimmering reflection of the sun in the little creek ahead. When he leapt over the water, landing on the opposite bank, his shoes sunk into the mud and gave a sucking sound when he pulled them free. As he continued walking alongside the winding brook, he was mostly content with life.

For the second time that day, Cuddy stopped suddenly in his tracks, uncertain if he was awake or dreaming. In any event, he was pretty certain that what he was seeing, sitting there up on a rock, was indeed an angel. The fact that this particular brightly glowing spectacle wasn't wearing any clothes did seem quite odd, but, there again, he wasn't sure what angels were supposed to wear—or look like.

A breeze cooled Cuddy's face, carrying along with it the musky fragrance coming off the nearby brook. Momma had talked about such things in the past, sometimes when she read to him before bedtime. Things like *heaven*. And *angels.* Sometimes Cuddy would dream of the things she'd read to him about.

Standing up, the angel was nearly as tall as Cuddy was—over six feet tall. Cuddy remained perfectly still—he held his breath. Suddenly, the angel looked around, as if he'd detected another presence. A rabbit ran into view and just as quickly disappeared into a nearby thicket. The angel stared after the critter for a while—then, slowly he walked away—going deeper into the woods.

Cuddy felt a chill run up and down his back. He wished he'd worn his sweatshirt and that he'd wake up from this strange dream.

Chapter 1

More and more of late, Tow had a tendency to be cynical. He already knew that. It wasn't news to him. Soweng's dying words, two months past, had told him as much. She'd said, *"Don't you see the irony, Tow? Of those who still see the promise of things to come … a future for our kind … one that is better than the past … it is you who will become, after everything we've endured together, the one … the final torch holder."* She coughed and blood appeared at the corners of her mouth. Her smile was genuine and her eyes misty—her fate so tragically sealed many months before. As Tow held her in his arms, she reached up a hand and gently touched the side of his face. *"… stay the course … take us home."*

She died then. Not five minutes later, or two minutes later, but right then. Tow wondered if she'd known how he felt about her? That he'd loved her ever since the first time he watched her walk, more like glide, onto the *Evermore*'s bridge, three years ago.

An audible alarm tone began to reverberate throughout the ship. "We're being shadowed, Captain Tow," the AI orb said. "It is one of the three Howsh vessels."

His gaze snapped away from the forward observation window and the view out to open space. He looked expectantly to the empty captain's chair. With renewed urgency, he strode to the other side of the bridge to check the helmsman readings. His heart sank; this was not how it was supposed to be—the captain dead, the helmsman dead. Everyone dead. Loneliness pressed in around him—an avalanche of lonely despair. How could he continue on alone? He wondered, for the hundredth time, if he was up to the task—its sheer enormity weighing on him.

Back at the forward station, he found his drink and brought the half-filled cup of *xicachan* nervously up to his lips. A good portion of the lukewarm stimulant sloshed down his chin and onto the controls in front of him. He badly needed to relieve himself. Attempting to stand, he instantly was reminded his left leg was injured during his most recent clash with the Howsh.

White-hot searing pain shot up his leg—spikes starting in his foot and ending in his upper thigh. Pounding on his leg with a clenched fist wasn't helping any, so he waited a moment for the pain to subside before awkwardly hobbling out from the oppressive bridge. Hesitating, something occurred to him: *it just might work* … He glanced over to one of the unmanned consoles, mentally *willing* an environmental system's configuration menu to download, and it immediately popped into view, six feet away.

Tow raised a hand, distantly manipulating the virtual menu settings. Immediately, the ship's gravity generators reconfigured, and he felt the heavy weight on his leg subside somewhat. Feeling new relief, he thought, *why didn't I think to do that before?*

Tow ceased limping his way toward the ship's stern and turned back toward the bridge. "How close are they?" he asked, speaking aloud into the empty compartment.

"Within seven hundred twenty million clicks," the anthropomorphic voice came back. The AI orb then appeared around a partial bulkhead. Seventeen inches long and eleven inches tall, the orb was shaped like an elongated sphere. Black as obsidian, the orb was the AI's singular outer connection with the physical world. It silently hovered nearby. At the sphere's apex was a concave circular section, an aperture of sorts, from which a faint blue light emanated—the orb's ever-watchful eye. Its opposing ends had two mechanical articulating arms—each with four finger-like appendages.

Tow weighed his strong urge to urinate against saving an entire species from extinction. He grudgingly hobbled back toward the bridge. Hurrying, he miscalculated the effects from resetting the gravity generators and found himself bicycling his legs—now being nearly weightless—two feet off the deck.

"Now seven hundred and five million clicks."

Tow didn't reply, waiting for his body to slowly drop down, and to again feel solid decking beneath his feet. By the time he reentered the bridge, taking the same seat he'd extricated himself from only moments before, he could see the cloaked outline of the trailing vessel on the virtual *viewscape* display, off to his left. After grabbing ahold of opposing diagonal corners, he pulled the virtual display—making it larger. He leaned forward to study the image.

"Yes … that is the same one that fired on us before!" he said aloud.

"I suspect they have been there all along, Captain Tow. It was well cloaked."

Tow still felt uncomfortable being called captain. A position he'd risen to by default—not because he'd earned it. Looking at the viewscape, he felt the familiar churning in his stomach as sour bile rose, burning the back of his throat. What he was feeling now was beyond fear—beyond anger—beyond hatred; only the natural instinct to survive remained, transcending all other emotions and propelling him forward.

"Now, six hundred and eighty-five million clicks," the AI

updated, its bucolic tone grating, as usual, on Tow's nerves.

He chewed on the inside of his cheek, while continuing to stare at the viewscape display, and briefly wondered what the captain would do in the same situation but then thought better of it. Doing things the way the captain once did could very well get him where the captain was—dead.

"Now, six hundred and sixty-five million clicks," the AI orb said.

"Do you know how annoying that is, AI?" Tow asked.

The AI orb then descended several feet, not responding.

"We have only a matter of hours, if even that, Captain Tow. The enemy's vessels are closing in on us fast."

"I know, I know, just tell me where the closest Class-A analogous sister planet is."

The AI went silent, checking.

As far as Tow knew, all worlds within the universe had a certain number of analogous sister planets. It only made sense. Out of the trillions of heavenly bodies encompassing the cosmos, there were only a select few matching a Class-A's pre-defined criteria, including such specifics as atmospheric conditions—a correlation of nitrogen and oxygen. While nitrogen needed to be between 75% and 80% of the total atmosphere, oxygen needed to be between 20% and 24%. The remaining percentage mainly consisted of argon. The size and weight of a sister world directly corresponded to its gravitational properties. Then there was the amount of water available—ice formations, lakes, and oceans. Finally, the planet's indigenous life forms, where the aggregate, similar-planet numbers dropped through the floor. A Class-A sister planet would not include gargantuan prehistoric beasts, running around looking for their next meal. Nor flesh-eating microbes that either lurked in dark crevices, or under rocks. No, a Class-A sister planet would be very similar to home—*Mahli*—where the *Pashier* civilization once flourished. A Class-A sister planet would have on it a species with a similar genome, not too dissimilar to their own.

Startled, Tow watched the AI orb unaccountably zip across to the far side of the bridge. Another annoying tendency of the autonomous bot, on a growing list. "We are relatively close to a Class-A world."

"That is good … how close?"

"Approximately six billion clicks."

Unconsciously, Tow rubbed his aching leg again. "Can we make it … before we are overtaken?"

"The answer is indeterminable, at present. I would say the odds are not in our favor, Captain Tow, unfortunately."

Tow began to scroll through the volumes of information provided by the AI orb. Slowly, then more rapidly, he began to shake his head. "No … no … no… that one is not Class-A!" Exasperated, he made the universal *what were you thinking* gesture—his shoulders raised, his palms up. "Look! There's nothing more than war-mongering savages running around in that world. I mean, sure, they've progressed beyond loincloths and rubbing sticks together to light a fire … but—"

The AI interrupted his tirade: "It's either that world, or travel another twenty-seven billion clicks to the next Class-A world."

"How long would that take?"

"It does not matter how long that would take. Both you and the ship would be destroyed long before then."

Tow noticed the AI had gotten progressively more *snarky* over recent weeks and idly wondered if one of the crew's now-deceased tech-heads had pre-programmed its alteration. Perhaps, as a parting gift to those who'd endured? Though Tow had been the first officer, not one of the tech heads, everyone—at least to a minimal degree—was somewhat adept doing another's job. When there was time, he'd look into the ship's systems coding.

"Set the course. I also want you to enrich the *sampian*-flux mixture entering the pre-burn manifold. No more than three percent should do it." He was grasping, he knew, but they needed to get some serious distance between themselves and those three relentless Howsh pursuers, even if it was short-lived. When they'd left Mahli, three years ago, there were fourteen vessels in the armada. But over the years, they'd been picked off, one by one, by their enemy—the Howsh. Now only one ship remained—the *Evermore.*

★ ★ ★

On approach, Tow stared at the bright-blue planet as it grew in size outside the forward observation window. His breath caught in his chest—his eyes suddenly brimmed with tears. *How? It was Mahli!* But then, as oceans began forming, the contours of continents more defined, he realized this blue planet was indeed a different world. That Mahli would no longer look anything like this, thanks to the dispersion of organic genocide. Genocide instigated by the Howsh. No … the oceans back home were no longer blue; the continents nothing more than dingy-brown wind-blown wastelands.

The alien turned to look at the *viewscape* display then to the many ancillary console indicators just beneath it—especially those that provided long-range scan results. Their pursuers had been evaded, at least for now. The AI had done an admiral job. *But for how long?* Long enough to make needed repairs? He didn't know. Tow felt, more than saw, the AI drone's presence.

Tow assessed the blue world's *demography*: where the planet's population centers were located; where military facilities were situated; and where technology, what there was of it, seemed to exist minimally. He instructed the AI orb to tap into their worldwide communications. Into their rudimentary, spider-like, network.

The orb followed the curvature of the bulkhead—then slowed to a stop. "There is an *Amazon* region—what is referred to as South America. Almost completely uninhabited," the orb said.

Tow studied the environmental data. "Looks … muggy. Hot. Place will be filled with insects, and I hate insects!" A series of popping noises erupted from his *donifer* glands.

"What about there?" Tow asked, leaning in toward the display. "It is called … Woodbury, in what is called North America. The Tennessee region … it seems fairly desolate. The population of local savages is close to three thousand and is spread across a wide area." He sat back. "We'll go there. Find a place to land … as hidden a location as possible. Make sure it's where we'll go unnoticed by the locals. Maybe there," Tow said, zooming in and turning to an area with a mixture of towering trees, distant mountain peaks, and open prairie lands.

★ ★ ★

It was late evening when the *Evermore* descended out from a moonless, star-filled sky. Nearly soundless, the wedge-shaped vessel skirted the tall treetops.

Tow, gazing downward through the forward observation window, had resumed manual control of the ship. He pointed. "Over there. Looks like there's some open terrain among those surrounding trees." *What had the AI referred to them as*—coniferous plant life? Within the genus Pintos, commonly referred to as *pine trees*.

"That site should be adequate," Tow said.

The AI orb said, "There are three agricultural habitats, called farms, and a small township. All are within—"

"It is fine," Tow interrupted. "We need to hurry up and land … to shut down. Our propulsion system needs to go dark. We'll just have to avoid making too much noise when initializing the drop thrusters. Who knows who or what is out there," Tow said, gesturing to all that was beyond the forward observation window.

The *Evermore* hovered over the clearing below—pivoting on its center axis thirty degrees. Tow watched the outside world around them spin around. After long periods of seeing nothing but open space, he had to admit it was exciting to be here. Whatever lay in store for him would be a relief from the constant monotony. The ship's soft-glowing running lights illuminated the closest tree branches, even though the dense foliage beyond them seemed dark and foreboding.

The embattled *Evermore*'s landing struts settled onto the soft forest soil. Once the propulsion system finished winding down, total silence ensued. How long had it been since there'd been such stillness? A year? Longer?

Tow knew he should sleep now—his fatigued body was demanding it. He leaned foreword, thinking he saw something moving around out there. "Stay vigilant, AI … we're not alone here … I suspect this place is hostile."

Chapter 2

Tow awoke just before dawn. Three times during the night, he'd awakened as the AI's proximity sensors went off—alerting him that various creatures had approached the *Evermore*. Cross-referencing them, they were catalogued as a coyote, a brown bear, and something called a fox. After the third such alert, Tow instructed the AI orb that unless it was one of the indigenous savages, creeping up around them, or the Howsh, or that another advanced spacecraft was en route … not to wake him up again.

Now, yawning, he swung his legs over the side of his berth, placing a limited amount of weight on his injured leg. It hurt, but no more so than it did the night before. The pain seemed manageable, until it once again spasmed.

The AI orb hovered into view within the berth's narrow compartment.

"What is it, orb?" Tow asked.

"I apologize, Captain; I have had to conduct a hard reset to each one of the *Evermore*'s systems. Apparently, during the last spatial attack, the Howsh were in close enough proximity to transmit a nearly undetectable systems-level virus."

Tow closed his eyes and shook his head. The *Evermore* was a complex myriad of numerous interconnecting intelligence systems. No single system was capable of bringing down the whole ship. The AI orb interconnected with each of the ship's systems, while internal firewalls kept the orb guarded from that very issue.

"Captain … two systems have been cleared and have come back online, but others are infected. Infected beyond repair. They have been wiped and are in the process of reloading from backups. After that, they must be rebuilt to the latest configuration modifications."

"And the wellness chamber?"

"Offline. And like the propulsion system, physical repairs will still be needed to get the chamber up and running. I know you are in pain, Captain. I have made that system's rebuild the highest priority."

"I was going to get working on repairs first thing this morning, starting with the chamber. When will all systems be ready to come back online?"

"I apologize, Captain Tow. In my estimation, it will take sixty-three hours and twenty-two minutes. I can assist you with manual repairs, if you would like."

"Sixty-three hours! We don't have that kind of time. What were you thinking? And without getting my permission first!"

"There really was no alternative, Captain."

Tow knew the orb was probably right, but he needed to vent his frustration. "What is the current status with the Howsh?"

"Thus far, they have not entered this planetary system. That is hopeful … yes?"

Annoyed, Tow shrugged, and watched the orb leave the compartment.

So … repairs will have to wait, he thought, looking around the claustrophobic space. For now—for his own sanity's sake, he needed off this ship.

★ ★ ★

Hobbling down the extended gangway, Tow experienced some of Earth's peculiarities for the first time. Breathing in the fresh atmosphere, he filled his lungs to capacity—then exhaled slowly. Immediately, an abundance of strange smells—some pleasant and others beyond disgusting—confronted his senses. Also, there was a larger insectile presence than he would prefer. Waving away an encircling swarm of annoying gnats, he used his telekinetic powers to thrust them upward—into the treetops.

He figured, after examining the exterior of the ship, he would venture no further than a click away; maybe a click and a half, if his leg could handle the exertion. Any farther, and he may lose sensory contact with the AI.

Tow stepped off the gangway onto the planet's surface. Looking about his feet, he saw an assortment of leaves, pine needles, and tree bark, along with something soft and brown. *Hmm … remnants of animal excrement?*

The ground was soft, making walking far more comfortable than on the hard decking throughout the spacecraft. He walked into a beam of warm sunlight, shining through the trees, and stopped—appreciating the magnificent sensation. *How I'd missed this.* He tilted his head back, letting the sun's radiant energy revitalize his entire being.

Three paces in front of him lay a four-foot-long branch. Tow casually raised an arm, willing the tree limb off the ground and up into his waiting hand. Tightening his grip, he felt the roughness of the wood against his palm, then thrust its woody point down into the soil. *Sturdy.* It would make a good walking stick. He continued on for several paces before spinning around, one hundred and eighty degrees, to look back over the *Evermore* in her entirety. He reflected back in time to when he'd first seen her, back on Mahli. He was beyond enamored with her sleek lines—her advanced technological capabilities. Close to two hundred feet long, she was fifty feet across at her widest beam, toward the stern. Enough sleeping berths on board for a crew of fifteen and with two *emersion*-type energy drives, she was fast. No other Mahli vessel had every exceeded FTL by a factor of twenty.

Inspecting her now, the craft appeared nearly unrecognizable—scarred and charred by too many enemy plasma strikes to count. Her stern and starboard aft sections were in the worst shape. Tow drew closer, until he was within arms' length of the large starboard thruster cone. One of two, it was twice his height. Using his walking stick for leverage, enhanced by his telekinetic powers, he levitated himself into the orifice. Needing to duck down the farther in he went, he looked deep into the propulsion system's exhaust. Although he spotted plenty of damage, if he was honest with himself, it wasn't nearly as bad as he'd anticipated. Still, much work needed completion here. He used the end of the stick to pry off a dangling section of scarred metal. Picking it up, he examined it, then flung it out through the wide opening of the thruster.

★ ★ ★

He breathed in Earth's heavy, pine-scented air, while observing nature's rawness surrounding him. *So much life here!* Walking off, he slowed down to relieve his aching leg, a click's distance away from the ship. From his recollection, the edge of the forest should be close by, and he needed to be careful. Being spotted by one of the local savages would not be good. He heard the sound of trickling water and soon came upon a small stream. More like a brook. He lowered to one knee and touched the swirling, cold, liquid surface. Like feeling that ray of sunshine on his face, the sensation here was remarkable too. He cupped his fingers together, bringing up enough water to taste. It was sweet and perfect.

A noise. Tow's eyes surveyed his surroundings. Perhaps a twig stepped on in the trees ahead. He stayed where he was—not moving—and waited. Movement came off from the side. A brown, fur-covered animal stood between two trees. The AI transmitted the genome of the creature to Tow: *a Whitetail deer.* He watched as it approached, coming for water. At ten paces out, the deer stopped and raised its head, and they made eye contact. The deer seemed to assess its options: venture on or run to safety. *Come on … I won't hurt you.* As the deer took a hesitant step forward, Tow had a realization—this was his first *actual contact* moment on planet Earth. His cynical side wanted to say, *so what?* His better self acknowledged the gift and gave thanks. The deer moved to the edge of the brook and lowered its head to drink. Apparently, a glowing white, six-foot-tall *Pashier* didn't register as something it needed to be afraid of. Slowly, Tow raised a hand. From ten feet away, he mentally reached out and petted the animal's fur. The deer's two ears twitched in unison as it stared back at Tow. It lowered its head back into the brook, and Tow gently scratched the animal's neck—right behind the ears—and smiled. The first time he'd actually smiled in many, many, days.

He waited for the animal to finish drinking and scamper off before moving forward, where bright sunlight filtered in through the trees. At the tree line he stopped. Lowering down to his haunches, Tow studied one of the agricultural habitats he'd flown over the night before. A farm, they called it here, that wasn't so different from the ancient structures known to exist back on Mahli, many hundreds of years ago.

Close by was a split-rail fence. Gray in color, it looked old—bowed in places from the passage of time and extreme temperatures.

Tow weighed his options, wanting to see more—but cognizant of the potential dangers. It was all so fascinating. Here was a sister world that hadn't been ravaged by ill-intentioned enemies. It was like stepping back in time—back into a world the *Pashier* hadn't known for generations.

Keeping low, Tow moved along the fence line. Stepping through a grassy, golden-colored meadow, which reached high above his knees, he approached a tall structure as gray and bowed as the fence surrounding it. Ragged openings pierced the roof. A wide door had been pulled open and Tow peered into the darkened space. There was a strong smell of excrement—not overly unpleasant—and the aroma of dried grasses—*hay*. Once he dared venture within he realized he was not alone. A loud snort froze Tow right where he stood, as two pointed ears bobbed up and down over a tall wooden wall. His query to the AI told him he'd found a creature called a *horse*. Tow came around the stall to its opening and took in the giant, four-legged black beast. He then learned that horses were herbivores, so there would be no attempt to eat him. *Fascinating.*

New sounds, off in the distance, dragged his attention away from the horse and the barn. *Savages*!

* * *

Tow discovered another door, narrower, at the opposite end of the barn and it too was open. From beyond it, the savages' voices emanated. He looked back the way he'd come—well aware he'd already pushed the boundaries of what was safe—what was prudent. He decided to quickly peek out to see what, *or who*, was out there before heading back.

Tow veered away from the wide rectangular band of sunlight, streaming in from the outside, and approached the door's opening along the back wall. He peered, with one eye, around the corner, noting another structure. He guessed it was some kind of domicile. Smaller than the barn, and lower to the ground, it too was made of timber, just like the barn. Rickety—it looked like it could be pushed over in a strong breeze. Tow's eyes widened when he saw them together—two of Earth's savages conversing. Strange looking, they also wore odd-shaped garments.

Then another four-legged creature strode into view. Tow was instantly informed it was called a dog. He tilted his head and listened, trying to understand the primitive speech spoken by both savages. It took several minutes to construct a working vocabulary database to draw from. Apparently, theirs was a familial relationship—a mother and son.

Tow's breath caught in his chest as the searing pain in his leg returned. A new series of spasms produced unintentional gasps and the dog's ears perked up. The dog was staring directly at him.

Chapter 3

"Cuddy … stop squirming around. These are sharp," she scolded, holding the scissors in front of his face. "I nearly trimmed off the tip of your ear."

"Sorry, Momma."

Repositioning herself, she looked him over—from one side of his head to the other. "Well … it's not even all around this time."

"That's okay, Momma."

"Got to cut the bangs, so stay put in that chair!"

As Momma hurried off, Cuddy heard the screen door squeal open, then, just as quickly, slam shut against the door jam. He looked at Rufus, lying outside in the dirt, and smiled. Making a kissing noise with his lips, he tried to get the dog's attention. But Rufus seemed more interested in something out in the barn. Cuddy wanted to play with the dog. He hated getting his hair trimmed. Looking down on the porch decking, he noted the accumulation of loose hair lying by his feet.

The screen door opened again before slamming back shut. When Momma placed a heavy bowl over his head, he smiled. He kinda liked this part. Sort of like wearing a football helmet, though he wasn't allowed to play football. Not with his injury.

"Don't move! Not even one little bit … okay, Cuddy?"

Cuddy nodded, rocking the bowl atop his head up and down, smiling with mischief. Momma rolled her eyes at his little prank, just like the last time … and the time before that.

He stared through the thin strands of hair—now pressed flat over his eyes—as Momma started to snip, beginning at his left ear then scissoring across to the front. He watched the strands fall away as she scissored over toward his right ear.

"Are you done, Momma?"

"No. Doing the back now."

He felt the pressure of her hand atop the bowl—and the *snip snip snip* of the scissors behind his head. Then, removing the bowl from his head, her hand brushed some loose hair from his shoulders.

"Good for another month! Go play. Stay close … lunch soon."

"Okay, Momma." Cuddy scurried to his feet and jumped off the wood-planked porch. Startled, Rufus yipped. With his tail tucked low between his legs, he scooted away. Cuddy, grabbing him, tackled the eighty-five-pound yellow lab and flipped him over onto his back. The wiggling dog twisted his head back, attempting to lick Cuddy's face.

★ ★ ★

Momma stood in the cool shadows—obscured behind the grimy mesh of the screen door. She watched the boy play with his idiot dog. A bittersweet scene. Her chest swelled—nary another morsel of love would find any room in her already overfilled heart. It wouldn't be possible. A part of her felt guilty, as well as unfathomably lucky; fortunate that her boy would never leave her. *Boy!* She inwardly scoffed at what that word implied. Cuddy was nineteen years old, six foot three, and near 'bouts two hundred pounds. But he would always be seven—have a young child's mind in a grown man's body.

The kitchen wall phone began to ring. Startled, Momma's back turned rigid. *Another bill collector?* She continued to watch her youngest son for another three rings before breaking away and picking up the receiver. "Hello?"

"Hello, this is the Whiteville Correctional Facility. Will you accept a phone call from inmate Kyle Perkins?"

Momma hesitated, then said, "Yes … yes, of course I will." She used her fingers to press down on an errant flap of faded wallpaper peeling up from the wall.

She listened to the canned message, explaining that all calls—into and out of the prison—were being recorded. That first year, she'd gone to the penitentiary every other month to see Kyle and found it difficult. He appreciated her visits, but Momma found it emotionally draining. Also, she could ill afford the gas expense for those two-hundred-mile round trips. She glanced at the center of the kitchen table where a stack of opened, unpaid, utility bills occupied the space. Now guilt weighed heavily on her shoulders—she hadn't seen her eldest son in nearly five months.

"Momma? Are you there?"

"I'm here, son. It's good to hear your voice. Are you doing okay? I'm sorry I haven't been by to see—"

Kyle cut her off, "Momma … that's okay! Look, I'm getting out of here."

"Getting out?"

"Early parole. Good behavior and the place is *way* overcrowded."

"That's … wonderful, Kyle. When will—"

"Tomorrow. I'm out tomorrow. I've got a ride. No need to make the drive all the way up here."

"That's fine, dear. Then we'll see you tomorrow."

"Yeah … tomorrow. Momma? How's Cuddy?"

"Cuddy's the same as he's always been. He'll be happy to see you."

"Okay … well, see you tomorrow, Momma."

"Goodbye, son." Momma hung up the phone, continuing to stare at it for several seconds. She should be happy. Kyle's coming home would make things easier. He'd be able to help her around the ranch, maybe get a job. They certainly could use the money. But still, she was more concerned than happy. Trouble followed Kyle—it always had.

She contemplated telling Cuddy the news, but getting his hopes up, then later dashing them—like times before—wouldn't be fair to him. This wasn't the first time he'd called to say he was being released early and was coming home. No … she'd believe it when she saw him.

She walked back into the foyer and looked out through the screen door. Cuddy was still playing with his senseless dog. To Cuddy, the world revolved around his older brother Kyle. Two years his senior, Kyle hadn't been home in a year and a half. Momma's expression changed. Kyle caused it—that accident in the barn. The three kids were roughhousing—Kyle, Cuddy, and Jackie. A pretty one … that Jackie; she was now away at college. Cuddy's age, she was his protector growing up—far more so than Kyle. Their relationship changed over the years, as of course it would; from childhood friends to something else. *A shame*, Momma thought, diverting her attention away from such possibilities; the ones that might have been—but would never be.

Opening the screen door, she peeked her head out. "You're getting filthy rolling around out there! Did you forget what I asked you to do this morning?"

Cuddy stopped wrestling with the dog and sat up. Dirt clung to his cheeks where the dog had licked him. "This morning?"

She waited.

Cuddy puffed out his cheeks and made a bewildered expression.

"The store …"

"Oh yeah … I'm supposed to bring back flour. Or was it sugar?"

"Both. That is if you want me to make *someone*'s favorite dessert."

"Cobbler?"

"Uh huh … peach," she added.

Cuddy released his grip on the dog's tail and climbed to his feet.

"Dust those dungarees off before coming inside. And that dog stays outside!"

She let the screen door close and watched him do as told, then returned to the kitchen. Opening up the first cupboard on the right, she double-checked the shelves. She had plenty of canned Del Monte peaches stacked up there. She next located a bottle of McCormick's ground cinnamon and shook it. Only a quarter of an inch of the brick-colored granules remained. Needing more of that as well, she added it onto the list for the grocer. Cuddy wouldn't remember the flour or the sugar—much less the cinnamon.

She closed the cupboard and stepped over to the large kitchen window. She noticed another small hole in the barn's roof. The ranch was literally falling apart before her eyes. How was she going to pay for needed repairs when she was already six months behind on her mortgage payments? Soon the bank would be taking action, but she couldn't think about that right now.

★ ★ ★

Tow quietly backed away from the barn door. The spasms in his injured leg had subsided. He moved through the barn, past the horse, and followed the same route back. Looking first to see that all was clear, he exited from the barn's other side. The sun had risen higher and, along with it, so had the temperature. He watched a flock of birds flying in unison—first going left, then turning and making a right angle, which took them directly overhead. Birds were fascinating creatures. He'd never seen anything like them. This world certainly had its mysteries.

As Tow hurried into the tree line he ducked behind a large pine, hearing the approach of a noisy vehicle along a nearby dirt road. The AI informed him that the vehicle, with its internal combustion power source, was something called a *pickup truck*. Blackish smoke puffed out from the rear of the vehicle and hung in the air like a dark cloud. Two male savages were seated inside. As the truck approached, he saw that the occupants were drinking from long-necked brown bottles and were conversing in loud tones; louder than the other two at the farm. Not as mature in age as the gray-haired female, they were closer in age to her large offspring. Twenty paces away, the truck came to a stop. He wondered at first if his presence had been noticed, but watching them, he knew it had not.

Tow continued to watch them. He could see a bizarre kind of posturing taking place, and feel a raw aggressiveness emanating from them both. One had long unkempt hair and a cluster of pimples—*called whiteheads*, he was informed by the AI—on his cheeks and forehead. Instinctively, Tow didn't like him. Didn't like either of them.

★ ★ ★

Once back within the *Evermore*, Tow's presence was requested on the bridge. The AI orb was waiting for him there. He directed him to the viewscape display where he recognized the symbolic representation of the Sol planetary system.

"They're here … here within the system?" Tow asked, his

voice elevated.

"Yes, Captain Tow … unfortunately."

Tow saw four sets of winding, curved vectors; each set was in a different color. The green vector symbolized the path the *Evermore* had taken, prior to landing on Earth. The other three—red, yellow, and violet—showed the pursuing Howsh, which were apparently scouting from one planet to another. Circling planets multiple times, landing and taking off—over and over again—they were hunting.

"What is that planet there?"

The AI said, "That is Saturn, Captain."

Tow wanted to leave, make a run for it right then.

"Saturn is a large planet. Based on the area already systematically traversed, they won't move on to Jupiter for another ten hours and nine minutes. It's clear they know we are close … within this system."

"How could they know that?"

"Residual energy markers."

Tow knew exactly what the AI orb was referring to—the turbulence left behind a moving spacecraft. An energy wake, of sorts. "This vessel is not supposed to leave those kinds of markers," Tow said.

"The *Evermore*'s sole remaining drive is malfunctioning. Out of alignment. On the positive side, the markers are undefined. They may not point directly to our current location. There is no way to know, for sure, though."

Suddenly feeling trapped—that the Howsh were again closing in on them—he felt the muscles in his abdomen go taut. He said, "I need to get the repairs started as soon as possible. Determine what can be worked on in spite of the hard systems reset. We must hurry, get systems back online. Am I making myself clear, orb?"

Chapter 4

Cuddy and Rufus walked along the old two-track road leading into town. Cuddy couldn't understand why his dog was walking so slow today. As he waited for him to catch up, he adjusted the brim on his baseball cap. "You know … I'm going to have two helpings of Momma's peach cobbler pie. But you're not allowed to have any. Momma says it makes you farty." Cuddy laughed at that.

Rufus glanced up at him. Panting, his long tongue curled; moisture dripped from his mouth.

Cuddy knew the way to town—two miles there and two miles back. On the way, they would pass three farms, a set of train tracks, an abandoned junkyard, and a school. Cuddy had never gone to a real school, though someday he thought he might want to. Momma called his schooling—home schooling. He was learning to read. He knew certain letters, but had trouble stringing them together.

As they approached the second farm, Cuddy hurried his pace—leaving Rufus to lag behind. Elma and Rutherford White lived there. They liked to sit on the porch in their rocking chairs. Cuddy stood tall and raised his chin, craning his neck in the process. A rusty, beat-up old tractor—parked next to a large mound of dirt—blocked direct views to their house, but he was tall enough to see over the dirt and even the grassy clumps atop the dirt.

"I see Elma!" Cuddy glanced back to see if Rufus was still behind him and ran ahead. He turned the corner at the leaning mailbox post, and half-ran, half-walked toward the Whites' house.

He saw Elma—not sitting, like usual, in her rocking chair but sweeping the porch instead. "Hi Elma!" Cuddy yelled, out of breath.

Elma turned, looking to see who was coming down her dirt drive. Cuddy liked Elma better than Rutherford. The old man never said much. She smiled and waved but didn't stop what she was doing. Elma was a big, solid woman—both wide and tall. Her dark chocolate skin glistened with perspiration. As Cuddy reached the porch, gasping for air, he leaned over—hands on knees—and asked, "Where's Rutherford?"

"I don't know … might be in the shed. He's been looking for something for the last few days, but he won't tell me what it is. I could help him find it, if only he'd tell me." She watched as the dog dropped down by Cuddy's feet. "That dog of yours looks all worn out, boy."

Cuddy patted Rufus's head. "Maybe he's thirsty."

"Take him round the side of the house … the spigot there has a hose attached."

Cuddy, taking ahold of Rufus by the collar, steered him around the corner and into the shade. He turned the spigot knob and waited for some water to drip from the faded green hose. As water slowly trickled out, he put his mouth to the nozzle and drank some before lowering the hose down to Rufus. The dog lapped up the water; then, suddenly losing interest, sat back down.

"Better?" Cuddy asked.

* * *

By the time they reached the edge of town, Rufus seemed to be back to his peppy, playful self and ran off ahead, knowing exactly where they were going. Woodbury was not a very big town. There was a much larger city, called Evans, right off the interstate—a few hours' drive away. Cuddy had only visited the city twice—first, when taken to the hospital, at age seven, and again, when his molars were pulled out, at seventeen.

It usually took Cuddy a long while to walk up the street, since he knocked on most of the storefront windows, waving to each proprietor as he passed by. He typically would wave his hand until they waved back. Gordon's was the only grocery store in town, though no one named Gordon had ever worked there. He had asked. No one seemed to know where the store's name came from. Momma called it a general store because it had all kinds of things for sale—like milk, and loaves of bread, and snow shovels, and eggs, and hats. It was where Momma had bought the hat he had on now.

Rufus anxiously pawed at the door as Cuddy approached the store. Letting him enter first, he followed closely behind. The dog ran to the back of the store, disappearing down a hallway.

The store was square built. Five parallel aisles ran down the middle, and a U-shaped counter ran around the store's periphery. Mr. Maxwell, helping a lady at the cash register, said, "Help you in a minute, Cuddy."

"Okay, Mr. Maxwell."

Cuddy strode toward the rear of the store and turned into a hallway. Passing three closed doorways, he found Rufus—lying on the cement floor next to Trudy. Trudy was another yellow lab, belonging to Mr. Maxwell's daughter, Rita. The two dogs were brother and sister. Cuddy, sitting down on the floor between the dogs, gave Trudy a pat and a kiss on her nose.

Mr. Maxwell entered and, looking down at them, said, "Give me your daypack, boy, and I'll go fill it with your Momma's grocery list items."

Cuddy had forgotten he was even wearing the pack. Slipping one arm out and then the other, he handed it to the store proprietor. Mr. Maxwell, unzipping the pack's zipper, fished his hand around inside and brought out a piece of paper. *That's Momma's grocery list*, Cuddy thought. He'd forgotten all about that, too.

"Cuddy … there's um … no money in here. No means of payment. I'm assuming this is going on Momma's tab again?"

"Um …" Cuddy wasn't quite sure what a tab was. "Maybe," he said.

"Well … come on … let's go get your supplies. I think I may have some ropes of licorice about … let's go see."

Cuddy jumped to his feet.

★ ★ ★

They'd reached the halfway mark back home. Cuddy knew it because he was standing on the railroad tracks. Halfway to town going—halfway to home coming back. He pulled a red licorice rope from his pocket, filling up his mouth. An old Beatles song kept ringing in his head—actually, only a small part of the song. He sang the one line he knew, over and over again: "*Hey Jude, don't let me down. Take a sad song and … na na naa na na na naaaaa …*"

Rufus was walking close by his side and he could feel the dog's warmth leaning in against his leg. Cuddy said, "Too close … Rufus," and gave the dog a soft nudge to back off a tad. Up ahead, he watched as a truck approached, music blaring out through its open windows. He saw two large figures in the front seat but couldn't make out who they were. He didn't recognize the truck as it drove closer. Moving to the side of the road to let it pass him on his left, Cuddy noticed it was an old, faded green, F150. It was riddled with rust along the fender, and also low along the side door. The two guys inside were laughing at something one of them had said to the other. The music was loud. Airborne dust swirled around him as the truck came to an abrupt stop nearby.

Momma didn't like him to talk to strangers. She said people didn't understand. Cuddy knew what she meant. That he wasn't smart, like most other grown-ups, because of the accident. She said people could be mean and to just ignore them.

The two fellows looked to be about his same age, though Cuddy was bad at guessing ages. But looking at them now, they seemed happy enough. Liking to laugh himself, Cuddy smiled and waved. "Hello … I'm Cuddy and this is Rufus. She's a yellow laboratory retriever. She has a sister in town named Trudy."

Their smiles were gone. The driver of the truck looked angry and Cuddy wondered if he'd said something wrong. He did that from time to time. The truck driver secured a greasy strand of black hair behind his ear; his face was riddled with pimples. Cuddy wondered if he washed his face often enough.

"What … are … you?" the driver asked.

"Huh?"

Rufus growled.

"I said … what the fuck are you?"

"Um … I don't know," Cuddy said, avoiding eye contact and looking down at his feet. He remembered Momma's warning.

"He's the town retard," the one in the passenger seat said, sporting a crew cut and a scar over his left eye.

"Is that right? You the village idiot? I think I heard about you. Got dropped on your head, or something, as a kid. Your brother pushed you off a hayloft." They both laughed at that.

Cuddy shrugged, not knowing how at first to respond, but then said, "He didn't mean it."

"He didn't mean it … he didn't mean it," the long-haired teen behind the steering wheel repeated.

Cuddy heard the engine turn off. Both doors opened wide on rusty hinges, and he took a step back.

Climbing out of the truck, the driver glanced over to his friend as both moved closer. The dark-haired teen puffed out his chest and raised his chin, trying to make himself look taller. But Cuddy was nearly a foot taller than either of them.

"You need to stay the hell off this road. Matter of fact, I don't ever want to see that big melon head of yours around here again. Understand that … retard?"

Rufus growled louder.

"I'm not retarded. I have a learning disa … disability."

The slap came fast and hard to Cuddy's left cheek. He'd never been struck like that before. Not ever. He didn't understand what was happening and looked down at the guy through tear-filled eyes.

"You didn't just back-talk me … did you, retard?"

Cuddy rubbed at his cheek. It still felt hot where he'd been slapped. "I want to go home."

Rufus growled and bared his teeth.

The one wearing a crew cut looked down at the dog, and said, "I think that dog of yours has the mange."

Cuddy tried to find his voice. "The mange? What's that?"

"It's like rabies. Your dog's got rabies. You know what they do with those dogs?"

Cuddy shook his head.

"They put them down."

"Put them where?"

"They kill them, retard!"

Scared, Cuddy looked down at Rufus, finding it hard to breathe. He suddenly became fearful he might pee his pants.

The crewcut-haired teen took a quick step backward, then moved forward even faster—kicking out with a boot that connected hard with Rufus's ribs. The old dog yelped and tried to run, but couldn't—something had broken inside. Cowering now, Rufus lowered to the road, trying to wrap himself around Cuddy's feet. Trembling, the dog looked up at him.

Cuddy reached for his dog, wanting to hug him. Let him know he was there. That he would protect him and give him love—at the very least.

The teen with the crew cut punched Cuddy in the face—hard enough to knock the cap from his head. Shocked, Cuddy staggered, seeing stars dance before his eyes. The pain was intense. Next, a kick came to the back of his legs and Cuddy's arm whipped upward. Unintentionally, his knuckles connected hard with the long dark haired teen's face. Cuddy heard a cracking sound—like the sound of a pencil snapping in two. Blood spurted from his nose. The teen screamed something then, bending over, clutched his face.

The crew cut teen then came at Cuddy with a vengeance. Lips pulled back in a snarl, he struck out, first with his left fist then with his right. Cuddy took the new blows to his cheek and chin, and cried out as he toppled to the ground. Quickly curling into a ball, he did his best to cover his head with his arms. Momentarily, Cuddy thought of the glowing angel he'd seen in the woods. *Was he a guardian angel? Could he help me now?*

Next came a series of merciless kicks—each one harder than the one before it—to his stomach, his back, and to his face. He'd never felt such pain before. He heard Rufus whimper nearby—for the first time in his life he wanted to hurt another person—he no longer regretted breaking the dark haired teen's nose. As the unrelenting kicking continued, he began to lose consciousness. He felt the daypack being pulled from his shoulder. Slipping into darkness, he heard one of them say, "Shit … I think we killed him. Let's git!"

Chapter 5

Tow had been working for four straight hours, trying to feed power back into the wellness chamber. Damage caused in that last attack by the Howsh, when the Howsh plasma strike hit the aft section of the *Evermore*. The ship had lurched, violently propelling him off his feet, and into an adjacent bulkhead. He knew right then his leg was broken. The plasma strike took out several key mechanisms—including the wellness chamber.

Tow concentrated on the electrical panel before him, where much of the ship's power conduits were junctioned together. The problem—much of this ship section was heavily damaged; primarily, the starboard berth compartment, not more than five feet away. The compartment had suddenly decompressed, crushed in on itself, flattening the sleeping berths. Seven lives were lost within a split second and the bodies were still in there, with no easy way to recover them. There had been no easy way to retrieve their essences for the heritage pod.

Tow, presently, hung upside-down between two bulkheads near the ship's stern. He'd give it another few minutes' effort before giving up, turning his attention instead to the propulsion system. What he really wanted most was to return to space … quickly.

Holding a test probe down onto the tenth series of contacts, he asked the hovering nearby AI orb, "Reading anything here?"

The orb said, "No … that terminal is dead."

"That one should be energized," Tow said, moving the tip of the probe down to the next series of contacts. "How about these here?"

"Yes, activated."

"They are supposed to be nominal!"

The AI orb said, "You could reverse them. I calculate you have a forty-percent chance of success."

"You do know that's less than even odds …"

"Yes."

At that point, Tow had little choice, since he wasn't an engineer. He swapped the plug-in junction cables between terminals ten and eleven.

The AI orb said, "That did it. The wellness chamber is now re-initializing. I believe you have alleviated the problem, Captain Tow."

Though I fixed one problem, I've most likely instigated another, coming down the road, he thought.

★ ★ ★

Aside from the emersion-matter drives, the wellness chamber had the most complex technology on board the *Evermore*. Another contribution by the *Kartinals*—the chamber was the advanced administrator of a completely independent, artificial intelligence medical treatment system; one that fundamentally changed the living conditions back on Mahli. The *Pashier*, as a race, saw life spans extend from an average of eighty to ninety years to twice that. Diseases, once terminal and inoperable, were all but wiped out. As far as Tow knew, there was only one exception: wellness chambers were ineffective in the treatment of the Dirth. The scientists—the *Kartinals*, required to make necessary modification updates to the wellness technology, which would diagnose the recent vile disease and treat it effectively—were all gone. They had either succumbed to the disease itself—before they could make modification—or were among the billions who died in the spatial attacks.

Tow sat within the wellness center's dome-shaped confined space, sited on the lower level of the ship. With hands clasped together behind his head, he let the warm, moist air soothe his injured outstretched leg, as well as calm his equally wounded psyche. Tow reflected back to the last time he'd been to the chamber, which was capable of administering to four individuals at once. It was with Soweng, when he'd first kissed her. *Or had she kissed him*? Why had they waited so long … two years? So much time wasted.

"Captain Tow."

Tow sighed, "Yes … go ahead."

"One of the Howsh vessels has moved on from Neptune and is currently en route to Uranus. The other two vessels will be completing their terrestrial scans shortly then moving on."

"Terrific. Don't you ever have any good news for me?"

"It is a very large planet. It will take them much longer to traverse—"

Tow cut the AI off: "I'll be out shortly. You can update me then."

Tow tried to mentally retrieve the image of Soweng, the feel of her lips upon his. The way she'd looked at him with such intensity. But the moment quickly passed. More pressing issues now clamored for his attention.

He raised his leg, probing it with outstretched fingers. He increased finger pressure downward, at the location of the injury, where a hairline fracture had made his life miserable for so long. Bones don't set well in space. The pain now was significantly less, and he figured he'd need only one or two more healing sessions.

★ ★ ★

By the time Tow entered the bridge, it was getting dark outside. *Dusk.* Looking through the window, he watched with fascination at what the AI orb had referred to, pointing with one of its articulating arms, as *fireflies.* Magically, they glowed on and off, with no determinate rhyme or reason. *Perhaps some kind of mating ritual?* he wondered. Tow was finding it harder and harder to keep within the confines of the *Evermore*'s hull. The outside world beyond was just too compelling—calling to him. It wasn't as if he'd forgotten his mission—the importance of setting off for Primara: to again set her roots upon her furtive soil, unfold the heritage pod's wide fronds, and commence *the awakening.*

Tow brought his attention back to the view-scape display—the crisscrossing of colored vectors. "All right, AI, talk to me about the Howsh's scouting progress."

"The Howsh have made sufficient progress. Engaging the *Evermore*'s propulsion system to make repairs will, beyond any doubt, alert them to our location."

Chapter 6

Cuddy awoke to darkness and pain.

He remembered the two attackers. He remembered Rufus trembling at his feet and tried calling out for him: "Rufus? Here boy …" His voice sounded strange, like it belonged to someone else. He then was aware he was no longer outside. No longer lying on the ground near the train tracks.

"Rufus? Are you there?" Cuddy, trying to make a kissing sound, instantly regretted it. His lips were split. He touched them with his fingertips, finding them swollen and cracked. He felt a bandage on his cheek and another one on his ear.

Cuddy tried to raise his head but found it too painful to move. He was in his bed, he knew, with his own pillow and the soft blanket Momma had made for him, using long needles.

"Rufus? Here boy … are you there?"

He tried again to turn over on his back and, even though it hurt a lot, he did manage to roll over. He heard voices—Momma's voice and someone else's. Cuddy's heart began to race. His eyes turned to his bedroom door as it slowly opened.

Cuddy watched the tall figure—his form silhouetted in the hallway light—approach his bed. It was the smell that gave him away first: cigarettes and the musky body odor on his Army jacket that needed washing.

Kyle sat down on the edge of the bed and stared down at Cuddy. "Are you alive, little brother?"

Cuddy laughed at that, then cringed in pain. "Of course I'm alive … how else would I be seeing you?"

"Who did this to you, Cuddy?"

Cuddy heard the seriousness in his brother's voice. "I'm glad you came home, Kyle. Are you going to stay here? Do you live here now?"

"I don't know … maybe. Who did this to you, Cuddy?"

"Um … I don't know their names."

"There was more than one?" Kyle's voice rose, and he sounded angry.

Momma's voice came from the hallway, "Don't you be upsetting him, Kyle. There's plenty of time for all that tomorrow. He needs to rest."

"Kyle?"

"Yeah?"

"Where's Rufus?

Kyle hesitated. "He's hurt, Cuddy. Hurt pretty bad."

Cuddy stared at his brother's face. "Is he … dying?"

Kyle smiled his familiar crooked grin. "I don't think so. But you won't be able to wrestle with him for a while. He should be okay in a week or two … maybe three."

"Okay … let him rest now. Out with you," Momma ordered.

Kyle stood and headed toward the door. Then, glancing back, he smiled.

Momma took Kyle's place on the edge of the bed. Leaning over, she kissed Cuddy on the forehead. "You gave me quite a scare, boy."

"Momma …? I don't remember … walking home."

"That's because you didn't. Kyle got home while you were gone. When it started getting dark I called the grocer.

He said you'd left hours earlier so I sent your brother to go find you. He came back with you and Rufus in the car. You both were in a bad way."

"I don't remember any of that."

"Do you remember Doc Sanderson stitching up your lip and cheek?"

"No."

"He says you're going to be fine, but you have *bruised ribs*. You're all wrapped up around your chest." Cuddy noticed his chest did feel constricted and, placing an open palm there, could feel the bandaging beneath his pajama top.

"I'm tired, Momma … I'm going to go to sleep now."

★ ★ ★

Three days later, Cuddy sat at the kitchen table, chewing on a mouthful of syrupy pancakes. Pancakes were his very favorite and he was already on his second batch. Fresh off the griddle, Momma carried over three pancakes atop a wide spatula and slid them onto Kyle's empty plate. His brother sliced off a large pat of butter and spread it across the top of the stack. "Pass me the syrup, little brother."

Cuddy, doing as asked, looked over at Momma, who seemed tense. His brother also looked tense. Cuddy wondered if it had something to do with an earlier phone call? He noticed them exchanging serious glances.

"Aren't you going to eat, Mom?" Kyle asked.

Sitting down at the table, she said, "I'm not hungry," using a paper napkin to swipe at Cuddy's sticky chin. She then glanced out the large kitchen window behind Kyle, toward the long winding dirt drive that led down to Beacham Road.

Cuddy smiled. Happy that Kyle was back home again. Happy too that he was eating his favorite breakfast, and that Rufus was sleeping in his bed in the far corner of the kitchen. The lab had bandages wrapped around his chest too.

Momma sat forward with her elbows on the table, her joined hands supporting her chin. Suddenly Rufus's head came up and barking only once, he looked toward the front door.

Momma said, "Ahh shit." Cuddy was surprised. He'd rarely heard her cuss.

Momma, after exchanging another long glance with Kyle, rose from the table and headed for the door. Glancing out the window, Cuddy noticed a plume of dust approaching from the distance, and watched as a black and white police SUV turned onto their drive. Eventually rolling to a stop in the front yard, the car parked next to Momma's old Maxima.

Cuddy rushed to his feet and hurried after his mother. Exiting through the screen door, he waved, "Hi, Officer Plumkin."

Momma stood on the porch, wringing her hands in a dishtowel, as Officer Plumkin extricated his large bulk up and off the front seat of the police cruiser. Wrangling the gun belt that was out of position around his protruding belly, he tapped the brim of his cap. "Morning Cuddy … Mrs. Perkins."

Kyle, followed by Rufus, came out too, and the screen door banged closed behind them. Officer Plumkin's chin came up, and he warily eyed Kyle.

"When did you get out?" Plumkin asked, his smile faltering.

"Few days ago."

Momma said, "That's all behind him now. He's been helping me around the ranch and with Cuddy." She raised the dishtowel in the direction of her youngest son.

Plumkin's mouth twisted into a snarl. "Make sure it stays that way, boy."

Cuddy knew Kyle had spent time in jail, that he'd, again, stolen a car. Momma always said Kyle hung out with the wrong people. Officer Plumkin and Kyle were the same age, both twenty-two. They'd grown up together—went to the same high school. Cuddy didn't understand why Officer Plumkin called his brother *boy*. Kyle didn't like to be called *boy*.

"Stay out of trouble, Kyle. Nobody wants a repeat of past events."

Kyle shrugged. "That's not what your wife told me last night—after you fell asleep in your tighty-whiteys in front of the TV."

Cuddy laughed at his brother's comment.

"Knock it off, Kyle!" Momma said, giving him a serious glare.

Plumkin stared at Kyle for several long beats—then turned his attention to Cuddy. "Cuddy, I understand you had an altercation with some local fellas the other day."

"What's an altercation?"

Kyle said, "When those two guys beat you up, Cuddy."

"Well, hold on there … that's not exactly how I heard it," Plumkin said, dramatically holding his palms up in mock surrender. "There's a hurt young man with a broken nose. He's pretty upset. Says he wants to press charges."

"That's bullshit … and you know it!" Kyle took a step forward on the porch.

Momma said, "Officer Plumkin, you know Cuddy. He'd never hurt nobody. Not ever. It just ain't in him."

"Not my call, ma'am. Tony Bone wants justice for what happened to his nose. Says it was a vicious attack."

"Oh … come on! It was two against one," Kyle said. "Two hoodlums against someone who can't defend himself."

Plumkin made an exaggerated expression of astonishment. "Have you looked at this bubba lately? What are you, boy … six two … six three? Two hundred … two twenty?" Plumkin continued on with, "Cuddy may have the small brain of an imbecile, but he's a full grown man just the same."

Kyle was off the porch in two strides, heading straight for Plumkin—his balled fist coming up fast. Startled, Plumkin took a stumbling step backward, his wide ass falling against the door of his cruiser as he fumbled for his pistol.

Momma yelled for Kyle to stop.

Kyle held up short—his fist raised and clenched. "Don't do this, Plumkin. We were friends once. That should account for at least something."

Plumkin, fingers working on the holster on his hip that held the unyielding pistol, nervously stared into Kyle's face.

Holding his breath, Cuddy watched them, as they stood glaring at each other for several seconds. Finally, Officer Plumkin's tense face slackened some. His shoulders lowered and his hands came away from his still-holstered weapon.

"You do know who Tony's dad is, right?"

"Yeah, I've met the sheriff … a few times," Kyle answered back sarcastically.

"And there's more," the portly policeman said.

"What … what else, Plumkin?" Momma asked.

Officer Plumkin's eyes moved off Kyle to up on the porch. He gestured with his chin, and said, "Both boys say your dog attacked them. Said he was rabid … foaming at the mouth."

Cuddy hurried over to Rufus then dropped to his side. Putting his arms around him, he said, "Mamma … they said he had the mange. That they were going to put him down. Then they kicked Rufus hard … in the side."

Plumkin watched as Rufus relentlessly licked Cuddy's face.

"Looks pretty rabid to me," Kyle said sarcastically. "Maybe you should have brought some backup … for old Rufus."

For the first time, Plumkin cracked a smile. "Let me see what I can do … about Cuddy. I'll talk to the sheriff, but no promises. But if so ordered, sorry, I'll be back to take him into custody."

"Those boys were more like grown men … the ones who did this to my son and to his dog. It's them you should be hauling off to jail," Momma said angrily.

"Look, I don't completely believe their story, but there's still a procedure I have to follow. The sheriff's looking for retribution for what happened to his son. For now … I do have to take the dog … it's a formality. Let the vet check him out for rabies. He'll be in quarantine for a few days … maybe a week."

Cuddy didn't know what quarantine meant. He didn't like the thought of being away from Rufus for a whole week.

Officer Plumkin's cap suddenly flipped high into the air, almost as if it had wings. Since there was no big gust of wind it was totally unexpected. Plumkin's fumble to try to catch it made Cuddy laugh out loud. The cap landed on the top of the police SUV—well out of Officer Plumkin's reach.

Chapter 7

Staying out of view, the alien, Tow, watched and listened from the barn's open rear door. Some of what was being said he didn't understand, but he was mesmerized by the course of events going on just the same. His suspicions about the one called Cuddy were now confirmed. He was a simpleton. A childlike mind in a grownup human's body. The dark-haired male with the beard, wearing a green coat, was Kyle, his older brother. Apparently, Cuddy was attacked a few days before. From the looks of his face—the nearly closed right eye, the bulbously swollen lips, and the bandages—he'd been severely beaten. The uniformed, portly male Cuddy called Officer Plumkin seemed to hold some kind of power position. He mentioned two other humans. Tow suspected he knew who they were. The same ones he'd observed several days earlier, while walking along the tree line, sitting in the pickup truck. He didn't like them then, and he liked them even less now. He watched as the uniformed male, wearing a weapon on his hip, opened the rear door of his vehicle. The brother named Kyle attached a long leash to the dog's neck collar and led him up into the backseat. Tow watched as

Cuddy become emotional, pleading for Officer Plumkin to reconsider—to let him keep his dog.

With the animal secured in the vehicle, the door closed, Officer Plumkin continued to speak to the three family members. Tow didn't like the tone of Officer Plumkin's voice. He'd known plenty of similar *Pashier*—windbags who liked to hear themselves talk.

Watching Cuddy's face, Tow felt sympathy for the odd, childlike young man. He found himself getting angry—drawn into their situation. Cuddy had already been beaten and humiliated and now that fat savage was taking his dog away, too. Ignoring his own better judgment, Tow—with a casual wave of his hand—flipped Officer Plumkin's cap away from the top of his head. Rising into the air, it landed atop the black and white vehicle. Officer Plumkin spun around, confronting the three onlookers and giving each an accusatory stare—perhaps thinking some kind of elaborate prank had been performed but unsure how that was even remotely possible. Flustered, he climbed into his vehicle and drove away.

★ ★ ★

Tow chastised himself for getting involved—being noticed by those humans could have serious ramifications. He walked back through the dense pines, leaped over the babbling brook, and ten minutes later saw his ship, parked within the clearing ahead. The walk back had given him enough time to think; to take a hard look at his situation. Now that the pain in his leg was significantly lessened—a little self-evaluation was not only timely, but necessary too.

As he approached he asked the AI orb for an update.

"Four of the *Evermore*'s systems have been reloaded and are currently being tested, including those for the propulsion system and the wellness chamber's artificial intelligence system," the AI orb said.

"Just keep me apprised of your progress," Tow said, well aware any physical repair made to the damaged emersion drive would take him the most amount of time.

With little else to do but wait, Tow made the same short trek to the farm a daily occurrence, sometimes several times a day, and he knew why. Unconsciously, he was developing a bond with this strange world and, in a limited way, to its human inhabitants. How long had it been since he'd last had direct contact with another living, sentient, being? Six months? Leaving here quickly meant spending additional time in space; returning to the same lonely monotony. If, and when, he reached Primara, he had no idea if other beings actually existed there. It was a destination derived from ancient legends and fables—touted to be a grand expedition, a pilgrimage—when in reality it was a last ditch attempt to save a dying race. *Once I leave this world, I will probably never see another living being again,* Tow thought, deciding to cut himself some slack. Although not yet exhibiting any of the disease's telltale symptoms, the Dirth was inevitable—would probably kill him before he even reached Primara.

The AI informed him the Howsh had moved on from both Saturn and Jupiter and were finishing up with Mars. They would arrive here on Earth shortly. *So why am I wasting precious time concerned with these human savages?* He had no answer for that.

Stepping into the clearing, the battered *Evermore* was a sorry sight. Still, it was his home and it represented something far more important to him than that. It was what was beneath the lower deck—secured within an environmentally controlled compartment—that gave him the most hope. Tow found it utterly amazing that it hadn't been destroyed over the past three years. It alone gave him sufficient motivation to complete his mission—or die trying.

Tow stared at the aft starboard section of the ship and the charred, six-foot-long gash in its hull. He'd procrastinated long enough. Before starting in on the repairs to the emersion-drive, he'd need to deal with the dead crewmembers. No longer entombed in the frigidly cold vacuum of space, the bodies had begun to putrefy—to decompose. He could smell them from outside. Caring about them all still, he dreaded what was to come next.

★ ★ ★

Access to the aft-starboard berth compartment was only possible via the outside hull. Months earlier, crossing deep space, he'd contemplated cutting into that damaged section of the ship through the inside primary aft corridor, but there were issues of cabin depressurization. Namely, far too much of the *Evermore*'s breathable air would be vented out into space. With what air had already been lost, during the last Howsh attack, it left barely sufficient atmosphere for recycling: first pulled through big environmental filters then through the complex, carbon dioxide / oxygenation conversion process.

The *Evermore* was well stocked with a variety of specialized tools and equipment. Each ship within the armada was required to be totally self-sufficient unto itself. The same philosophy extended to ship areas, like functioning food replicators, a wellness chamber, and the capability to make virtually any repairs to the ship—on the fly.

★ ★ ★

The stench had quickly become intolerable. Wearing a lightweight environment suit, it took Tow most of the afternoon to remove the damaged four outer hull panels. Later, prior to his reinstalling them, the open gash—where the plasma strike had occurred—would need to be resealed with a high-strength bonding mixture. He'd have to check the ship's storage hold to see what was available for that.

One by one, hundreds of cap-bolts were removed with a tool not too dissimilar from any number of hand-held power tools utilized on Earth. The individual outer hull plates came away easily and he stacked them into a nearby pile. With the outer hull plates removed, the inner, far thicker bulkhead wall was clearly visible. Multiple long wavy *stress-creases* traversed horizontally through its metal siding. Beyond that was the actual berth compartment, comprised of much lighter, less rigid materials that had folded inward from instantaneous depressurization.

The inside bulkhead was one huge piece, comprised of a high-strength metallic compound. Using a hand-held plasma torch, Tow started at the upper left corner of the section, cutting a seven-foot-long vertical swath downward. Completing that, he moved up to the top and initiated a sideways horizontal cut—close to twenty feet long—that took him close to an hour to execute. Halfway done, he stood back, admiring his handiwork.

Annoying flies were everywhere, buzzing and circling. A thought occurred to him: What was he going to do with the crew's remains? Typically, he would quote a prayer then release them out an airlock into the vastness of space. Tow queried the AI, "What do Earth humans do with their deceased beings' bodies?"

"The two most popular methods are ground burial and cremation."

Tow expected as much, for it had been the same on Mahli. He needed to find a nice location, somewhere deep in the trees, then dig seven deep holes.

The last two plasma cuts went faster than the first two. As he neared completion of the fourth cut, the nearly separated one hundred and forty square foot sheet, pushed outward, sagging down. He'd wondered if it would simply drop away, but it stayed put, just barely secured.

Tow moved his tools and equipment out of the way. The

next task would require some heavy lifting: Not the physical kind—but the mental kind. The combined weight of objects did matter. He estimated the cutaway piece of metal was easily three hundred pounds. That, and it was an awkward size. Taking five paces back from the *Evermore*, Tow flexed his fingers and rolled his shoulders. Raising both hands, he concentrated. For close to a minute nothing happened. He was out of practice; couldn't remember the last time he had to *move* something this substantial using only his mind. And like any unused muscle, it too can atrophy.

Suddenly, there came the sound of metal scraping against metal. And then, finally, the large hull section began to pull free, making a distinct sucking sound. Almost immediately, loose debris within the compressed compartment began to fall onto the ground. Tow continued to mentally levitate the section another five feet away from the ship's fuselage, moving it off to the left. Its weight was daunting. Tiring, he needed to quickly set it down before it dropped. He then lowered it onto its bottom edge, letting it lean vertically against the trunk of a large nearby tree.

Up until then, Tow had managed to keep his eyes averted from looking into the now-open, multi-berth compartment, and what he surmised would present a most horrific sight. He opened his eyes and gasped. Burning bile retched up from his already queasy stomach. He could almost make out the seven blue-colored individual berths within the distorted and twisted mass. Almost. But it was the entangled appearance of sporadic body parts that hit Tow the hardest. His eyes unwillingly focused on one after another—a seemingly unattached arm—a patch of long brown hair swaying back and forth—as if the congealed mass of metal and berth bedding had somehow sprouted it from somewhere deep within the wreckage. Tow stepped forward, unsure of what he was now looking at. He stopped and brought a hand to his mouth. Two, side-by-side eyes, blankly staring back at him—the crewmember's face so unimaginably compressed to where it was no more than two, maybe three, inches wide.

Chapter 8

8 across and 10 down: A nine-letter word for *Repeated to perfection.* Jackie Hansen brought the eraser end of the pencil to her lips and thought about it. Then wrote in, *Practiced.* She dropped the crossword puzzle to her lap as a middle-aged nurse, wearing light pink scrubs, entered the room and moved to the other side of the bed. The nurse checked the heart monitor, flicked her middle finger several times against the bottom of the hanging IV, before turning her gaze over toward Jackie and smiling.

"You should go home and get some rest, honey. We'll call you if there's any change. He's stable now … there's nothing you can do here."

Jackie nodded. Truth was, she was exhausted. Totally spent. Had driven like a bat out of hell to get back here. Seven hours straight behind the wheel. Hadn't even locked her dorm room door—only grabbed her backpack which doubled as her purse, and her keys, and ran to her car.

Her eyes leveled on the old man's face. Propped up with several pillows behind his back, he looked different here. The florescent lights exaggerated the etched lines around his mouth and eyes—lines cultivated from working too many years beneath a relentless overhead sun and smiling a broad, contagious-type grin that was present far more often than not.

According to the doctor, her father had suffered a massive myocardial infarction—a heart attack. More precisely, an ST-segment elevation myocardial infarction—referred to as a STEMI. She knew what that was.

Feelings of guilt and self-loathing washed over her. He'd been living alone on the ranch far too long—her mother gone ten years now—with no other children, siblings, to help out. Three years ago, she left for college, only returning on breaks and holidays. Down at her feet, her eyes momentarily held on the corners of two pre-med-school books peeking out from the top of her backpack. She instantly felt the pull to dive back into her molecular and cellular biology studies. She could ill afford a day away from her coursework, let alone a week or more.

Looking at him, now, he was still a bear of a man, filling the confines of the narrow hospital bed—looking like a gnarly giant lying asleep there. Still unconscious, he shifted in bed. He'd insisted she follow her dream of becoming a doctor, stating, *what good is having a full-ride scholarship if you're not going to use it?* There was so much she wanted to tell him. As a pre-med student, she was graduating a year early from the University of Tennessee. Accepted into the prestigious Vanderbilt School of Medicine—on track to be a licensed MD in less than four years and hopefully a practicing neurosurgeon two years after that.

But now, she had to figure out how to balance both her obligations to her dad and school. She was the only family her dad had. He'd be laid up in this small, sixty-bed hospital for a week or two, then be convalescing at home after that. He'd need her help—cooking meals, walking to the toilet—*shit,* taking care of the damn farm animals. *Cows don't milk themselves*, her father used to say. *Oh God …* Frustrated, she kicked out at her backpack.

"Tomorrow we'll get him up and walking around a bit," the nurse said, ignoring Jackie's obvious mini tantrum.

"Um … you can do that, with all the damage done to his heart?" Jackie asked. She quickly glanced at her smartphone and saw two more missed calls had come in. Glancing at the caller I.D. she saw that it was Brian, again. She didn't have the mental bandwidth to deal with him right now.

"Well, spending weeks lying around in a hospital bed isn't going to help him recover faster either. Nope … we get our patients up and moving about as quickly as possible."

Jackie nodded and stood, placing a hand on her father's foot. Feeling warmth beneath the blanket, she said, "I'll be back in the morning first thing. You have my cell number …"

They both looked up as the ceiling lights suddenly flickered then went out. As if on cue, heart monitors, including her father's, began to chime loudly. In the distance, Jackie could hear auto alarms going off, one by one. Then, just as quickly, everything returned to normal—electric lights came back on, heart monitors normalized, and car alarms went silent.

"Been happening like that since last night … more and more often, too. Heard one of the maintenance guys talking about it. Says it's some electrical issue, external to the hospital. Saw it on the news. Cosmic interference—something like that. He mentioned something about solar flares, you know … from space, the sun. It's downright disconcerting, is what it is," she added, looking flustered.

Jackie remembered her own car radio acting up on the drive up from Knoxville.

The nurse motioned she should leave, and said, "If there's any change … we'll call. Go on home now, hon … get some rest."

★ ★ ★

Jackie headed for the hospital's front lobby exit, suddenly conscious she was wearing black, form-fitting gym pants and a purple Lycra sports top. A top revealing more than what was probably appropriate for these conservative southern surroundings. She repositioned her large handbag over her partially exposed cleavage. It hadn't been intentional garb. Hell, she was on her way to the gym—to work out—when she'd gotten the call from the on-duty nurse at Stone River Hospital.

She felt multiple eyes tracking her progress. A man, covered head to toe in mud—his arm held high up at an awkward angle—smiled a toothless grin in her direction. *Dislocated shoulder*, she thought. *Five will get you ten … the idiot was thrown from his ATV.*

"Jackie!"

She turned to see another Tennessee hayseed in the hospital lobby, waving enthusiastically at her, and figured it was someone she'd probably known in high school. She had zero interest in reconnecting with anyone from Woodbury. Flanked by an older, gray-haired woman, there was something about the young man's manner—his smile. His shirt was neatly buttoned to the collar, his face a mess. The guy had obviously been beaten within an inch of his life. *Wait … Could it be?* "Cuddy? Is that you?"

He awkwardly ran ahead of his mother, his arms outstretched. Jackie mirrored his smile, prepared for what was about to come. Taking her in his arms, he raised her high off the floor then swung her around. Giving a sudden grunt, he quickly set her down, wincing at the pain he'd caused himself.

"Cuddy … is that really you?" she asked with genuine excitement.

He nodded sheepishly. "I saw you. I knew it was you. I said to myself … that's my best friend in the whole world. That's Jackie!"

Joining them, Mrs. Perkins looked pleased to see her, too.

She gave Jackie a hug, then pushed her an arm's length away and held her there. "What are you doing back here? Why aren't you at school, dear?"

Jackie let out a sigh. Looking back down the hallway that led to the room her father was in, she explained, "Dad … had a heart attack. I drove back here right from school."

"I'm so sorry. How is he doing? Is he going to be okay?" she asked.

"I think so. I hope so." Jackie's eyes became moist and she found it hard to swallow. She looked at Cuddy, who was still beaming at her. He'd gotten so big. Normally, she knew, he'd be handsome, except for that ridiculous, bowl-type haircut and those far too short *high-water* pants. Jackie wondered if it was no accident he looked like he did. That Mrs. Perkins helped dress him this way, sending a message to anyone who came in close proximity: *Back off, people—this boy is severely mentally challenged. Don't mess with him.*

"Where are you off to now, Jackie?"

"Home. To sleep."

"Tomorrow, you'll come over for dinner."

"Oh no, I'm not …"

"I insist, sweetie. I'm making pork chops."

"And smashed potatoes and leftover peach pie," Cuddy added.

Jackie smiled, then changed the subject. "What happened to you, Cuddy? Get run over by a herd of buffalo?"

Cuddy's face turned serious. "I got mugged. That's what Momma calls it. Mugged."

"By whom?"

"By Gary Wallahan and Tony Bone."

"I remember them both, went to my high school. They were bullies … mean bastards back then. Guess they still are. Is that why you're here … your injuries?"

Cuddy said, "I was bleeding … so I got a few more stitches added to my lip." He pointed to his still puffy-looking lips and the black Frankenstein-looking sutures. Jackie tried to remember the last time she'd seen Cuddy. It was years ago, when she'd first entered high school. Before then, for close to ten years, she'd been his best friend and protector. Her thoughts traveled back to the barn incident, when she was seven, and she, Kyle and Cuddy were playing up in the loft. Kyle was showing off, acting rowdy. She remembered him pushing Cuddy, who was seven, out of the way, as if it happened yesterday. Like seeing it again, taking place in slow motion, as Cuddy stumbled then fell backward, out into open space. His arms outstretched, as if he were reaching for her. She watched him land hard on his back, unmoving in front of the stall. He looked dead.

Seeing him now, she wondered if things would be different if he had grown up *normal*—what their relationship would be now? *Would they be friends? Something more?*

"We eat at six o'clock. Oh … and Kyle's back home. I'm sure he'd be happy to see you too."

Jackie was about to decline but thought better of it. She hated cooking for herself and being home alone at the farm didn't appeal to her in the slightest. "I'll try to make it. Thank you, six o'clock tomorrow. What should I bring?"

Mrs. Perkins shook her head. "Nothing. Just bring yourself. Maybe you can wear something more fitting; you know … for the ranch."

Jackie felt her cheeks flush and tugged her handbag higher across her chest.

Those around looked up as lobby lights again began to flicker, and car alarms resumed blaring noisily in the parking lot.

Chapter 9

Tow, spewing and retching, had vomited eleven separate times and counting. He wished there was a way to erase the last three hours and ten minutes from his memory. Even though the bodies were more like gelatinized masses—their internal, skeletal remains still gave them some physicality. Lormin, the captain, had been the worst to see—suffering the least amount of decomposition, he was the most recognizable. But he'd done it all, nevertheless. Scraped and cleaned up the remains of the seven entombed crewmembers, then buried their bodies in separate unmarked graves. Just thinking about it, he felt bile burn the back of his throat. Once inner and outer repairs to the starboard berth compartment were completed, Tow removed his fouled environmental suit and incinerated it.

Returning to the babbling brook site, Tow sat naked on a flat rock, watching the stream as it gently flowed past—errant twigs or leaves caught up in small, twirling eddies, only to be freed moments later to continue their journey.

A breeze suddenly kicked up and he felt its light coolness against his skin. Tree branches, thirty feet above, swayed and made a rustling sound. Tow was aware of the AI's subtle presence—always lurking within his psyche. He knew that the automated brain wanted to remind him of the impending disaster—one that would most assuredly occur if he didn't get himself moving.

He'd been alerted by the AI only the previous day that the Howsh's lead ship had entered into high orbit around Earth. Feelings of dread swept over him. Sitting there—nestled within the lush forest—he'd almost forgotten about his terrible plight. The other two Howsh ships, currently completing their terrestrial scans around Mars, would be following within the next day or two. Their hunt for the *Evermore* now elevated to a new level. If he kept the ship's propulsion system inactive, quieted, the odds of being discovered were lowered somewhat. On the other hand—to continue onward with his journey, his mission, while still able—he needed to hastily make the necessary repairs, which meant reinitializing the propulsion system.

Tow, inwardly musing and *stuck* in his head—approaching concerns from different angles—didn't notice a new presence nearby.

* * *

Cuddy missed Rufus. Looking down, expecting to see him by his side, he was reminded he'd been taken away—in the back of Officer Plumkin's police cruiser. Momma gave him some easy chores to do this morning—ones that didn't require heavy lifting due to his bruised ribs.

With breakfast eaten, his chores all done, he was now walking in the woods alone, and it wasn't the same. Typically, Cuddy liked talking to Rufus, even though the dog couldn't say anything back. He'd point out things that he found interesting, funny, or weird, and Rufus would look up at him like he understood. Rufus was a smart dog.

So right then, when Cuddy came upon the strangest oddity of all, he looked down to get Rufus's reaction. Disappointed—not seeing his dog's friendly face staring up at him—Cuddy brought his full attention to the oddity before him. Now remembering, he had seen him before … *the sad-looking angel in his dream? Or was it a dream?* It occurred to Cuddy that he might be in danger. The recent encounter with those two tough men near the railroad tracks had taught him a good lesson. One Momma had reminded him of only this morning: *Stay away from strangers!* But was this, *whatever it was*, a stranger? Strangers were people. Was this oddity an actual person? That didn't seem likely.

The *odd being* was sitting on a large rock, staring down at the water. Cuddy studied the glowing figure, keeping perfectly still, like when he watched a deer family's approach. The trick was to become quiet in both movement and thought. Cuddy watched the odd one's face, whose features weren't that different from anyone else's. But there seemed to be some sadness about him, and Cuddy wished he could alleviate his unhappiness. He wondered what was making *whatever it was* feel so sad.

"I get sad, too," Cuddy said. "Officer Plumkin took my dog."

The ghostly oddity looked up at him with surprise—with almost panic in his eyes. His mouth moved to speak but no words came out. Cuddy hadn't expected him to talk, any more than he did Rufus. Taking a tentative step forward, he said, "I sometimes sit on that same rock. Yup … right where you're sitting." Cuddy came within several paces then plopped himself down onto a patch of accumulated leaves and pine needles. He looked around the ground and plucked up a small twig. Using it to stir the water, he added, "My name is Cuddy. I think it means donkey in another country."

The oddity, seeming to have settled down a bit, nodded at that. "My name is Tow … from the lineage of *Pon*. You can call me Tow, if you like."

Cuddy stared at Tow for a long time. First of all, he wasn't one hundred percent sure that what he was seeing was real. Second, how could a ghost even speak to him? He said, "I didn't think ghosts could talk."

Tow pondered that one over. "I am not a ghost, Cuddy."

"Are you a person … like me?"

Tow shook his head no.

"Where are you from?"

Tow seemed to find that funny, because he smiled then looked upward, pointing to the sky.

Cuddy said, "An alien? Are you *funnin'* with me … because of my disability? My accident?"

"No Cuddy, I would not do that."

"Can I take you to meet my Momma? She's not far …"

"No, Cuddy. I do not want to be discovered … or found. Your presence here changes things. It puts me in danger."

"I'm sorry."

"I am too."

Cuddy nervously played with the twig for a while then looked over at Tow. "Where do you live? Do you have a house? Maybe underground … or up in a tree?"

Again smiling, Tow said, "I live in a spacecraft. One that has traveled many many miles before landing here on your world."

Cuddy's eyes went wide. "A spaceship? Seriously? Where is it? Can you show me?"

"Maybe later, but Cuddy … remember, I do not want to be found. If you told anyone, even your Momma, it would be very bad for me. People here would not understand."

"People don't understand me, either," Cuddy said. "Do people make fun of you, Tow? Do they say mean things? Laugh at you?"

"No, not for a long time. You see … I'm all alone now."

★ ★ ★

Tow's mind raced. He'd been reckless—reckless and selfish—jeopardizing the entire mission by his lackadaisical response to news of the approaching Howsh. The lack of pressure he'd placed on the AI orb to get the various ship systems up and running, so he could get the ship's propulsion system again operational. *And now he knew why.* He didn't want to leave this place. He wanted to stay—to simply give up—and become part of this world. Find his own unique place here amongst the white-tailed deer, the fox, and even the strange humans. But that would not be possible. Could never be possible. Looking across at the strange humanoid, with the childlike mind, he knew that.

Tow coughed, then coughed again. His chest burned somewhere deep within. Coughing again into his open palm, he studied the phlegm, noting its bluish mucous. Inexplicably, the time clock had started: the *Dirth.* Suddenly, he'd become symptomatic, with mere weeks to live. No, he would never reach Primara now—that was a certainty. Tow's mind turned to Soweng—as it often did when he was faced with his own mortality. Oddly enough, he found himself strangely at peace. Soon he would be with her again. *Or would he?* He was the last of his kind, the last *Pashier.* With his demise, who would add his essence to the heritage pod? For that matter, who would deliver the heritage pod to Primara?

With finite resolution, Tow's eyes settled onto Cuddy's inquiring face. There was much work to do and little time to do it in.

The human spoke again, "Are you … are you an angel?"

"No, Cuddy, I am not. But what I can be is your friend."

Chapter 10

They walked together in the forest. Birds sang their musical tweets and hidden insects chirped in unison.

Cuddy pointed. "That's a squirrel … up there on the tree branch. Do you have squirrels where you come from?"

"Something similar … called *yeemics*," Tow said, watching the small rodent scurry up the tree to a higher branch. He found the human to be both earnest and likable, and wondered if he'd ever encountered another being so void of malice—such a genuinely good soul. But he would have to tread carefully here. Push too hard and he'd alienate the simpleton—jeopardize not only himself, but all *Pashier* to a bleak fate. He thought about the word … *fate*. What he was contemplating would dramatically alter the life of this young savage. *Would it be for the better?* There was no clear answer to that. His life would become far more complicated, that was for certain.

Cuddy stopped in his tracks with an audible inhalation of breath, spotting the *Evermore* up ahead, nestled in the clearing.

"A spaceship!"

"That is right, Cuddy. It is called the *Evermore*."

"You were telling the truth! And it's so … big!"

Tow watched Cuddy grow somewhat hesitant to move closer.

"Perhaps this is close enough,"Tow said."If you are scared that's perfectly fine, Cuddy."

"I'm not scared. I'm …"

"It's all right, Cuddy.You are looking at something, I suspect, no one else on your world has ever seen. It is okay to be overwhelmed. Now could be the time for you to return home." Tow inwardly hoped the human would rebuff the suggestion.

"Maybe you're right. I am kinda getting hungry."

"Yes … good idea. I'm going to have my lunch, as well," Tow said. An AI-derived suggestion informed him the humanoid would be inclined to stay if a certain type food was offered him."I will be having grilled cheese sandwiches and tomato soup. Have you heard of such a meal … here on Earth, Cuddy?"

Cuddy looked at Tow with astonishment."That's my very favorite. Momma makes the best grilled cheeses. Do you want to come over to my house for lunch?"

"No, Cuddy. As I told you before, no one can know of my existence here. It would be dangerous for me."

Cuddy's expression relayed the fact that he'd forgotten that but now remembered."Can I eat lunch with you … in your spaceship?"

"Well, I don't know. I guess that will be all right."

⋆ ⋆ ⋆

Tow set upon the AI orb the task of configuring the galley food replicator for making the ultimate grilled cheese sandwich and tomato soup. A meal that sounded ghastly to the alien—but seemed a small price to pay.

As they approached, the side hatchway slid open then

disappeared into the hull as the gangway extended outward toward them. This was a crucial point—the human could decide to reconsider entering the alien ship.

Tow said, "I hope you don't mind. The way I make a grilled cheese is with strips of cooked bacon. Have you ever tried that, Cuddy?"

Again, Cuddy's eyes went wide.

* * *

Cuddy followed the glowing white figure up the angled plank, noticing for the first time the alien limped. Stepping inside, Cuddy hesitated—finding it hard to take everything in at once. The spaceship's futuristic interior was different from any he'd seen on TV, or in space movies, but then again there was some similarity. It was very spacious. He wondered how it could be so much bigger on the inside than it appeared on the outer. He also wondered if he should leave right now, as Momma would probably disapprove of him being here.

"I wish Rufus was here to see this," Cuddy said, as he panned the space before him. A myriad of soft blinking lights glowed, and much of the spaceship's interior seemed to be made of chrome and glass. What looked like floating television screens hovered in the air, and everything was so clean. Self-consciously, he glanced down at his mud-caked Keds.

"They are fine, Cuddy. Your soiled shoes will not be a problem. Come this way … lunch is ready. I hope you like vanilla ice cream, too; it is my favorite dessert," Tow casually added.

Cuddy, becoming overwhelmed—to the point he didn't really know what to think, or say, or how to act—followed Tow through the interior of the ship that he figured was nearing the back. Tow then motioned that he should follow him down a circular series of glass steps. Hearing Tow cough several times, he wondered if the alien was catching a cold.

Momma would smother his chest with that awful-smelling Vicks VapoRub and send him to bed.

"This is what's called the ship's galley, Cuddy. It's like a kitchen. Go ahead and have a seat at the table and I'll bring your lunch over to you."

Cuddy eyed the flat, crystal-clear surface and, leaning sideways to see beneath it, said, "There's no legs!"

Tow followed Cuddy's gaze and smiled. "You are correct, there are no table legs—they are not necessary on this spaceship. Sit!"

Cuddy did as told and watched the alien move around the strange-looking kitchen. Bringing a tray over, he placed it in front of Cuddy, who watched Tow's expression—he looked unsure of himself. The tray held a plate with a large golden-brown sandwich atop it. Sliced in half, corner to corner, the toasted bread was thick—bright yellow cheese oozed out from inside. Cuddy spied the ends of bacon strips poking out the two halves. On a separate plate, a bowl contained what looked like steaming hot, dark red-orangey tomato soup.

Cuddy didn't hesitate. Grabbing one of the halves, he bit into the center of the sandwich. He chewed for a moment, as if assessing it. It was perfect—the most perfect sandwich he'd ever tasted. Even better than Momma's, but he wouldn't tell her that.

Tow left, returning with a strange-looking spoon that he placed next to the bowl of soup. "You are going to need that, I imagine," he said.

The alien stood by and watched him eat, which was kinda weird. But then Momma did that pretty often too—so he let it go. "Are you going to eat, Tow?"

"Not right now." Tow took a seat next to Cuddy and made a serious face then asked, "Would you let me do you a favor?"

"I don't know. What?"

"It would only take fifteen minutes."

"What kind of favor?"

"Would you let me heal the injuries on your lip and cheeks? After you finish your lunch."

"I don't know … they'll get better on their own. I hurt myself all the time. Things get better if I don't pick at them, or do something stupid to re-hurt them."

As Tow continued to stare back at him, it became apparent this was important to the glowing alien. The truth was, his split lips almost always hurt, especially when he laughed or tried to whistle for Rufus. And even now as he bit into the sandwich. "I guess it would be okay."

Tow brought over a small bowl of ice cream drenched in hot chocolate syrup.

★ ★ ★

Tow felt as if he might throw up again. After tasked with the collapsed sleeping berths, the smell of the foul human food was enough to put him over the edge. He quickly tried to think of other things, like what was at stake here. He looked across the wellness chamber to where Cuddy now sat.

"What am I supposed to do?" Cuddy asked.

"Simply sit there."

"Why?"

"I told you, so your lip and cheek can be repaired."

"By just sitting here? That's ridiculous!"

"It may seem that way to you, Cuddy."

Cuddy reached a hand up and touched his lip. With a furrowed brow, he pressed his fingers down somewhat harder. Looking over to Tow, he said, "I guess it hurts a bit less than it did before."

"Yes … we'll give it another ten minutes, then we're done until next time."

"Next time?"

"Yes. Your face will be all better today, but I wanted to ask you an important question."

"Okay … just ask me."

"You'll need to think long and hard before answering," Tow said.

Cuddy waited for the question.

"What would you say if I told you I could make you really smart, like you never had that accident happen … when you were younger?" Tow watched the young human's expression. Cuddy's eyes looked away—unfocussed—as he thought about the question. Balancing things out the best he could in his growth-stunted mind. Earlier, Tow had decided this deception would only go so far, and that hereafter he would attempt to be ethical. He wouldn't be like the Howsh—a wrecker of divergent life forms.

In truth, the healing process to Cuddy's brain began as soon as he took a seat within the wellness chamber. Invisible manipulations were occurring—faster than thought—faster than the speed of light. His brain matter was being reconstituted; first to a reference point dictated by human DNA indices, then to that of the superior *Pashier* physiology. But Cuddy would need several other sessions. The effects from a single session would hardly be noticeable. But with that said, Tow was unfamiliar with human physiology, knowing only that humans had large brains. Even larger than Pashier's.

Tow watched Cuddy fiddle with his untied shoelaces and sadness tugged his heart. This man-boy child was actually no longer completely human. Even now, he had become a different being and would never again be quite the same. Tow instantly regretted his subversive action. In principle, was he any different than the Howsh? *What have I done?*

Cuddy suddenly straightened up and leaned back in his seat—his brows pulled together. "I don't know what is happening to me … I don't like what is going on … in my head. I want it back the way it was, Tow. Make it the way it was!"

Tow watched as Cuddy brought his fists up to both sides

of this head and started to pound against his skull in a staccato rhythm.

Tow moved quickly—kneeling down in front of Cuddy. He took hold of his fists. "Stop … Cuddy … it will get better … I promise. Just give it a little time." But Tow wasn't sure his words were, in fact, true. *What have I done?*

Tow watched as Cuddy's anger turned to fear—fear along with a confluence of other emotions. Tow hadn't thought he could feel any worse, but now seeing the tears streaming down Cuddy's cheeks, he realized he was wrong.

Abruptly, Cuddy stood up. Seemingly disoriented, he looked around the confined space—panic increasing with each hurried breath. "I want out … I want out!"

Tow hurried to the control panel and got the hatch open. Cuddy ran like a scared wild animal released from a cage.

Chapter 11

Tony Bone gave it one more shake and left the toilet bowl unflushed. Turning around, he came face to face with himself as he studied his reflection in the dirty mirror. Two long strips of medical tape were on his nose—one high up at the bridge, one lower, near midway. His nose was purple and looked twice its normal size—both nostrils plugged with gauze. Now, in order to breathe, he had to inhale through his mouth, so his jaws were always ajar. He knew it made him look retarded and instantly thought of Cuddy Perkins. He felt anger rise up and hatred. *That big mother fucker is going to die for this …*

He exited the bathroom, zipping up his fly.

"I can't even look at you without getting annoyed, boy."

"Christ … come on! Leave it alone, Dad," Tony said, plopping down into the middle of the sofa.

He watched as his father in the kitchen tilted his large head back, swallowing the last dregs in his coffee cup. Setting the cup down in the sink, he gave Tony a sideways glance. "Hey … you don't take the Lord's name in vain in my house." His father buckled his thick black holstered belt around his hips then continued, "… I'm just saying, boy, it's all over the damn station."

Tony shut his eyes and groaned. He'd already heard the same shit the night before. How the Woodbury Police Station buzzed with what had happened. How the retarded Perkins kid broke the sheriff kid's nose. The problem was the station did double-duty—was both a police station and a jailhouse. So the inmates, mostly drunks sleeping it off from a night-before bender, wouldn't shut up about it. The one person you didn't want to taunt in the town of Woodbury was Sheriff Bone, his father. He had no sense of humor. None.

"I sent Plumkin out there to collect the boy, but he came back with the damn dog instead. I want you and Gary to submit formal, written complaints, so get your asses into the station this morning, understand?"

Tony watched the Sheriff of Woodbury collect his uniform-matching, khaki-colored wide-brimmed hat from the countertop, then secure it atop his bald head. Without the hat, he was already tall—close to six-five. With it on, he looked like a freakin' giant.

"Did you hear me, Tony?"

"I heard you, Dad. I'll call Gary. See what's happening."

* * *

Tony listened as his father's cruiser drove away. There was no way he was going to file any kind of written statement. He was already the butt of too many jokes. Putting in a formal police complaint would label him the world's all-time biggest pussy. A pussy smacked around by the town idiot who then went crying to his daddy. No thank you. Tony had his own, far more effective, plan in the works.

A knock came at the door.

"Come on in … dickwad."

Gary opened the door, sauntered in, and sat down in a

chair opposite the couch. Tony's friend said, "You look like shit on a stick."

"Thanks. Bring what I asked?"

"Yeah … but why my dad's?"

"Because your dad's not the fucking sheriff. Your dad won't even notice it's gone from his closet. How often do shit-haulers use a gun?"

"Don't call him that! He's a Septic Engineer."

Tony laughed out loud. "That's the funniest thing I've heard all day. Septic Engineer!"

"Screw you," Gary retorted back. "And why do we need it? I'm not going to prison because you have a hard-on for the Perkins kid."

"I told you, it's just for backup. To scare him a bit."

Gary shrugged. "I don't know about this ... Tony."

⋆ ⋆ ⋆

They knew he wasn't home. Earlier, they'd snuck onto the property—crept up to the back of the Perkins' house—and peeked in the windows. The old lady was inside and so was the older brother, Kyle. Tony remembered he'd just gotten out of jail. But the idiot boy was nowhere around.

After that, they drove up and down the winding two-track lane, looking for the big moron. Leaving the sleepy town behind, they drove south along the road, eventually slowing down at the high school. Both were drunk as skunks and hazy-eyed. Gary burped, letting the truck's engine idle as they sat for another ten minutes in the faded-green F150's hot cab. When Tony moved his feet empty Keystone beer cans clanged together. "It's hotter than hell in here," he said, "maybe we should just forget it."

"Wait … I think he sometimes hangs out with those two old blackies down the road. I think I've seen him there when I'm driving by."

"Well, what are you waiting for? Cruise on by … we'll take a quick look."

Gary moved the gear selector into Drive and slowly eased the truck forward, unsure which house was theirs.

"Slow down … I think it's that one there on the left with the leaning mailbox."

Gary, pulling into the drive, did a wide U-turn so his truck would face back in the same direction. Then, after shutting the ignition off, they climbed out of the truck.

Tony looked around the cluttered-looking property then did a double take, spotting a corrugated steel shed off to the side—its sliding door opened-up wide. Tony liked old cars and he was surprised to see the front end of a true old classic, sitting in there with its hood up.

Tony and Gary, neither one capable of walking a straight line, moved closer to the house. An old black man with a crown of silver hair sat on the shaded porch in a rocking chair. He stopped rocking as they approached. "What you two want?"

Tony said, "You know who I am? You know who my father is?"

The old man answered, "No and no. Should I?"

A screen door swung open and a ginormous black woman, wearing a bright red apron, stepped out. "What the hell you want? Get your skinny white asses off my property now!"

Tony recognized her—Elma White. The elderly man was her husband Rutherford, or something like that.

She towered over them, holding an industrial-size metal dustpan clenched in her fist. Raising it higher, she snarled, "Go on … get off my property. I'm not going to say it again!"

Gary said, "Easy there, Elma … we're just looking for a friend of ours. You know Cuddy? Cuddy Perkins, don't you?"

"What you need that boy for? He wants nothing to do with the likes of you two. Now go on … get going before I call the police."

Tony didn't particularly like Negros. Or Mexicans. Or the Asians. And don't get him even started on the camel jockeys. Or anyone not white. Especially when they didn't know their proper place and got uppity, like this big black bitch.

Tony lifted the front of his shirt, revealing the butt end of a Smith and Wesson .45 tucked into the waistband of his pants. "I am the police and I've had as much lip from you as I'm going to take." He watched as Elma took in the gun; seeing it finally shut her up. *Good.*

"I don't know nothin'. That boy ain't come around here for a few days now."

Tony said, "What about you, Uncle Tom? You see the boy around here lately?"

The old man spat something brown onto the porch and leaned back in his chair. Staring down at it for a few moments, he said, "I ain't seen nothin'."

Tony's head hurt. Too many cheap beers drunk in the hot sun and now one too many people disrespecting him: First his father this morning and now these two spooks. He pulled the gun from his pants, letting his arm hang loosely at his side. Gary eyed him warily but didn't say anything.

Tony said, "The next time I come around here, you're going to show me a bit more respect." He lifted the nickel-plated semi-automatic pistol and pointed it at the old man's face. Closing one eye, he lined the gun's sight between Rutherford's staring eyes. Tony smiled, *finally* the old man looked frightened. *That's a start.* He moved his aim slightly to the left, toward a closed window, and pulled the trigger. An incredibly loud *crack* echoed outward onto the distant plains. Elma screamed, and the old man flinched as he twisted away sideways from the now-shattered window. His eyes were tightly clenched shut and Elma was whimpering. Tony had another idea. "Come on, let's just go," Gary said.

Tony pointed at his nose. "I told you, I can't allow this to go unanswered." He smiled—discovering one more way to screw with the Perkins … the retard's family. "Old man, that car over in the shed."

The old man stared back at him. "What about it?" he said, then glanced toward the old shed and his pride and joy—a fifty-year-old Ford Mustang.

"It still drivable?"

When Rutherford hesitated Tony raised the gun. "Uh … somewhat; rear brake shoes need replacing."

Tony, still feeling exhilarated after pulling the trigger on Gary's father's gun, smiled. "We're gonna be borrowing it … for a day or two. You don't mind, do you?"

"Like hell I don't," Rutherford said, getting to his feet.

"Sit back down!" Tony barked. He looked up toward the second story, counting five small windows. He raised his arm and aimed at the one farthest away, then pulled the trigger five times: *bang* … *bang* … *bang* … *bang* … *bang* and all five windows across the front of the house exploded into shards. Elma dropped her dustpan and screamed into her hands, "Stop! Please stop! What do you want? What do you want from us?" sobbing in fear.

With no other word, Tony headed toward the shed and the old Mustang. Over his shoulder, he said, "You can report the car stolen but don't mention our visit today. You have no idea who took it, understand? I'm sure you don't want us coming back here."

Elma was still sobbing, clearly terrified. "Just take it. Leave us alone."

Gary hurried after Tony and grabbed him by the arm. In a hushed voice he asked, "What the holy fuck are you doing?"

Tony, walking toward the old car, slapped the gun into Gary's stomach. "You take the truck. Oh … and did you bring any more bullets for this thing?"

"Yeah … some. But why'd you take the old man's ride? We already have transportation."

"Don't be such an idiot, Gary. This is the exact same model … maybe even the same year that retard's brother, Kyle, stole … guy's got a hard on for old mustangs. Just try to keep up, man … we'll take the Mustang and drive it into Crowley Lake. I'll text my dad that I saw Kyle driving it around town. Put big brother right back in jail again."

Chapter 12

Jackie was running behind—started doing the chores too late around the farm. She actually managed to crack the books earlier this morning, but it had been a feeble attempt. She couldn't concentrate. Everything she read, she knew she'd have to reread again later.

Her chores included gathering eggs from the chicken coop, milking the fatter-than-remembered cow Hilda, and cleaning out Dad's disgusting refrigerator. After taking her third shower of the day, she almost called Mrs. Perkins to decline her invitation for dinner—explaining that she wasn't up to socializing—with her dad in the hospital, and all. But her dad was doing surprisingly well and she really wanted to see Cuddy again. Over the course of the day she found herself thinking about him on and off. How losing touch with him over the last seven or eight years—ever since she'd entered high school then gone off to college—how she'd unknowingly lost a part of herself. What that was exactly … she wasn't sure.

The drive over to the Perkins' ranch was a ten-minute trek across mostly packed dirt roads. She had the top down on her yellow 2011 Volkswagen Beetle and wore an Atlanta Braves baseball cap to hold her long hair in place. A warm Tennessee breeze flowed nicely in and out of the convertible. It was times like these when she most appreciated coming home to the small town of Woodbury. Sure, it was poor and backwoodsy, with practically nothing to do for a modern Millennial like her … yet there was something decent here. Woodbury was true and honest, had never claimed to be anything it wasn't. Cruising down the one stop-sign town, you could get a sense of its humble Americana roots, and there was something comforting about that. Its lack of pretense—*take me as I am* sentiment.

The early evening sky had turned brilliant amber and pink atop darkening cornflower blue. From horizon to horizon, a pallet of vivid colors excited her vision. She couldn't recall anything even close to being so beautiful. Her analytical mind knew that the colors were derived from refracted light, coming off particles in the atmosphere. Since there was no real industry around there to speak of … no smog … where did those lofty particles come from? *Perhaps blown in from Memphis?*

Slowing, she turned off Beacham Road onto the Perkins' rolling, cratered driveway. Twice, she felt the Bug's undercarriage bottom-out—*clunk … clunk.*

Up ahead was the old ranch house, and the dilapidated barn off to the left. Coming back was like going back in time. She recalled a hand pump for watering next to a horse trough, just beyond the wraparound front porch. Skirting a massive pothole, she remembered there used to be chickens running around all over the place, and even a few goats. Now, the old ranch looked deserted. If it weren't for Momma's old car, parked in front of the house, Jackie could have sworn nobody lived there anymore.

Momma Perkins did what she could with what she had, which wasn't much. Jackie suspected they lived on whatever the state doled out to her. Having a disabled child maybe helped with that some, she supposed, and she knew Momma also took on odd jobs, using her old Singer sewing machine. Six years ago, her late husband, whom everyone called Hash, was struck by lightning while standing on the barn roof during a rainstorm, leaving family members to pretty much fend for themselves. Jackie wondered how they'd even managed—by the looks of things *not very well.*

Jackie braked to a stop and turned off the car. She grabbed the basket of eggs from the passenger seat, opened up the door and climbed out. Waving away disturbed-up dust and dirt, she headed for the house.

"And she comes bearing gifts too," a deep voice said from the porch. She'd expected to see Cuddy. Child-like, she remembered him in past years, waiting at the end of the drive, waving like a maniac.

"You're back," she said, handing Kyle the basket of fresh chicken eggs. He looked as she remembered—a little older, perhaps, and a little rougher around the edges—still wearing the same old olive-green Army jacket he always wore, with his first initial and last name stenciled in black letters on the upper left pocket. His hair was longer and his eyes portrayed a young man who'd lost hope in ever finding a meaningful future.

She watched his eyes rove up and down her body. Found buried in a drawer, she'd pulled on a pair of old faded jeans, unworn since high school, but pleased they still fit her. Suddenly self-conscious, she gave Kyle a friendly punch on the shoulder suspecting that he too was reflecting back on their one night of intoxicated wild abandonment. She had that single indiscretion with Kyle years ago, which she instantly regretted. Regretted, because she felt she'd somehow betrayed Cuddy—her childhood friend who loved her. Loved her in a way that was purely innocent, but nevertheless just as real. She'd made it clear to Kyle that their intimate time together was a one-time mistake, which she wished had never happened. Hurting Cuddy would never be an option for her.

"Yeah … back after one year, seven months, and three weeks, but who's counting?"

Jackie glanced back toward her car. "Should I hide my car keys?"

He gave her a crooked smile. "Truth is, I wouldn't need 'em. But I think you're safe. There's not another car on the planet that screams chick-mobile more than a VW bug. I bet you even have a flower sticking out of the little bud vase on the dash."

"Well, yes I do, as a matter of fact. A plastic daisy."

"Is that Jackie?" a woman's voice asked inside the screen door.

"It's me. Something smells awfully good in there." Jackie added, "I'll have you know, I've been doing ranch work all day long and the only thing that kept me going was the thought of some good ol'-fashioned Southern cooking."

Momma Perkins swung wide the screen door, propping it open with a foot, then spread out her arms to give Jackie a hug. "Come on in, dear …"

Jackie caught her tight, artificial smile. The tension reflected off the older woman's face was unmistakable.

* * *

The two women stood at the kitchen window, looking outdoors. Momma Perkins had turned down the burners on the stovetop. Tinfoil loosely covered an assortment of pots and pans.

"When he didn't come home for lunch I started worrying. Especially in lieu of what happened to him a few days back." Her arms were wrapped about her.

Jackie put a reassuring arm around Momma's broad shoulders and squeezed. "I'm sure the big goofball's simply lost track of time."

"Don't think so. Last few days … without Rufus … he's been moping around something awful. Seeing you was the most excited I've seen him get. He wouldn't be late, not with you coming here tonight. No … I'm afraid he's met up with those two wretched boys again …"

Jackie was worried too but didn't let on. She glanced over at Kyle, sitting at the kitchen table in the process of lighting up a cigarette. He didn't look particularly worried.

"Put that out! You know there's no smoking in the house," Momma scolded.

Kyle shrugged but did as asked. "I went looking for him, but Cuddy's been wandering around this countryside since he first learned to walk. Could be anywhere."

"Get out there and look again!" Momma shouted.

Kyle looked up, startled, his eyes shifting between his mother and Jackie. "Fine …" he said.

"No wait," Momma said, "I see him. And I have a good mind to take a switch to him, damn worrisome child."

Jackie, the first one out the door, watched Cuddy hurrying. He looked up and smiled. Smiling, ready to wave back, her hand stopped mid-motion as Cuddy drew closer. There was something peculiar about the way he looked, though it could be her imagination.

Chapter 13

While Momma stood at the stove, filling each plate with a pork chop, a mound of mashed potatoes, and a scoop of steamed sliced carrots, Jackie carried the plates over and set them around the table. She heard Cuddy, cleaning up in the bathroom. The faucet then turned off and the bathroom door opened. She wondered if Momma too noticed something different about Cuddy.

The screen door opened, then slammed shut as Kyle walked in. "That sky … it's … crazy weird-looking. The nag is acting skittish, too … something's got her all riled up."

Jackie turned around, gazing out the window toward the barn, and caught the last vestiges of dusk before nighttime took hold. The sky was still ablaze with color—with added hues now of sparkling gold and violets.

"She'll settle down. What she needs is to be let out of that stall tomorrow. You know animals can go stir-crazy too … just like people," Momma replied, wiping her hands on a dishtowel.

"Claustrophobic."

At first, Jackie thought it was Kyle who spoke, then realized he was already seated at the table, using a fork prong to clean a fingernail. Curious, she looked at Kyle, then toward the entrance into the hallway. No, it was Cuddy; he'd spoken from the hallway.

Momma said, "That's disgusting! Stop doing that at the table, Kyle." He merely shrugged and winked at Jackie.

Jackie looked up as Cuddy entered the kitchen and noticed his face was washed and he was wearing a clean plaid shirt. He then took a chair directly across from her own.

"Hi Jackie," he said, giving her a broad smile.

"Hi Cuddy … good to see you again. So where did you go off to today?"

"I just goofed around … out in the woods," he said.

"He's always in the woods," Kyle said. "Never understood what's so fascinating about it."

Momma, sitting down at Cuddy's left, took his hand in hers then reached over and took Jackie's hand, who then took Kyle's, and he took Cuddy's—completing the handholding circle.

"You can give thanks to the Lord tonight, Kyle," Momma told him, though he wasn't paying attention, staring at his brother instead. Irritated, Momma glanced at Cuddy.

Jackie took it all in. Cuddy's bowled haircut no longer formed a straight line across his forehead, since he'd moistened it and pushed it off to the side. His multiple injuries—the sutured split lips and cheek, all the bruising—were almost completely healed. *How is that possible?* Jackie thought back to the day before, seeing him at the hospital, when he looked like he'd been run over by a truck.

"I think I can say Grace tonight," Cuddy said, looking over to Momma. She hesitantly nodded and said, "Well … okay …"

Cuddy swallowed, and then began, "God, we thank you for this food. For rest and home and all things good. For wind and rain and the sun above. But most of all for those we love."

He smiled—looking pleased with himself. "That's the prayer Momma almost always says. Before, I never *remembered* the right words to say … before today."

Momma stared at Cuddy, speechless for several moments. "That was … beautiful, son. I'm proud of you." Somewhat unsettled, she reached down for her knife and fork as Kyle did the same, every so often glancing over at his brother.

Jackie knew Cuddy's face well, but something seemed *different* … She took in the two-or-three-day stubble on his cheeks and chin, also his open shirt—now unbuttoned at the neck—exposing a few errant chest hairs. From what she could remember, Cuddy always buttoned his shirts up to the neck. Had that habit *changed* over recent years? Then she thought back to how he was dressed yesterday. No, he never left buttons unbuttoned. Not thinking some miracle had occurred, nothing like that, but the Cuddy she now sat across from no longer seemed, at least mentally, seven years old.

★ ★ ★

"I'm beyond starving!" Cuddy said, putting an oversized slice of pork chop into his mouth. As he chewed, he thought about the afternoon he'd spent in the woods, about his promise to the alien man. He really wanted to tell them—Momma, Kyle, and Jackie—all about him. Keeping the secret inside was driving him crazy. He wasn't upset anymore, and now felt bad about how he'd acted—had overreacted. His brain—his thoughts seemed to have calmed down substantially. Cuddy smiled as he thought about first seeing the white glowing man, standing by the brook, and then his experiences within the … *what did he call it? Oh yeah, the wellness chamber.* Truth was, they wouldn't believe him anyway. No way.

Cuddy looked out, over Jackie's left shoulder, to the darkness beyond, wondering if the alien was still out there—somewhere—right now, maybe watching them eat their dinner?

Cuddy noticed Jackie studying him across the table. Her narrowed eyes were searching his face. He smiled at her, noticing how pretty she was. No, she was beautiful.

"Boy … is everything all right?" Momma asked, her voice almost a whisper.

"I'm good, Momma. Why?" His mouth full of mashed potatoes, he stared back at her, then asked, "Why are you all staring at me that way? Is something on my face?" Setting his fork down, he swiped at his cheeks with his palms.

"There's nothing on your face, Cuddy," Jackie said. "You just look very handsome tonight."

★ ★ ★

Within the confines of the musky-smelling barn—where it was dark and the big horse repeatedly hoofed at the ground—Tow watched the four humans eat their meal.

Cuddy's session today, within the wellness chamber, had been brief, but the physical transformation would not go unnoticed by the others. *How could it?* But Tow was even more concerned with Cuddy's altered mental state. He didn't know the human well enough to make a comparison—*before, and after,* the session. Perhaps the chamber did not affect humans in the same manner.

Tow closely watched their faces, trying to interpret their expressions. He wondered if Cuddy was acting differently now than what was expected? Acknowledging the AI's voice in his head, he listened to what it had to say:

"Looking at the relevant data, human physiology is quite complex. Their brains are larger than the Pashier's … much of it still not utilized at this point in their evolution."

"That sounds encouraging," Tow said.

"Yes, but you took a risk … taking this one called Cuddy into the wellness chamber. How he will respond, over time, is indeterminate. You are assuming much. Session times …

intensity levels … more testing would have been wise."

"You are right. But there is no more time. The Howsh are here."

"Their scans may not detect the *Evermore*'s whereabouts, at least not for some time," the AI said.

Strobing blue and red lights were approaching in the near distance—two internal combustion vehicles. Tow watched as first one, then the other, turned into the driveway and headed toward the human's domicile. After coming to a stop, with the engines turned off, the bright lights continued to flash.

Chapter 14

"What the hell do they want?" Kyle asked, getting to his feet.

Momma and Cuddy came around the table to peer out the window. They watched as Sheriff Dale Bone climbed out of his four-door Crown Vic while Officer Plumkin Richards, simultaneously, climbed out of his SUV. Both vehicles had large italicized blue letters—POLICE—stenciled across their sides.

Jackie said, "Ugh, I knew plumpy Plumkin back in high school. He was always a bit creepy … always the tough guy. Maybe it's something to do with his height." She looked over to Kyle, "Don't police departments have a height requirement?"

Kyle shrugged. "If they don't they should."

"Yeah, I mean, don't they have a strong image to project?" she added.

Cuddy watched the two policemen come around their vehicles to speak to one another. The voice of a woman dispatcher could be heard, coming from inside both patrol cars.

"Sheriff … third call tonight. Ruby Johnson insists she's

seen a UFO. Wants to know when you can send a car over."

Plumkin tipped his head sideways and spoke into his shoulder mic: "Gale, we're on important police business here. Just tell Ruby to cool her jets. Unless little green men are coming through her doors and windows, it might be morning before we can get back to her."

"Ten Four … I'll let her know."

Momma looked at Kyle accusingly. "Why are they here? What's this about?"

Kyle said, "How the hell should I know? I've been here since I got out of bed this morning. You know … I'm not always up to no good …"

Three heavy knocks pounded on the door.

"Stay right there. Let me deal with this," Momma said, taking a deep breath and squaring her shoulders—exchanging her irritated expression for one of innocent bewilderment. She then walked out of the kitchen.

Cuddy heard the screen door open and Momma say, "Sheriff? Plumkin? What brings you two out this time of night?"

"Ma'am … sorry for the late hour. I need to ask, is your son here?"

"Cuddy? Of course he's here. Been here all day."

"No, I mean Kyle, ma'am."

"Well, he's here too. But I don't understand what you'd want him …"

"Mrs. Perkins, I'm sorry, but we're here to take Kyle in for questioning. Into custody. Please call him to come on out, we're not looking for trouble. This can go as easy as he makes it."

"Not until you tell me what's going on, Dale," Momma demanded.

"Another car's been stolen," the sheriff said.

" … A sixty-five Mustang. Same make and model Kyle snitched from Dr. Howard over a year ago. That's a pretty big coincidence, don't you think?" Plumkin asked.

"I don't know anything about cars. Why don't you come inside? I'm sure there's a simple explanation."

"Sure … for a minute, Mrs. Perkins, but we're taking Kyle into custody. Please go get him. We really don't want any trouble," the sheriff said.

Still seated at the table, Cuddy and Kyle exchanged a questioning glance. Jackie said, "I've got an idea!"

Both looked at her, somewhat startled. Kyle shook his head. "What are you going to do?" he whispered, with a sideways expression, attempting to look menacing.

Jackie hurried over to the sink, wetting down her hair under the faucet. She pointed to Kyle and mouthed the words: "*Hurry … get your hair wet.* You too, Cuddy, and maybe button up your shirt."

⋆ ⋆ ⋆

Hair wet, Cuddy came around the corner into the foyer, wearing his most engaging smile, and enthusiastically waved at both the sheriff and Officer Plumkin. The sheriff, as tall as Cuddy, though fifty pounds heavier and forty years older, did a poor job hiding his annoyance.

"Kyle and I went to Hollow Pond today, Sheriff," Cuddy said. "Taught me how to do the dog paddle. Ya know, like a dog does when it swims. Have you ever been to Hollow Pond, Sheriff? Do you like to swim? Have you swung on the rope with the stick tied on the end?"

The sheriff held up his palms. "Cuddy … we're here on police business. Maybe best if you go to your room for a while. We're here for your brother Kyle."

Kyle chose that moment to come around the corner, with Jackie right behind him. Both heads of hair were dripping wet, though she was drying hers with a towel.

"Oh … hi there, Sheriff and hi, Plumkin," Jackie said,

giving an easy smile. Her wet shirt revealed the outline of her breasts and two erect nipples. Innocently, she raised her brow, "What's all the hubbub about?"

The sheriff averted his eyes while Officer Plumkin stared unabashedly at her chest. It seemed the sheriff, finally, was getting it: Pointing his finger at Kyle like a pistol—his thumb straight up and his forefinger extended—he asked, "What? You're telling me you were all together this afternoon?"

Cuddy, portraying only simplest innocence, watched Kyle and Jackie give Oscar-worthy performances. Momma, who Cuddy couldn't remember ever being anything but totally honest, simply stared at the Sheriff—not taking a stand either way. By the way he tilted his head and pursed his lips, Cuddy could tell Officer Plumkin wasn't buying it.

Plumkin pulled a set of handcuffs from the back of his utility belt and said, "Look, we have zero doubt you had something to do with this, Kyle. You've been spotted out and about joyriding in the missing car. Add to the fact, the last time a car got stolen around here was when you nabbed it. Today, another car, the exact same make and model ..."

Momma jumped right in and said, "I don't care what kind of car was stolen, Kyle had nothing to do with it. What in God's name do you have against my family?" she asked indignantly. "First my youngest son is accused of something and now my eldest. Sheriff ... Dale ... My family, seems clear to me, is being harassed by your department. I'm telling you, you're barking up the wrong tree. And let me tell you this ... we live in a real small town where everyone knows everyone else. We stick together, Dale, and if I'm not mistaken, the Canyon County Sheriff is an elected position. Isn't that right?"

Deflated some, the sheriff then steadied his gaze on Jackie. "Miss, you willing to make an official statement down at the station that Kyle was with you today, between the hours of 1:00 p.m. and 3:00 p.m.?"

"Sure. Can I do that tomorrow?"

"That'll be fine," the sheriff said.

"Sheriff … I think they're lying. This is a cock-and-bull story if ever I heard one. We should take Kyle into—"

The sheriff turned on Plumkin. "You see this star here, Officer?" pointing to the tin badge on his chest.

Plumkin reluctantly nodded.

"Then put a sock in it and go get the dog. We've taken up enough of this family's time."

"Dog?" Cuddy asked. Coming from outside, he heard Rufus's familiar bark.

Chapter 15

The good news for Tow was that he hadn't gotten much worse. Physically, he was at least managing the disease, though emotionally his life was a different story. He had lapsed into a funk—an emotional, constricting struggle that continued to weigh heavily on his shoulders. As a *Pashier*, he was a pacifist. It was the way of his people. It was why no weapons would be found on the *Evermore*. Evolution of the *Pashier* race, over countless generations, had taught them violence only begot violence. He silently cursed himself for manipulating the young human. Tow reflected back several days to his wellness chamber session with Cuddy. In a sense, that too was a violent act; a conscious decision to alter the course of another being's life. What right did he have to do that? No one individual—no race of people—withstands the ravages of time indefinitely. In the end … there must be an end. Tow thought about the many thousands of individual essences constrained within the heritage pod below deck. What would they think of him now for his actions? He briefly wondered if that single act of selfishness was done more for his own gain, or for theirs. *Did it even matter?*

Sitting within the confines of the bridge, Tow turned in his chair and looked at the viewscape display. "Is this updated?" he asked.

The AI orb silently hovered around into view. "Yes, of course it is."

The icon-based representation of Earth also provided evidence of the encircling three Howsh warships, leaving little doubt they were closing in on a specific southern section of North America—the area where the *Evermore* had landed. The same three vessels had already traversed the planet numerous times. Their long- and short-range sensor scans had disrupted the planet's electrical fields. One effect—the atmosphere at dawn and dusk had blossomed into a kaleidoscope of beautiful colors. UFO sightings were becoming more and more commonplace. The alien vessels were mostly invisible to Earth humans' rudimentary technology, but when one of the Howsh ships swooped down low toward the surface—to investigate and make possible verifications—they were very much, albeit momentarily, visible to the naked eye.

Today, Tow planned to power up the ship and begin repairs on the damaged drive, aware he would have to deal with repercussions from his decision one way or another.

"Captain Tow?"

"Go ahead, AI."

"I have a suggestion … a temporary accommodation."

"Accommodation?"

"It may provide you with more time."

"Just tell me what you are referring to?" Tow said, his patience running thin.

"There are several nuclear power generating facilities in relatively close proximity to our current location. My suggestion is to instigate an emergency radioactive vent into the atmosphere. I can do that by interfacing directly with their Internet network."

"That sounds dangerous. No, I am not going to jeopardize the lives—"

"Captain Tow, the amount of radiation dispersed would be insignificant … miniscule; just enough to thwart the Howsh's sensor readings. Health risks to the population should not be a concern."

"I will consider the option. Basically, you are suggesting camouflaging the *Evermore*'s drive power signatures long enough for me to make repairs … to bring them back into balance."

"Yes, that is correct, Captain Tow."

Tow closed his eyes. More manipulations, with the possibility of harming local humans. He knew there was no way the AI orb could safely guarantee the non-effect of fallout long term. Yet there was still a bigger threat he had purposely avoided considering—the threat of Howsh ships attacking the planet the way they had Mahli—*relentless plasma strikes; dispersion of the Dirth.* No, he had to risk it—take the orb's suggestion, then leave this planet quickly, if only to save it.

Tow's musings were interrupted by the *Evermore*'s proximity alarm. Looking out the bridge observation window, he noted movement outside.

★ ★ ★

Rufus ran ahead into the clearing, barking nonstop upon seeing the spacecraft. The yellow Lab ran from one end of the vessel to the other, then back again. Cuddy called out to him but the dog kept barking.

"No! Rufus … stop that!"

Cuddy stepped away from the trees and into the morning sunlight, his eyes focused on the rectangular shape he knew to be the closed hatchway he'd entered the day before. Rufus, finally tiring of barking, joined Cuddy's side and sat down. "So, what do you think of that, boy?"

The gangway began to extend as the hatch door slid open.

Cuddy watched, waiting for the glowing man to appear, and then there he was, waving back.

Cuddy approached the ship, stopping after several paces to look back. Rufus hadn't moved—was staring intently at Tow.

"It's okay, boy … he's a friend. Come on …" Rufus then joined Cuddy, staying close by his side.

Tow waited for them at the bottom of the gangway. Cuddy took in Tow's face—his reaction to Rufus and to himself—so much had changed in such a short time.

Rufus, keeping low, edged forward and began sniffing Tow's feet.

Cuddy smiled. "It's okay—you should pet him; let him know you're not going to hurt him."

"Pet him?"

"Yeah … like this," Cuddy gave Rufus a couple of firm pats on his flank then petted his head.

Tow slowly moved his hand toward the dog, giving him the same combination of pats and pets. Rufus enthusiastically licked Tow's fingers.

"He likes you. You can tell by his wagging tail."

Rufus darted off to the right to grab a stick off the ground, then came back with it, dropping it at Tow's feet. Tow looked from the stick to the dog.

"He wants you to throw it."

"Throw it where?"

"I don't know … wherever you want. It's called *go fetch*."

Tow picked up the saliva-covered stick and tossed it twenty feet away. Rufus chased after it, grabbing it in his jaws, then ran back and dropped it at Tow's feet barking twice. Tow looked at Cuddy with a questioning expression.

"That's basically it. You throw it … he brings it back. For some reason, dogs find it fun. People do too."

Tow reached down for the stick but Rufus grabbed it first and ran off.

"He wants you to chase him," Cuddy said.

Tow stood tall and held Cuddy's stare. "Tell me about you, Cuddy. Tell me how things have been since you were here last."

Cuddy figured Tow would ask him something like that, and he had questions too … many questions. He felt bad for how he acted the last time he was here. That he had yelled at Tow. He had been scared and unprepared for his increased mental abilities. He had so many new thoughts now. Thoughts he'd never had before—different kinds. Part of him already missed the *old* Cuddy, the one that lived a far simpler existence. Living an unquestioning life, for the most part. Perhaps because he knew, on some level, that he wouldn't understand the explanation anyway. He understood better now, and he remembered things too. Not just events happening now, but also those in his past … as if all the broken wiring in his head had magically reconnected. But his new access to old thoughts and memories had come with some humiliation and embarrassment. Not knowing for sure if his mental disability was now a thing of the past, he only knew he never wanted people to look at him the old way again. With either annoyance or tolerance or, worst of all, pity. He'd come today for a reason, so it was important to say what needed to be said.

"I'm glad you are still here, Tow, and that you hadn't left in your spaceship."

Tow nodded at that, seeming to find it humorous, for some reason. Cuddy continued, "I want to thank you. I don't know exactly what you did, or how you did it, using that chamber thing, but you've given me a different life. A life I didn't know I even wanted."

"Is it a life you want now, Cuddy, or have I pushed you into some sort of new existence that was never meant to be yours? Does my question even make sense to you?" Tow asked.

Rufus was back, again dropping the stick at Tow's feet. Cuddy watched as the stick slowly rose into the air—all the way up to eye-level—then remained midair for several seconds before flying off. It was as if an invisible hand had tossed it into the trees. Rufus chased after it.

Cuddy could hardly believe what he'd just seen. He knew the alien was an amazing being, but this … "How did you do that, Tow?"

"The *Pashier* … have the ability to move matter with their minds. For two thousand years, my people—the Pashier—had continued to manipulate what is called our genome code, by enhancing a once-thought useless tiny organ, buried deep within the right section … what humans would call the parahippocampal gyrus. The Pashier have a very similar organ found, strangely enough, to influence psychokinetic abilities. What followed were thousands of subtle tweaks—over millennia—by the Kartinals. Revered—they were more like Gods than scientists to the Pashier."

Cuddy could see the sadness on the alien's face. "What happened to them?"

"The last of the Kartinals are gone. Massacred many years ago … but their essences were added to the heritage pod. At least, that is something."

"Well … maybe you can you teach me to move things with my mind, too?"

"Maybe, but I don't think your physiology would support …" he cut himself short. "We'll see, Cuddy. But now back to my question. Do you feel I have gone too far … repairing your disability?"

Cuddy could see that the question was important to Tow by the concern on his face. That he was having second thoughts—some doubt. "You have done a good thing, Tow, I promise. A really … *really* … good thing." Cuddy smiled and Tow smiled back.

"Can I ask you a question?"

"Of course, Cuddy, anything."

Cuddy looked up at the colorful sky. "Does what's happening up in the sky have anything to do with you?"

Chapter 16

"Indirectly, yes, Cuddy," Tow said, gazing up at the beautiful spectacle above the treetops. "I did not come here alone. I was pursued by three other spacecraft. By other aliens."

"Do they look like you … or maybe like me?"

"Neither. They are larger and covered with fur … like Rufus over there. And they are not friendly. In fact, they want to destroy the *Evermore*, me, and what lies within the lower deck of the ship."

"How come?"

"Their beliefs are complicated, Cuddy. For them, there is no room for both the *Pashier* and the Howsh to exist together in the universe. To exist anywhere."

"That is what they are called … the Howsh?"

"Yes, that is right."

"Then we should figure out a way to strike them first."

"That is not our way, Cuddy. It's not the way of the *Pashier*. We are pacifists. Do you know what that means?"

"No … not really."

"It means we do not use violence to resolve issues."

Cuddy seemed to consider that, then said, "Well, I'm not a

Pashier. I'm a human and I'm pretty sure it's always been our way to fight back when others are out to hurt us."

Tow, for some unknown reason, found that funny. He laughed out loud, and the more he thought about it the funnier it became. There was so much this savage human didn't know—didn't understand—but in an off-handed remark he said something fairly profound. Soon the Howsh would no longer be Tow's problem for he would be dead, like all the other Pashier. That was inevitable, and the Earth humans would be left to deal with the Howsh alone. He wasn't justified—passing over a particular ethical reference to pacifism, which was a conscious decision made by his people over millennia. One they were willing to adhere to even though it led to their eventual demise. The humans were free to act as they saw fit in their own world.

Tow, after regaining his composure, said, "I apologize. You said something that struck me as funny."

"It's fun to laugh. I laugh all the time," Cuddy said, looking at something over and beyond Tow's shoulder.

Tow turned to find the AI orb hovering within the open hatchway and his first reaction was immediate irritation. Until then, Tow hadn't shared the outside world with this hovering artificial intelligence orb, and he didn't wish to do so now. He didn't want to corrupt this beautiful place with the cold, calculating machine.

"Proceed no further, AI. Tell me what you want."

Tow listened to the orb's reply before dismissing it with the wave of a hand and turning his attention back to Cuddy.

Wide-eyed, Cuddy asked, "Was that a robot?"

"Of sorts."

"I heard you talk to it but I didn't hear it talk back to you."

"Yes … well, that was another ability the *Pashier* developed over many years. The capability to converse or command non-organic beings by using only our thought … like

I just did with that AI orb. Based on Earth's evolutionary progression, the same ability will probably present itself to humans over the next one hundred years."

Cuddy only nodded.

There was so much for this human to digest in such a short period of time. But Tow did feel less guilty now since Cuddy seemed surprisingly well adjusted to his new, altered state of beingness.

"Will the Howsh hurt us?"

"Maybe. I am truly sorry. It is my fault … I led them here."

"But when you leave, they'll follow you. Right?"

"Cuddy … I am sick. I am dying. I have a terrible disease caused by the Howsh. I may not live long enough to—" Tow stopped speaking, seeing tears stream down Cuddy's cheeks. He was taken by surprise; causing the human such distress was the last thing he wanted, and guilt over what he had done returned. "I am sorry, Cuddy. I probably shouldn't have informed you in such a casual manner."

Cuddy wiped his runny nose on the back of his sleeve, then lowered down to the dog and wrapped his arms around him. Burying his face in the animal's fur, he seemed to find comfort there. The sadness of the entire situation became less abstract to Tow at that moment and he too felt himself become emotional. Placing a comforting hand on Cuddy's shoulder, he said, "I'm so sorry, Cuddy."

Tow watched the dog lick tears off Cuddy's face and thought about the brief time Cuddy had spent within the wellness chamber. Though some remarkable things had been accomplished, this human, clearly, still had farther to go. Remembering Cuddy's actual age was nineteen in human chronological terms, Tow surmised he was now, both mentally and emotionally, somewhere around twelve or thirteen years of age, up from age seven.

The orb roved back into view within the open hatchway

and hovering there, said, "The humans have a saying—*in for a penny, in for a pound.* I suggest the human spend additional time within the wellness chamber."

* * *

Cuddy wanted to bring Rufus into the wellness chamber along with him, relaying the fact that Rufus, too, had recently been injured, but Tow would not allow it. He also said he would not be joining Cuddy this time since there was a limit to the amount of time anyone could undergo such treatment. So now Cuddy sat in the chamber alone.

Cuddy's thoughts wandered back to early that morning when, eating breakfast, he'd purposely acted dumb—like how he was before meeting Tow. *Why did I do that?* He suspected it was because he felt he'd done something wrong. That he was not supposed to be like other people—wasn't intended to be smart—and wondered if Momma would still love him in the same way. Cuddy's thoughts then turned to Jackie, who'd spent the night. Momma had put sheets on the family room couch and Kyle gave her a big T-shirt to sleep in. Cuddy didn't like the way Kyle looked at her. *Has he always looked at her that way*? He suspected so, but Jackie had ignored Kyle—was looking at him instead with the same narrowing of eyes. Like she was trying to puzzle something out. Jackie was the smartest person he knew—next to Tow.

Ten minutes into the session, Cuddy was thinking with far more clarity than he could ever remember. He looked about the curved enclosure—the soft surfaces within the sterile chamber—and took in the blinking, multi-colored lights on the control panel that were positioned midway up and to the right of the entrance hatch. Wondering what parameters Tow had set for him to undergo, he then puzzled about the word itself ... *parameters*. How he knew what that word meant. It occurred to him that he'd heard Tow use the word earlier and now Cuddy made the mental correlation that it meant something similar to the word *settings*.

He then thought about Tow—that he would be dying soon—and the thought made him sad as he looked across at the three vacant seats within the chamber. *Why did Tow bring me into the chamber for a second session?* Tow would soon be gone, but he had mentioned something about a mission … about returning some kind of pod to a distant planet. Would this ship then need a new captain or would the hovering robot be sufficient for that? Cuddy didn't think so. He may not be as smart as Jackie, but it didn't take a genius to connect the dots. Tow was making him smarter for a reason.

Another five minutes' time elapsed before the wellness chamber hatch slid open. Tow, standing in the opening, said, "Tell me, Cuddy, how much did you figure out in the last fifteen minutes?" Cuddy saw Rufus, standing at Tow's side.

"I think … quite a bit of it."

"Are you angry with me?" Tow asked.

"No … not really. But you've made a few assumptions. Namely, that I would agree to help you. That I would risk my life to further your cause … or the cause of the Pashier."

"They are one in the same, Cuddy. You, your family, Earth, are now entangled in this drama. Again, I apologize for coming here but one fact still remains … this planet is in grave danger."

"I know that."

"I want to show you something. Something no one else … no other race of beings in the universe has ever witnessed before. Please … follow me."

Cuddy stood and instantly regretted he'd risen so fast. He felt dizzy and somewhat nauseous. Tow put out a steadying hand, and said, "I apologize, I extended your session slightly longer than the recommended timeframe. It may take several hours for your equilibrium to fully adjust." *Equilibrium*—another word Cuddy was fairly certain he'd never heard of, or used before, yet he knew its meaning just the same.

Tow guided him through several lower deck passageways, moving forward toward the bow. With Rufus by his side, Cuddy felt the dog's warmth press against his leg. They entered what seemed to be a storage hold area. Until then, Cuddy wasn't aware the flying robot—what Tow referred to as the AI orb—had followed them in.

Tow said, "AI … open the sub-level hatch."

"Captain Tow, the human is not authorized. I am tasked with protecting—"

"Update your authorization list so that it includes Cuddy. Do so now!"

The orb went quiet. Cuddy had the distinct feeling the orb did not trust him, and the feeling was mutual. A hidden section of the hold's deck paneling suddenly descended several inches, then slid to one side. Staring into the blackness below, Cuddy could barely make out the first few steps that led downward.

Chapter 17

Tow coughed several times into his hand and, seeming to be in some pain, cleared his throat. Composing himself, he said, "Please respect the space you are about to enter, Cuddy. No loud noises—whisper instead of talking—and you may need to duck your head somewhat; vertically, the ceiling's height is limited."

Tow walked toward the opening, then halted before heading down the stairs. "Cuddy … you may not fully understand yet, but bringing you down here is a great honor. An honor and a responsibility." Tow continued to descend the stairs until he was out of sight. Cuddy heard him say, "You may bring Rufus along with you."

Cuddy hesitated as the AI orb silently hovered around him before it too descended into the blackness below. He looked around the hold area, unsure if proceeding forward would be such a good idea. He had the uncomfortable feeling that this moment in time was somehow important. A crossroads of sorts, and he wondered why him? Why was he, someone who, until a few hours ago, could scarcely read or write, or remember his address or phone number—singled out by this alien called Tow? Surely, there were far more qualified people … like Momma, Kyle, or Jackie, who were smart; far better—

Cuddy heard Tow's soft voice emanate up from below. "Please … come down, Cuddy."

Cuddy, complying, then proceeded to go down. Halfway down the stairway, he felt a breeze gently buffeting his pant legs. Stepping off the bottom step, he leaned forward, hoping not to bang his head, then slowly stood upright to find about an inch of clearance above him. It took several moments for his eyes to adjust to the darkness. The breeze down below was cool and smelled fresh—a scent he'd not encountered before that was pleasing. He wondered why it was kept so dark down there; it would be too easy to walk into a bulkhead, or Tow, or the AI orb, if he wasn't careful. He held out his hands, slowly moving forward, then noticed his two, barely perceptible, glowing hands. *Why are my hands glowing?*

"This way, Cuddy."

Cuddy looked to his right, hearing Tow's voice, and saw the glowing alien gesturing for him to follow. The AI orb was all but invisible—only tiny blinking red and green lights, which gave away its hovering location.

Down there in utter darkness, Tow's form looked even more beautiful. What Cuddy thought was strictly a bright, glowing-white iridescent form, instead showed subtle hues of blues, pinks, even green. He looked again at his own outstretched hands. Certainly not quite as bright or vivid, nevertheless, the same pastel hues were also present within him. As the orb moved lower, the breeze picked up and a series of sounds—musical tones—filled the space around them. It was beautiful. He closed his eyes and felt something familiar—the feeling he often got when Momma put her arms around him and hugged him tight. The feeling of being protected—nurtured—that everything would be okay.

He opened his eyes and gasped. A sparkling white light was spouting upward, like a water fountain, but it was light glistening instead of water. Brighter and brighter it became and Cuddy could see the outline, just below the light, of what looked like a plant of some sort. He instinctively knew it was the heritage pod, which Tow had spoken about only days before. It looked like a pod—organic in shape and texture—that was slowly opening up at the top. Large leaves curled backward, one after another, then slowly extended outward to eventually come to rest on the lower deck. Layer after layer, the large leaves unfurled and lay flat. The breeze by now had turned into a steady wind. Tiny sparkling lights encircled them, in between them—more lights than he could ever count in a thousand lifetimes. Cuddy had never witnessed anything so beautiful. Kneeling, he put his arm around Rufus, then placed his other palm on his own chest—wanting to feel his own heartbeat. Certain his heart would soon burst. He was barely able to constrain the myriad of emotions springing forth.

Cuddy felt Tow's hand on his shoulder. "We will sit now." Cuddy and Tow sat down, and with Rufus's head in his lap, Cuddy looked left and right. And then he saw it: they were sitting within a spiraling galaxy of slow-moving stars within a massive universe. By squinting his eyes he could see more galaxies, even farther beyond. It was an infinity of stars. And—like the iridescent hues he'd seen in both Tow's and his own glowing forms—the dazzling, colorful brilliance emanated from out there.

Cuddy was mesmerized. He asked, "Tow … is this heaven? Are you showing me heaven?"

Tow didn't answer the question. Instead, he said, "I would like you to meet someone very special to me. Would that be all right with you?"

Cuddy, not understanding why Tow felt it necessary to ask his permission, replied, "Sure." A minute or two passed before Cuddy noticed it, and Rufus's head came up. A faint distant star—one out of millions or billions—was moving in the opposite direction of the others. Slowly it grew in size and intensity as it sped toward them. Cuddy glanced over to Tow and watched the anticipation register on his face. Smiling—childlike—Tow's eyes glistened with moisture.

The fast-approaching star took on a different shape. Not a star at all, it was a being—a *Pashier!* Cuddy watched as she glided toward them and noted she was beautiful. Her glowing form slowed, then stood suspended, only mere feet from them. Her eyes held steady on Tow's, and Cuddy knew they were silently communicating. They loved each other—no doubt of that. Eventually, her eyes turned toward Cuddy and he felt like he was being drawn into her. In an instant, he knew who she was, and what she was trying to communicate to him. Not knowing how to properly respond back upset him. She raised her palms in a gesture he understood … *all in good time, Cuddy.* She took another tentative step forward and he then knew her name was Soweng. *Thank you, Cuddy … we all thank you. You are very special. Know this … we have waited an eternity for you. Thank you for what you are about to endure and the sacrifices you will soon face. Know all is worthwhile, and that, in the end … it is just.*

Glancing down at Rufus, her bright smile returned. When she turned back toward Tow, they held each other's gaze for a long moment. Cuddy knew what was being communicated was strictly private, just between them. Eventually, she turned away saddened, as was Tow, and didn't look back. In due time, she merged into the universe—once again—a distant star.

He heard Tow's voice alongside him. "We have no right to ask this of you, Cuddy."

He didn't need to explain; Cuddy knew what he wanted. "How will I know what to do … when the time comes?"

"Soweng passed that knowledge on to you directly. It will come to you when the time is right. All *Pashier* instinctively know the *Shain* ritual of the *rejoining*."

Cuddy held up an arm and studied his softly glowing

hand. "Am I a *Pashier*, Tow … have you changed me?"

"Yes … I have changed you. You are no longer human, but you are not a *Pashier,* either. You are something else. You are something new."

"Will I come here … when it's time?"

"Would you like to?"

"I think so. Yes, maybe I would."

"Then we shall see … won't we?"

The spinning universe around them had suddenly quickened. Now, the great leaves that formed the heritage pod were rising off the deck and curling inward—slowly transforming back into the same, organic, pod-like shape as before. The fountain of sparkling light now flowed inward, instead of outward. As that whole order of events reversed themselves, Cuddy felt a release within his own heart and, along with it, the weight of his physical life's reality returning back. The sadness, the new sense of loss he felt, was profound. In that very moment, he understood why Tow rarely visited the heritage pod. It was far too painful.

Chapter 18

When Cuddy returned home, Momma was walking back from the mailbox at the end of the drive. Distracted, she glanced up as Cuddy approached, but quickly brought her attention back to the sheets of paper in her hands. He fell into step beside her, noting she'd torn open several envelopes and was reading what looked to be a bill of some sort. He saw the words *Final Notice* stamped in red at the top of the page—surprised he knew what it said. *I can read …*

"Hi, Momma … what's that?"

"It's a bill, what's it look like?"

"Where is everybody?"

Momma didn't answer right away, then said, "Your brother took the car without permission … so I don't know where he is."

Cuddy saw Jackie's bug still parked in front of the house. "And Jackie?"

Momma looked up, irritated. "Um … she took Ellie out for a ride. That poor horse needs exercise. Didn't I ask you to let her out into the corral this morning?"

"Sorry, Momma." He looked off toward the horizon and

thought he saw Jackie on horseback about a half mile off in an open pasture. He had been debating with himself what he should say to Momma. He didn't want to break his promise with Tow, but keeping secrets—not telling her—seemed even worse. "Momma, can I talk to you?"

At that very moment, a wailing sound could be heard off in the distance, carried aloft by the warm afternoon breeze. Cuddy knew it was coming from town; from the big metal cone atop the firehouse. Momma stopped reading and looked up, then hurried up the porch steps and flung open the screen door. Cuddy followed her into the house and into the kitchen, where she made a beeline for the little Sony TV, sitting on the counter, and turned it on. Again, Cuddy was surprised by his ability to read the screen's words. Bold white letters, atop a blue and red banner at the top of the screen, read:

State of Emergency — Two Nuclear Reactors Venting

A familiar-looking news reporter—his hair whipping around in the wind—stood with a microphone to his lips. In the distance, a large, concrete, hourglass-shaped structure dominated the background. Momma, momentarily, brought a hand to her mouth then reached for the TV's volume control.

"... the Soddy-Daisy, Tennessee nuclear power plant has had its share of problems over the years. But nothing like this. Both reactors ... Sequoyah Unit 1 and Sequoyah Unit 2 ... are currently operating within states of emergency, venting caustic radiation into the atmosphere."

Momma said, "Oh my ... that boy needs to get away from that place." She turned the channel and another reporter, with a slightly different perspective of the Soddy-Daisy nuclear power plant shown in the distance, was saying something similar to the guy beside him. Momma continued to switch channels. Each station broadcasted the same news but this one had a blonde female reporter, wearing bright red lipstick, who urged:

"... it's very important that everyone stay indoors. If you are outside ... stop what you are doing and find shelter immediately. If you are driving, keep your windows rolled up and stay clear of the Soddy-Daisy, Tennessee area."

Momma looked up and out the kitchen window. "Kyle's out there … and Jackie!"

Cuddy said, "I'll go fetch her."

"No … you're not leaving this house, boy!"

"But Momma …"

"I said, no!" She hurried to the hallway closet, sliding hangers left and right until she found what she was seeking—a bright yellow rain slicker. "Don't just stand there, help me on with this!"

Cuddy, grabbing ahold of the rubbery coat, held it open for her as she slid both arms into the sleeves, then tightened the belt snugly around her waist. She fumbled, reaching an arm back over her shoulder, so Cuddy lifted up the oversized hood so she could reach it. When she pulled it over her head, Cuddy almost laughed at her appearance. She rushed for the door, shouting, "Get out of the way, Rufus!" as she swung it open and hurried outside. As the dog ran inside, she said, "Close the inside door, Cuddy, right now!"

Cuddy did as he was told and returned to the kitchen. Like Momma, he spun the TV dial several times, finally coming to rest on CNN. Wolf Blitzer's bearded face dominated the screen. As Wolf continued reporting on the reactors' dangerously reduced coolant levels, Cuddy found he easily followed what was being broadcast.

He thought about current events now taking place, and had a new respect for the abilities of Tow's AI orb. In a matter of several hours, the hovering robot had breached the facilities' network somehow, riling up nationwide excitement. He wondered if the AI had miscalculated; if the radiation was more dangerous than anticipated. But he didn't think the AI orb made many mistakes. As he gazed up at the colorful skies out the window, he wondered if the marauding Howsh ships would actually be thrown off the hunt. Leaning sideways to get a better view of the open prairie, he saw Momma waving her arms above her head, yelling something unintelligible into the wind.

Eventually, Jackie, riding atop Ellie, trotted into view. Leaning forward, her head was angled to better hear what Momma was yelling. Strands from her whipping ponytail had strayed into her mouth. As Momma turned back, she raised an arm and pointed off toward the west. Cuddy silently acknowledged to himself that he knew where west was—as well as east, north, and south.

Jackie swung a long slender leg up and over the saddle, then slid to the ground. With Ellie's reins in her hand, she hurried toward the barn as Momma headed toward the porch. Cuddy, sitting in the kitchen, heard the door smack open as a gust of wind pushed its way into the house.

Momma rushed in, untying her slicker and pushing the hood off her head. Glancing at the TV, she asked, "Any more news?"

"It's a disruption of coolant flowing into the reactors. The overheating instigated the emergency venting into the atmosphere."

Momma simply stared at Cuddy for several beats with her brow furrowed—as though she was seeing him for the first time that day. As her eyes searched his face, Cuddy could see her, almost imperceptibly, shaking her head.

"Cuddy … do you understand what you just said, or are you parroting what one of those reporters said?"

"Um … I think both. The guy with the microphone explained that the disruption of coolant flowing into the reactors would cause emergency venting into the atmosphere. Made sense to me."

As the front door opened, another blast of wind found its way into the kitchen. Jackie, coming around the corner, halted when she saw Momma staring intently at Cuddy. "What … what is going on?"

Cuddy repeated what he'd said a moment before. "It's a disruption of coolant flowing into the reactors … the overheating instigated the emergency venting into the atmosphere."

Jackie stole a glance at the TV, then looked at Momma. "That's kinda weird, coming from his mouth … isn't it?" They stared at each other.

Cuddy said, "I've been trying to tell you things have changed. That I'm no longer simpleminded."

"I noticed something going on with you last night, Cuddy," Jackie said. "I don't think I ever heard of anything like this happening before. I hate to use the word *miracle*, but Mrs. Perkins … Cuddy's—"

Momma took a step closer to the table while reaching out a hand for support. "Tell me our street address, Cuddy."

"I think it's Number Three Beacham Road, Woodbury, Tennessee."

Momma gestured toward the battered old telephone, mounted on the kitchen wall. "Our phone number?"

He told her the correct number.

Jackie looked excited, they both did. "You really have … changed, haven't you, Cuddy?"

Cuddy nodded. "Yeah … but that won't be what will surprise you most."

Momma seemed overwhelmed. "As wonderful as this news is … it's a miracle from God … we still need to think about what's happening outside now. Kyle's out there. He's in danger."

"Sit down, Momma … you too Jackie. The thing is, it's all connected."

Momma, ignoring him, said, "Maybe we should take your car and go look—"

"Momma!"

He'd never before raised his voice at his mother—not ever. Jackie quietly slid into the closest chair without saying a word. Momma, reluctantly, sat down too.

"Okay, son … tell us what's happening with you, but please hurry."

★ ★ ★

Jackie couldn't take her eyes from Cuddy. There'd been other times in her life when she was aware—at some deep level—that something monumental was happening. A specific pinpoint in time she knew she would recall later—perhaps years from then. The air in the kitchen turned suddenly electric. She found herself smiling with anticipation at what this boy-turned-man was about to say next.

"I'm hoping that the changes you see in me, which you are experiencing first hand, will make what I say next somewhat more believable. I want you to know I'm not nuts; at least, I don't think I am."

"Just get to it, Cuddy," Jackie said impatiently. "I'm sure it's fine."

"Several days ago, the day after Officer Plumkin took Rufus away, I was walking in the woods where a brook runs deep in the trees."

Momma let a stream of air out through her puffed cheeks.

"Okay … I'm getting to it!" Cuddy said. "There was

someone there, sitting on a rock. I surprised him."

"A man … woman … who was it?" Jackie asked.

Cuddy shook his head, as though searching for some specific word. "Here's the weird part. It was an … um … alien."

Jackie felt the smile leave her face. *Okay, he's crazy—from retarded, to sudden genius, to crazy as a loon.*

"Son … I know you probably think …"

Cuddy nodded, his expression conveying an all-knowing *yeah, I knew this was coming* look. "He's from a planet called Mahli. He's a *Pashier*."

"Stop!"

"Momma … it's all true!"

"Stop, son, I don't know what's going on with you, but I can't listen to any more of this nonsense."

As Jackie loudly cleared her throat, Momma didn't acknowledge her. Instead, she reached out a hand and took one of Cuddy's in hers.

Jackie said, "I think I might believe him."

Momma's condescending smile faded. Sitting back, she studied Jackie.

"Let me at least ask him a few questions before we discount everything he's saying, okay? I mean, think about the odds of having a bizarre reactor event take place right now, and the sky is … well, it's like nothing we've seen before. And all of a sudden your son has made an amazing … miraculous really … mental recovery. Mrs. Perkins, I'm educated, a premed student. I like to think I have a fairly analytical mind."

"Go ahead, ask your questions, dear," Momma said.

"So … how did the alien get here, Cuddy?"

"A spacecraft. It's parked in a meadow deep in the trees. It's called the *Evermore*. It's damaged and Tow, that's the alien's name, landed there to make needed repairs."

"Okay, so what's going on with our extremely colorful sky?" Jackie asked.

"Tow's ship was chased across space by three other alien

ships. They are called the Howsh and they want to kill Tow … destroy his ship. They've already destroyed his home planet … Mahli. Their sensor scans are causing the atmospheric anomaly."

Momma and Jackie exchanged a glance. "And the nuclear reactors?" Momma asked.

"The alien has a robot that purposely caused the radiation to vent, giving Tow enough time to repair his spaceship. Radiation hides the *Evermore* from the Howsh's sensor scans."

Momma shook her head and stared blankly out the window. Jackie, still on the fence about Cuddy's tale, wanted to believe him, but it seemed so farfetched. She suddenly wondered if Cuddy was, in fact, highly delusional. Maybe the ginormous leap in intelligence had caused secondary, impactful, consequences.

"It's not like I can't prove what I'm saying. If the spacecraft isn't where I say it is—you can chalk it off to me being crazy."

Jackie smiled and said, "Well, at least you'll be smart and crazy."

Momma's stern look conveyed she didn't appreciate Jackie's comment. "No, I don't want you … any of us, going outside in this …"

"Mrs. Perkins, I'm sorry, but if you think these drafty old walls will protect us from radioactive fallout, you're highly mistaken. I think we should go take a look."

When the phone on the wall began to ring, Momma reached up for it without leaving her chair. "Hello?"

Jackie watched Momma. Showing growing concern on her face, Momma looked over at Jackie, and said, "It's the hospital, saying you gave them this number if they needed to reach you." She handed the receiver across the table.

"Hello. Yes, this is Jackie. Okay, I'm on my way." Handing the receiver back to Momma, she said, "It's my father … I need to get to the hospital right away."

"We're coming with you," Momma said. "And then we need to find Kyle."

Chapter 19

Kyle, leaving town, was driving much too fast on the narrow country road. With high winds buffeting the car, he twice veered off the road and onto the dirt shoulder. The second time, he barely managed to bring the old Maxima back out from a tailspin. He didn't care—he only wanted to get home, though he knew he was going to catch hell for taking Momma's car without her permission. Hell, he didn't even have a valid driver's license. Catching his reflection in the rearview mirror, he noted the crusted blood, now dried brownish, on the inside of his nostrils, and that one eye was already turning black and blue. Slowing down for a sharp turn ahead, he then pressed the accelerator to the floor when the road straightened out. With his fists clenching the steering wheel at ten and two, he took in his scraped red knuckles and smiled. At least he'd inflicted more damage than he'd received back. Fucking Tony and fucking Gary, after all he'd endured the past year! Kyle wasn't alone when he stole the car—one year, seven months, and three and a half weeks ago. In fact, it wasn't even his idea, it was Tony Bone's. Tony said Dr. Howard never drove the old Mustang, just kept it up at his cabin that he never visited. Their plan was to take it for a drive for an hour or two, then put it right back, and no one would be the wiser. But Dr. Howard wasn't as old and decrepit as they figured and had set up some kind of video surveillance system in the garage. The old codger, watching them take the car in real time, was on the phone to the sheriff within five minutes. They were friends. In fact, the sheriff was his best man at his wedding. That, apparently, went a long way toward the retired doctor reporting he only saw Kyle take the car, not the sheriff's son Tony.

Without knowing it, things went from bad to worse for Kyle. Held in jail, he found out old Dr. Howard was Judge Sorenson's brother-in-law. Kyle thought back to that next morning. Nervously shaking in his cargo shorts and flip-flops, standing in front of the tall judge's bench, he never had a chance. That shouldn't have been a big surprise, since everyone knew the little town of Woodbury was as corrupt a town as it could possibly be. Hell—the cronyism that went on there was a well-known fact. After three minutes and the bang of a gavel, Kyle was sentenced to two years behind bars. Later, in low tones, the sheriff promised him he'd be out in one, but only if he never, ever, brought up the fact that Tony was with him on that fateful night's joy ride. That he would do the time while Tony Bone skated—free as a bird.

Nobody messes with Cuddy and lives to talk about it. But he surprised even himself and kept his cool after that—for the most part. He owed Momma that much—not to be thrown back in jail just days after returning home. If prison had taught him anything, it was patience. So he bided his time and waited. But then Tony went one step farther, stealing old man White's mustang, making it look like Kyle had stolen that one too. Kyle still didn't know why Tony was going to such extremes to fuck with him. Hell, if anything, it should have been the other way around. In any event, that act was the last straw.

Kyle showed up at the sheriff's house early that morning. Noticing his police cruiser wasn't there, he went inside and found Tony and Gary sitting next to each other on the couch. As cartoons blared forth from the TV, they didn't notice his presence while passing a bong back and forth. Kyle, coming around the side of the couch, pulled Tony to his feet and saw his nose still taped up. But Gary was apparently less stoned than Kyle had estimated. He jumped to his feet and connected with two solid hits—one to Kyle's nose and one to his eye. As Kyle staggered backward, barely dodging a wild punch from Tony, he balled-up his fists until his knuckles turned white. With one year, seven months, and three and a half weeks of rage consuming him, he stepped in and elbowed Gary hard in the mouth. Two of his upper front teeth ended up somewhere on the carpet. Kyle next aimed for the two white strips of tape, striking Tony twice in his already ruined nose. As he doubled over in pain, Kyle kneed him in the balls.

"The second I get out of the joint you beat up my brother! What was that supposed to be, some kind of message?" Kyle yelled—infuriated. "What … you wanted to keep me quiet that you were there … along with me on that joyride? I should rip your head off your pimply neck!"

Both Tony and Gary were down for the count, though Tony was still conscious. Kyle knelt on the floor beside him and, putting his mouth next to his ear, said, "Can you hear me, Tony?"

"Fuck you … I'm going to kill you. My dad's going to—"

"No, Tony, you and that idiot friend next to you did this to each other. That's what you're going to tell your father."

"Fuck you."

"There's one thing I did gain in prison, Tony." Tony didn't reply.

"Friends. Friends like Olson Briggs. Remember big black Olson from our high school football days? He played right guard. Well, he's a lot bigger now … must be three hundred and fifty pounds. Anyway, Briggs was in there for, I kid you not, ripping a man's arm off. Tony … he ripped a guy's arm right off at the shoulder in a bar fight for teasing him about his damn lisp. You remember Briggs' lisp, right? I think you used to tease him about it too. Anyway, Briggs is out of prison now … got out a month before me. He and I are still pretty good friends. He liked me in there. I treated him like a regular guy. And he saved my ass, literally, while I was in there. Nobody messed with Briggs, or with me. Tony, I think I might want to give my friend a call. Have him drop by here sometime. But I have to warn you; he picked up some bad habits in prison. But we won't go into that right now."

Tony shook his head, his words coming out wet and nasally, "No … I remember Briggs. Yeah, Okay … Gary and I did this to each other. I promise."

"That's good, Tony. But if I even hear your name come up in a conversation, I'm sending *pile-driver Briggs*, that's what everyone called him in the big house, over here. He'll make both of you his bitches and you'll be sitting on stacked pillows for at least six months. I kid you not."

Kyle left them both lying on the floor. There was no guarantee Tony would keep his word, but he'd cross that bridge if and when he came to it.

Up ahead, he saw flashing red and blue lights coming off of the cruiser's light bar. He slowed under the speed limit as three cruisers sped past, their sirens blaring. Next, he heard the distant firehouse alarm come alive—bellowing out back in town. Kyle switched on the radio, hearing nothing but static. Even changing the station made no difference. He looked up at the colorful sky and thought he saw something fly past in a blur overhead, pretty sure it was a helicopter. He'd heard about the situation with the nuclear power plant. Someone *shit the bed*, a colossal screw up, and now radioactive steam was venting into the air. He thought about Momma and Cuddy and stepped harder on the accelerator. Then he saw it again, this time in the rearview mirror, approaching low to the ground, and coming from behind. It flew right over the top of the car and Kyle reflexively ducked his head. *What the fu* ... realizing that it wasn't a helicopter. No doubt about it, it was some sort of spacecraft. Not some kind of military secret project, or something NASA had come up with. The craft was dark and looked threatening with all its sharp angles and edges. Weapons were clearly visible—mounted on the outer wings and along the underbelly. The outside of the vessel was a complicated looking assemblage of what looked like interconnecting pipes and junction boxes. Everything about the vessel was ominous.

The craft continued following along in the same direction of the road. Kyle, too slow moving his foot from the gas pedal to the brake pedal, suddenly had all four tires lock, causing a painful screeching sound. Smoke from burning rubber billowed into the air. The Maxima finally slid to an angled stop. The spacecraft set down fifty yards ahead and he had almost plowed smack into it.

Kyle sat there, his hands still tightly gripping the steering wheel. The engine had stalled and he heard the *tic tic tic* of it cooling. Black smoke from the hot tires was slowly dissipating from around the car. Kyle continued to stare at the spacecraft and figured it was several hundred feet long—twice as wide as the two-lane road it rested on. Small jets of steam periodically spewed out from various points along the ship's hull. Kyle could feel heat emanating from the ship's stern, where two thruster-like cones faced the car.

"This isn't happening," he said aloud. He had forgotten to breathe and suddenly took in a lungful of air. The triangular-shaped craft was suspended on three metallic landing struts, and looked battered—beat to shit. At one time, it was probably orange in color but now was more a sooty gray.

"*What am I doing? I need to get as far away from this thing as ...*"

Suddenly, an underside section of the spacecraft began

to lower. Amazed, Kyle watched as events transpired—he was paralyzed with a combination of fear and stupefied fascination—which kept him sitting alert in the driver's seat—his hands gripped on the steering wheel. The lowering section of the ship seemed to be some kind of lift—a platform. It soon became apparent that three sets of legs were standing on the platform. Not human, they were thick as tree trunks—and furry. As the lift continued to lower, more and more of the three alien beings became visible and he found it difficult to breathe in. He'd seen pictures of *big foot* before and these three could pass for his much larger cousins. Except *big foot* didn't carry advanced weaponry, like these aliens did.

The furry aliens jumped from the lift just before it reached the ground and, moving fast, headed straight for Kyle.

This can't be happening …

Chapter 20

Captain Holg unconsciously coughed up a *galk* from the back of his throat with a guttural choking sound, then began chewing the congealed secretion. Primarily composed of thick phlegm—mixed with hundreds of strands of snarled hair—the habit was similar to a cow chewing its cud. All Howsh found strange comfort indulging in the practice.

With a bridge crew of seven, the captain paced back and forth behind them, silently fuming. The venting of radiation into the atmosphere had been an ingenious tactic, and one, he was certain, instigated by the hiding lone *Pashier.* The indigenous savages of this blue world simply weren't capable of that level of intelligence.

Captain Holg's baritone growl filled the small space. The others mimicked the sound, a practice customary among subordinate Howsh crewmembers. Holg, now standing behind the tactical officer, Tee Ro, assessed the console readouts and his growl intensified in volume. The ship was called the *Arm of Lia.* Its sensor array was practically useless. Both long- and short-range scans were indeterminate in providing the specific location of the *Evermore.* But Captain Holg knew they were close … of that he was certain.

I O stood tall, twitching his shoulders and upper back. "Tee Ro … continue the search. I will be in the Containment Lab …"

★ ★ ★

Coming around, Kyle had the distinct sensation of movement—like a pendulum swinging back and forth. He opened his eyes to an upside-down view of a dingy metal wall in a place he didn't understand. *Where the hell am I?* His head throbbed. With a profound sense of dread, he remembered driving Momma's Maxima when a strange craft—a spaceship—landed in the middle of the road. Like something out of a movie, aliens exited the ship and were approaching the car. Scared shitless, Kyle sat frozen. If only he'd put the car in reverse and hightailed it out of there. *Why didn't I do that*? Instead, one of them raised a weapon and shot him.

Kyle tried moving his legs, but couldn't. Hanging upside down, his legs were bound at the ankles to somewhere high above him, his arms bound behind his back. He found if he shimmied his hips left then right, he could build up enough momentum to spin his body around and face in another direction.

Snap … crack … snap … crack … crack … Instinctively, Kyle grimaced at the sounds. Unsure what they were, there was something familiar about them nevertheless. Perhaps it was the beastly grunts that came along with them—*grunt … snap … grunt …* crack. *Exertion grunts!* Like the sound you made removing over-tightened lug nuts changing a tire.

As Kyle's bound body slowly spun around, one by one other hanging forms came into view. Suspended upside down—their legs bound and secured to something high up out of view—were three women and two men of varying ages, all naked. He realized he was naked as well. Three wires were attached to their abdomens—secured to bloodied metal probes that penetrated their bodies. The other ends were tethered into a small box, which swung free. A grizzly sight. *Grunt … snap … grunt … crack.* One of the *big foot* furry beasts, Kyle realized, was the chief source of the sound, at least the grunting part. The other sounds were of bones breaking within limbs. The male being tortured looked rubberlike—like a big Gumby toy. Although he seemed conscious, his screams were eerily mute in contrast to his desperately pleading eyes. His gaping, wide-open mouth was the most frightening sight Kyle had ever witnessed, and one he would never forget. He tried to control his own hyperventilating, but it was no use. He was beyond terrified. *Oh God … when will they turn their attention on me?*

Then something *strange* strode into the compartment. Clearly some kind of robot, it also was covered with long fur—nearly identical to the alien *big foots.* They had made the robot in their own likeness … *sort of.* The *big-foot-like* creature grunted something at the robot, which then bent over and moved its mechanical head close to the man's ear. Its distorted robotic voice was beyond frightening. "Where is the spacecraft? Tell me … and your misery will come to an end." The robot then touched something on the hanging box and the man's bone-chilling screams reverberated all around. With a raspy voice, almost undecipherable, the man screamed, "Ahhh! ppplease stop … please … I … I don't know anything about any spaceship!"

The robot next touched something on the box and the man's screams mercifully silenced.

Another furry bastard entered, wearing a red angled sash, and both the torturing alien and the robot momentarily bowed their heads. *Must be someone in charge*, Kyle thought, and tried to say something—to tell the one in charge there'd been a terrible mistake. That he wasn't supposed to be there. But like the Gumby man, he was voiceless.

Kyle felt sick as he watched the alien in charge move from one upside-down prisoner to the next. Red sash hesitated then began to openly defecate, his excrement plopping down below onto a widely spaced metal grate. *Disgusting.* Kyle closed his eyes, the only aspect of his present life he had some control of, and trembled as the footsteps approached.

★ ★ ★

Deep in thought, Holg moseyed between the savages' hanging carcasses. As disgusting as the *Pashier* were, these humanoids were worse. Their lack of intelligence … their pink, now exposed, flesh … so *revolting.* He symbolically looked upward and silently asked Thonna, *the god of all gods*, what he should do next. Above and beyond finding the *Pashier's* ship—destroying the wretched heritage pod—and exterminating the one called Tow, what about this world? At some point, like the others, would it too require extinction? To be cleansed of these vile creatures—these ungodly life forms? Not lost on Holg was their similarity to Mahli. *Yes, dangerous to let the humans evolve much further.* He contemplated what another cleansing would entail—weeks, if not months, of eradications. Relentless plasma strikes into primary population centers. Dispersion of Dirth, of which only so much remained within their storage canisters. He needed to decide if this foul planet warranted using that limited supply up.

Chapter 21

As they sped through the town of Woodbury and passed in front of the firehouse—the noise coming from the wailing air raid siren made Cuddy want to cover his ears with his hands. He was folded into the bug's cramped back seat, while Jackie drove and Momma occupied the passenger seat. Every so often, Momma glanced back at him, looking concerned. And every so often, Jackie's eyes found him in the rearview mirror. Before the three of them had rushed out to the car, he had dropped the bombshell about the alien … and the spaceships. Cuddy couldn't worry about their concerns and doubts about his sanity—not now, anyway. He had his own issues to deal with at present. For one thing, his mind had continued to transform over the hours since he'd sat within the confines of the *Evermore*'s wellness chamber. Cuddy thought about Tow and his decision. One that fundamentally changed Cuddy's life. Perhaps Tow hadn't considered the ramifications of bringing a human into the chamber—the adverse effects that would ensue. Tow had told him that Pashier and human brains were so very different. Tow had contemplated on that—on the fact that, from a technological evolutionary standpoint, the Pashier were obviously far more advanced. Tow had said the human brain was much larger—with their hundreds of trillions of firing synapses and exponentially greater capacity for learning.

At the moment, Cuddy's cognitive processes were overwhelming him. The rapid transition—going from being an imbecilic child-like individual to … *whatever he was now*—had adverse effects. It was one thing to be smarter. But that hadn't compensated for the simple fact his emotional state was constantly in flux. He was spending so much time with self-talk—reining in the wild spikes of feelings—one moment joyful the next sorrowful. One moment angry the next something else. He wished Tow was here. He'd tell him how to cope … what he needed to do.

"What is it, exactly, the nurse told you on the phone?" Momma asked Jackie.

"Only that there had been a change in Dad's condition and I should get myself to the hospital as soon as possible. I don't think the nurse wanted to tell me over the phone. I'm worried sick that it's something bad … I just want to get there."

Cuddy felt the little car accelerate. He watched as Jackie took the next turn faster than she should have.

"Well, don't kill us all in the process," Momma said. "I'm sure he's fine, dear."

"You doing okay back there?" Jackie asked.

"I'm good," Cuddy said, giving her a more confident smile than he was feeling.

★ ★ ★

"For goodness' sake!" Momma said. The hospital was a madhouse of activity. An ambulance was dropping someone off as another was just pulling in. Dodging a stream of pedestrians, Jackie impatiently urged an old lady to move it along. It was quickly apparent the lot was full, and Jackie was forced to park on a nearby side street. Getting out of the car, Momma told Jackie to run ahead, she and Cuddy would catch up. He watched her sprint for the double doors beneath the big red Emergency sign. He felt for her, while mentally checking his emotions—one more time.

Momma took Cuddy's arm in hers—something she had always done. He had a tendency to wander off at the slightest provocation. Something he knew would no longer be an issue. He smiled at her—and he found the human contact was comforting—grounding.

"Let's hurry it up, Cuddy," she said, quickening her stride.

Up ahead he saw Officer Plumkin's SUV pull up to a red curb. He flung the driver-side door open and quickly got out. He repositioned his gun belt as he half ran half walked toward the hospital. He yelled, "Out of the way … come on … get out of the way!" opening a path for himself between the people moving too slow for him.

"Maybe it's the radiation," Momma said. "People getting sick from that damn power plant."

Cuddy didn't think that was it. Before Momma had turned it off, they had listened to the radio on the drive over, and the announcer had relayed the latest scientific information coming out of the NRC, the Nuclear Radiation Commission. The levels were significantly higher than normal, but not lethal. At least not for the short term. The news caster had made it clear, this was no Chernobyl or Three Mile Island situation. Cuddy wasn't really sure what those two references meant—but it did seem that things weren't as bad as they seemed.

So why all the activity here? he wondered.

Momma and Cuddy entered into the frenzy—all the emergency room seats were taken and hordes of people were standing around the periphery. Momma approached a middle-aged couple Cuddy recognized as two school teachers from the high school. He thought one or both of them may have been Kyle's teacher at one time or another.

"Catherine? … Don? … what in *God's* name is going on here?" Momma said, almost sounding angry.

The two, both looking distressed, glanced to each other. Catherine said, "Dotty … you must have heard … it's unbelievable."

"What is? What's unbelievable … the power plant?"

Don shook his head. "No … well not entirely that … Dotty … there's been sightings … hundreds of them all over the state."

Momma's eyes darted to Cuddy and then back to Don.

"They're saying everyone needs to get to safety … into protected shelter. That means the firehouse, which was already overflowing, or here at the hospital."

Cuddy said, "Sightings? You're talking about aliens?"

All three of them looked up to Cuddy, who wasn't supposed to be able to offer up this kind of question.

Catherine said, "Yes, Cuddy … exactly. We've seen it … the spaceship! Flew right over our house. Half the windows blew out. They're saying it may be an invasion! It's horrible."

Cuddy watched as Momma put a comforting hand on Catherine's arm and nodded several times sympathetically—but there was nothing Momma could say. It was all too preposterous. She pulled Cuddy away from them, her expression resolute.

She kept her barely controlled voice low so no one else could hear her. "Talk to me, Cuddy … tell me about … all this craziness."

"What I told you this morning is true. That ship they were describing is looking for the *Evermore* … they're looking for Tow … an alien."

"And you've had contact with this … alien?" Her expression was full of worry.

"Momma … the simple fact that I'm having this intelligent conversation with you should tell you things are different. I've been on the ship twice … I've been … modified. That's a stupid word for it. But know, I would never lie to you. That spaceship Mrs. Lampard was telling us about … it's looking for the *Evermore* … which is in the woods close to our ranch."

Wide-eyed, Momma put her hands to her mouth. "Cuddy! We need to tell someone … the police!"

"No, Momma, we can't do that." Cuddy hesitated while he tried to think of a way to tell Momma the situation so she'd understand … to believe him. "You need to trust me, Momma. I would never do anything to put anyone in danger. But the ship the Lampards were describing … the aliens … they are called the Howsh … they're very bad. Evil. Tow is good … a pacifist … he is the last of his kind. The Howsh destroyed his planet … they've been chasing him through space … for years. He just needs time to make repairs to his ship. I should be helping him."

At that moment, Officer Plumkin was hurrying through the crowd, making his way back toward the exit. Momma pointed to Plumkin. "But why not tell …"

"The authorities will think they are all together. Think about it, you yourself barely believe me. We need to help Tow …"

"Fine … but this is getting too much for me to handle. The way you've changed, the nuclear accident and now … aliens! Son, I feel like I'm losing my mind. It's like a bad dream."

A combined cheer erupted on the other side of the room where people had gathered around a TV mounted high on the wall. Cuddy saw that it was CNN and this time it was Anderson Cooper's face on camera. The feed broke away from him to what looked like a wide view of the sky. The picture changed and it was clearly a shot of five or six fighter jets flying in formation. Cuddy instinctively knew bringing in the military was the absolute worst thing that could happen. Earth did not want to go to war with the Howsh.

"Have you heard?"

Momma and Cuddy spun around to see Jackie approaching. Her eyes were locked on the distant television. When she joined them she said, in a lowered voice, "We've been invaded by aliens …"

Momma nodded, again looking as if she had no words to add to an already crazy situation. Finally, she said, "Your father … how is he?"

Jackie looked at Cuddy and gave him a strange look. She waved off Momma's question. "He's fine … they're putting in a pacemaker. Walking around the second floor last night he kept fainting. He'll be here for another week." She looked at Momma … "They say it's a very common surgery and it's nothing to be concerned with. I just needed to sign some papers." She turned her attention back to Cuddy. "You were telling the truth."

"Yes … and there's more you don't know. I need to get back to the ranch … right away. Can you take me?"

"We also need to find Kyle," Momma said. "I want us all to be together."

Chapter 22

"Stop!" Momma shouted, spinning around in her seat, startling both Cuddy and Jackie.

"That's my car ..."

Cuddy followed the direction Momma pointed at out the passenger window. And sure enough there it was ahead, parked on the side of the road. A Latino man in greasy gray overalls was connecting its front end to the rear of a tow truck.

Jackie pulled off to the side of the road, right behind the Maxima. Even before the ignition was turned off, the passenger door was opened wide and Momma was out, running toward her car. Cuddy, extricating himself from the back seat, exited through the open passenger door. He and Jackie reached Momma and the tow truck driver at the same time.

"... you don't understand, this is my car. I can prove it!"

The tow truck driver didn't stop, continuing to drag a heavy set of chains beneath the car.

"Stop what you're doing, George!" For the first time, annoyed, George looked up and around. "Cuddy?!"

Cuddy nodded. "That's my mother's car ..."

George finished attaching the chains to the Maxima's undercarriage then gave Cuddy an appraising look—like he had two heads, or something. "I have dispatch orders … you'll have to go pick up the car at the impound garage."

"No!" Cuddy said firmly.

"What do you mean no—?"

Cuddy took a step forward and, kneeling down, began to unfasten George's work.

"Hey … I'll call the police, if I have to. Now, let me do my damn job."

Momma and Jackie stood back, keeping out of it, though both looked apprehensive.

Cuddy tossed first one, then the other end of the big hooked chains onto the pavement. Standing back up, he slapped his palms together several times to remove some residual rust. Then, staring down at George, he asked, "Do you really want to do that, George? Call the police?"

George locked on to Cuddy's steady stare, then let his eyes move over to Jackie and Momma. Eventually, he shook his head.

"This is bullshit … I shouldn't even be out here. Radiation … fucking aliens. Go ahead, take it; keys are in the car."

Collecting both lengths of chains, he tossed them into the rear bed of the tow truck. Without looking back, or speaking further, he hurried to the truck's cab and climbed in and started the motor. They watched in silence as he drove off.

Momma moved to the Maxima's driver side and opened up the door. Leaning in, she peered around, as if looking for something, as Cuddy watched her through the dirty windshield. Her voice muffled, he heard her say, "There's blood … not a lot, but it's definitely blood."

Cuddy focused his attention on the landscape surrounding them, then stared up at the sky above.

"What are you thinking?" Jackie asked.

He looked toward the middle of the road. "See those tire marks?"

Since the two-lane road was void of traffic, Jackie walked over and straddled the double yellow line. He watched her as she took in the skid marks.

Cuddy said, "There are three sets of skid marks going back a hundred yards or so. Looks like three drivers all locked their brakes at the same time. Something was blocking the road."

Jackie tracked the black rubber skid marks into the near distance then turned around. "Did you see those … over there?"

At first, Cuddy didn't see them. Five distinct, circular soot marks. "Maybe landing thrusters?" he queried.

"You're asking me?" Jackie said. "I have no idea, Cuddy."

Momma yelled, "Get off the road … car's coming!"

Cuddy and Jackie moved just far enough away so the approaching car could get past them. Instead, it slowed down and came to a stop—the sheriff's cruiser.

"Sheriff!" Momma exclaimed.

All three leaned down to look inside the car. The sheriff's wide-brimmed hat sat next to him on the passenger seat. Cuddy noticed the sheriff's shiny domed head was just about touching the interior headliner.

"Whatcha folks doing, standing out there in the middle of the road? Are you nuts or just plain stupid?" Cuddy could see the sheriff instantly regretted his choice of words as soon as he looked at him. "It's not safe."

Momma said, "Kyle's missing, Sheriff. He left the car here … abandoned. I'm worried."

The sheriff first studied the Maxima, then his eyes tracked all the skid marks. Cuddy noted the tired resignation on his face before he looked up at Momma. Probably the closest thing to compassion he could conjure up. "He may have been taken. I'm sorry … this is … all … so unbelievable, Dotty …"

Momma, now angry, said, "Oh no, you're not going to tell me my boy's been taken by those …" her words died off.

The sheriff let out a long breath before answering: "Earlier, three cars were abandoned here. No one was in them when Plumkin arrived on the scene. But he saw it. A space craft … or whatever it was." His eyes lifted toward the sky back behind them. "He saw it up in the air … heading off."

Cuddy, Jackie, and Momma all turned and stared into empty open sky.

"Best you get indoors. I'm sorry about Kyle, I truly am, but I have my own family issues to attend to."

Momma, who'd begun to wring her hands, looked more kindly at the sheriff and asked, "What's happened, Dale?"

"It's my boy … Tony. He's been badly beaten up. His friend Gary, too."

Jackie glanced at Cuddy.

"Actually, talking to your boy here was on my list of things to do today."

Momma said, "Cuddy's been with me all morning, Sheriff."

Rolling his shoulders, the sheriff said, "No … since they woke up their story is … they got into it … beat the living daylights out of each other. That's their story, anyway."

Cuddy thought about that, but it didn't ring true. Tony and Gary were both cowards; more apt to pick on the disabled or a helpless dog. Thinking about it, he let a faint, lopsided smile cross his lips. *It was Kyle!* It made sense. Probably was only a matter of time before Kyle settled things with them … for what they had done to him and Rufus.

Jackie asked, "Can we get back to the aliens? Kyle might be … up there now, like a hostage, or a prisoner, or something."

Momma nodded in emphatic agreement, while unconsciously continuing to wring her hands—her face taut with worry.

"The latest reports say anything approaching that alien ship will get shot down. It has some kind of ray beam. Five of our F-16s were plucked out of the sky in only a matter of seconds. It's like the end of the world. People are scared.

Hell, I'm scared! And today things have only gotten worse. First Arnold Air Force Base was attacked … then with McGhee Tyson Air National Guard Base, and then Camp Frank D. Merrill in North Carolina … all have all been destroyed. So there's no one coming here to help us … we're completely on our own."

Momma stared at the sheriff, her temper again beginning to rile up. "Well, don't come all unraveled here, Dale. Everyone's counting on you to hold things together."

He took her scolding and nodded. "Best you all get out of the street … I'm sorry about Kyle," he said, and drove off in the direction of town.

Cuddy said, "I need to get back to the ranch … help Tow. Maybe he'll know how to find Kyle."

"Can I help?" Jackie asked.

★ ★ ★

They reached the ranch ten minutes later, Momma driving her own car while Cuddy rode with Jackie in the VW bug. Pulling alongside the already parked Maxima, she cut the engine. Momma was already hurrying toward the porch. Cuddy reached for the passenger door handle when Jackie placed a restraining hand on his leg.

"Cuddy … can you just wait a minute?" Feeling her hand resting on his thigh, Cuddy immediately felt his heart rate double. "Um … yeah … sure. What is it?"

"There literally is a world out there … filled with terrified people … and you are the only one that knows what's really going on. The only one! It's … staggering. Think about the responsibility!"

"Why? I'm already freaking out."

Looking across at her, Cuddy saw her smile at that. To him just then, she was breathtakingly beautiful. It was disconcerting, for some reason embarrassing, that after all these years he only now was coming to that realization.

She said, "I've been thinking about everything."

Cuddy looked at her and waited.

"That alien friend of yours, Tow," she smiled again, realizing how preposterous that sounded, "chose you. You know that … right?"

Cuddy looked away, letting his gaze drift toward the distant tree line, then nodded.

"Future actions will impact more than Kyle, your momma … or me. They will impact life as we know it today."

"I already know that!" he snapped. "I need to get to him now … to Tow."

"What I'm saying is I want to help. I want to go with you to the ship. I've got nothing better to do. It's not like I'm going to be able to take the MCAT this year."

"I promised him … Tow … that I wouldn't tell anyone," Cuddy said.

"Well, that ship pretty much sailed. Take me with you … please!"

Chapter 23

Momma was on the phone as Cuddy and Jackie prepared to leave the house. She covered the mouthpiece with her hand and said, "I don't like this … you two going out there on your own. Let me call the sheriff …"

"No!" Cuddy said, more sternly than he intended. "We'll be fine. Promise me you won't tell anyone, especially the police? Promise me, Momma."

She hesitated then nodded. "But, Jackie, you call me on that cell phone of yours. I need to know what's happening."

"I will, Mrs. Perkins, I promise." Jackie, smiling, gave her front jeans pocket a couple of pats. They left the house and headed for the barn, the late afternoon sun casting long shadows before them. Jackie asked, "Is there anything I should know … you know, before we get there?"

"Like what?"

"I don't know … I've never met an alien before." She looked nervous, perhaps even a trifle scared.

"He's sick … he's dying. Has the Dirth." Cuddy suddenly stopped in his tracks and looked hard at her. "He might not even be alive. Last I saw him he was pretty sick."

"Is it—"

"Contagious?" He finished her sentence. "I don't know for sure, but I don't think so."

Together, they walked into the cool darkness of the barn. Cuddy paused just long enough to give Ellie a few pats on the horse's nose, then, exiting the barn, he said, "I guess I should tell you the rest of it … the things Tow told me. About the Howsh … and his own people, the *Pashier.* The destruction of his home world, Mahli, and what's most important to him … something called the heritage pod."

Entering into the woods, they stopped at the brook. Cuddy, starting at the beginning, told her everything that had transpired since he first met the glowing *Pashier* alien only days before. Jackie interrupted him several times to get better clarity on certain events. She was most interested in, concerned with, the effect of the wellness chamber on Cuddy. He tried to explain what he'd been dealing with since.

"I guess what's most surprising is that, after all these years … since I was seven and fell from the hay loft … the memories I thought were lost … gone forever … were not. I just couldn't make the right mental connections to them. The problem is, Jackie, that I remember much of what's happened over my life. Even things people have said to me, or what I've seen on TV. But that doesn't mean I understand it all … there's a lot I'll need to learn. I can do that … over time … but it's overwhelming. But worst of all, the feelings I felt … way back then … I remember them now, too. I spend all my conscious moments trying to bury a ton of emotions."

"Doing that doesn't at all sound healthy, Cuddy."

"I'm dealing with it. Anyway, it's getting dark. We better keep going."

Ten minutes later, they reached the edge of the clearing. Cuddy watched Jackie's expression as she caught sight of the alien spacecraft.

She stopped and stared. "This is … un … fucking be … lievable!"

Cuddy smiled and focused on the closed hatchway, wondering if perhaps Tow was too sick to greet them. He regretted wasting so much time getting back, and then wondered if some of his concern was that he'd brought someone along with him. He'd brought Jackie.

"Are you absolutely sure you want to … you know … be a part of all this?" Cuddy asked, looking unsure.

"Are you kidding me? I want to help … to have a chance to protect Earth and humanity … I haven't had any sense of purpose since my father's heart attack. No … I'm a part of this, like it or not."

At that very moment, the hatchway began to open as the gangway descended toward the ground. Cuddy was surprised at the elation he felt when the glowing figure moved into view. He was alive! Tentatively, Tow raised a hand in a half-hearted wave.

Approaching together, they stopped at the bottom of the gangway. Cuddy said, "This is Jackie, Tow. She's my friend. And Jackie, this is Tow … he's also my friend. Can we come in, Tow?"

Tow lowered his head and leaned forward as he stared at Jackie for a long moment—as if examining her with his eyes. He then hobbled down the gangway and awkwardly held out his left hand. He tentatively looked over to Cuddy, "Is this the right gesture … how humans greet one another?"

Cuddy had to think about that. Was that the correct hand … should it be the right hand?

"Yes!" Jackie said. She took his outstretched hand in hers and shook it. "I am … honored to meet you … Tow. Cuddy has told me so much about you."

Grimacing, Cuddy gave Tow an apologetic smile.

Tow, nodding, gestured for them to come up the ramp.

Jackie hesitated a moment as she looked again at the ship

there before her. Looking excited, she glanced over at Cuddy.

"It's okay. I promise, you're safe here."

She smiled and, taking in a deep breath, headed up the ramp behind Tow. Last, Cuddy followed behind. The alien stopped at the open hatch, bowed his head and gestured for them to proceed inside.

Inside the ship, Jackie—with an expression of utter astonishment—looked around at the surroundings. When the AI orb hovered into view from the bow, she took a step back. Cuddy felt her body press against him.

"It's okay. That's the orb … the artificial intelligence for the ship." The orb hovered in close. One of its articulating arms began to extend, its claw—three finger-like digits—opened and closed. Cuddy tensed—his hands tightening into fists.

Tow ordered, "Back away, orb! Jackie is a friend. Amend your database to include her … do it now!"

"Database amended. Hello, Jackie … welcome aboard the *Evermore*." Cuddy noticed the orb was sounding less alien-like than before.

"Tow," he said. "… I think the Howsh took my brother."

Jackie was uncharacteristically quiet as she continued to take in the glowing and naked, as usual, alien.

"That may be true, Cuddy. I am sorry. It is my fault; I have caused unexpected turmoil on your planet."

"We need to rescue him. Find that ship … go get him."

Jackie said, "And I'd like to help too." Tow silently studied them both.

"The repairs to your ship … have you started yet?" Cuddy asked.

Tow nodded. "Yes, but I am quite weak. It is a slow process." He searched Cuddy's face and asked, "Tell me, how are you doing, Cuddy?"

"You mean since you used him like a lab rat in that chamber of horrors of yours?" Jackie interjected. Tow and Cuddy stared at her.

"It's not like that, Jackie," Cuddy said. "I thought you understood." He was beginning to regret bringing her along.

Indignant, she looked at Tow. "He's changed, you know. He's not the same person he was before. He's having a big problem adapting. Did you think about that before—"

"Jackie!" Cuddy snapped. "It's what I wanted. What's wrong with you, anyway? Stop attacking Tow. Remember, you're a guest here."

"It's all right, Cuddy. She is correct. I did not fully anticipate the physical and mental repercussions those wellness chamber sessions would have on you beforehand … on a human. I made some assumptions that have proven to be incorrect, and I have thought about little else ever since."

"Look, Jackie, I wouldn't go back … to the way I was before, not for anything. What Tow did for me … was a gift. He's changed my life for the better. I think you owe him an apology."

Jackie said, "Fine, then … sorry," crossing her arms over her chest.

Cuddy was well aware she could be tenacious—had spunk—but he'd never seen her be rude before. He chalked it up to her being overwhelmed. Any normal person would be freaking out about now.

"Tell me what to do, Tow; how I can help with the repairs?" Cuddy asked.

★ ★ ★

Tow was a good teacher—patient with Cuddy's lack of knowledge of even the simplest of concepts. But Tow provided the necessary information along the way, as well as the rudimentary principles behind them. Tow had commented multiple times how quick a learner Cuddy was … which in and of itself was super encouraging.

They were in a section of the ship Cuddy had not seen

before, and as far astern as they could go. Tow referred to the compartment as Engineering. The emersion-drives, each about twelve feet high by ten feet wide, took up the majority of the compartment's space. Tow pointed out a specific area, where a Howsh plasma strike had breached both the outer and inner hulls, striking the drive. A charred, blackened section on the drive appeared to be in early stages of repair. Several newer-looking components had been added, and a cluster of optical cables, of sorts, hung loosely from some kind of conduit. Again, it didn't go unnoticed on Cuddy that only a few days before he had no clue what an optical cable was, or of the basics of how a propulsion system performed. Now, his brain was like a sponge. He listened as Tow and the AI orb spoke, no longer attempting to speak in generalities, and found he had a greater affinity toward understanding—both the mechanical aspects of the propulsion system, as well as the physics that lay behind it.

Jackie was a hard worker. Her job, principally, was to carry various small parts from one of the nearby storage compartments, as requested, or hold items in place while the AI orb fastened them on, using an assortment of strange looking power tools. Cuddy mostly was tasked with using his brute strength wherever needed. One tool he used, looking nearly identical to the common crowbar, pried fried, welded-on components off the drive.

Tow leaned against a bulkhead, supervising only. Cuddy could see his friend was having a hard time staying vertical and then noticed something else as well—his beautiful white glowing radiance had significantly diminished. A sudden tightness gripped at Cuddy's throat. He remembered the conversation—where Tow had talked so openly about his impending, inevitable, death. Cuddy's heart felt heavy in his chest. He looked over to his alien friend and wished there was something he could do.

Chapter 24

Standing next to Tow, Jackie watched him work from the opposing bulkhead on the damaged emersion-drive. Using brute force, Cuddy jammed the end of the crowbar into a small gap on the last, melted-together, metal component. He put his full strength behind prying it off. It was steamy hot in the small compartment and Cuddy had removed his shirt an hour before. His back muscles were tense beneath his wide shoulders, his abdomen flat. He had the muscular build of an athlete, which surprised her since, before that day, Jackie had never witnessed him do any form of exercise.

Over the preceding hours, Cuddy had asked a never-ending sequence of questions—mostly directed toward the AI orb. Seeming to have an insatiable hunger for information, he needed to understand not only the *whats and hows* of everything, but also the *whys*. Questions like, why did the designers of the ship's propulsion system decide to install an emersion-drive system instead of some kind of anti-matter drive? It appeared that he was asking questions even Tow could not answer.

While Cuddy and the hovering orb conversed, Jackie

asked, "So, what's going to happen … next?"

Tow said, "Soon, the AI orb will attempt to initialize the drive. After that, the two drives need to be balanced … synchronized—"

"No, I mean with Cuddy. Will you be taking him away from us? Into space?"

Tow, watching Cuddy and the orb, said, "I no longer make those decisions, Jackie. Even if I could, I wouldn't. My time here is almost at an end." As if on cue, Tow began to cough into his open palm. Jackie waited silently for the deep hacking to let up. He then continued, "The question you need to consider asking is this: What will you do … go with him or stay here?"

"I don't know. He hasn't asked me to go with him."

"And he probably won't," Tow said. "Unfairly, he has taken on this burden by himself. No one should have such an enormous weight placed upon them … such as his now."

"You mean returning the heritage pod to Primara?" Jackie asked.

Tow looked surprised.

"He told me about it. But I'm not surprised that Cuddy would want to help. I've never known a more decent person," she added.

Cuddy gestured toward the emersion drive, with its myriad of newly mounted replacement parts. "Almost done." Then, pointing to the contraption Jackie had held in her hands for the last twenty minutes, he said, "I'll take that."

She handed the strange device across to him. "Here you go."

"Thanks." Cuddy held it up before the hovering orb, and gestured with his chin towards the side of the big drive unit. "How will this be oriented onto the *suspension-regulator?*"

Tow, his voice now barely above a whisper, told Jackie, "Cuddy's intelligence has continued to grow exponentially. Yet emotionally, he is still immature. I am sure you too have noticed as much. Those two aspects will continue to be at odds for him. For how long, I do not know. He will need help … to cope and understand."

"I have my own life to lead. Obligations … my father's recuperation … school …"

Tow nodded appreciatively. Then he and Jackie looked toward Cuddy, who was addressing them.

"Sorry, Cuddy, what did you say?" Jackie asked.

"Weapons."

Confused, Tow shook his head.

"Time is a crucial factor. Best if we do things in parallel. The orb here tells me the initializing and synchronizing of the repaired drive will take over an hour. Eventually, we're going to need sufficient weaponry on board this ship to even the odds with the Howsh."

Tow said, "Why would the *Evermore* have any weapons available? Pashier are pacifists."

"Look … you're going to have to get over that, Tow. I'm sorry, but there's no other option, now that humans are in the mix. And remember, you made that choice."

Impressed, Jackie watched Cuddy patiently hold strong—not backing down.

"Well, there are no weapons on board, although the vessel does have powerful energy shields."

"Obviously not powerful enough, since your thirteen other armada ships were all destroyed. That should be proof enough." Cuddy turned to the AI orb. "And are you a pacifist too?"

"I am programmed to be, that is correct."

Cuddy looked back to Tow. "I'm sorry … the orb needs to—"

Tow interjected with a raised hand: "AI orb, from this point on you will take directions from Cuddy Perkins. I am transferring my executive command status to him. Update your database to coincide with my orders."

"Database updated," the AI orb said.

Jackie was well aware something huge had just transpired, as Cuddy and Tow continued staring at one another.

"Cuddy Perkins, a Howsh vessel is quickly approaching from the north. The course vector is perfectly aligned with our current position."

"How much time—"

"None," the AI orb replied. "It is nearly upon us."

★ ★ ★

Tow, Cuddy, and Jackie, along with the hovering AI orb, hurried forward. Standing within the small bridge compartment, Tow showed Cuddy the symbolic representation of the landed Howsh ship on the virtual *viewscape* display. It took Cuddy several moments to make heads or tails out of the surrounding landscape.

"That's your ranch. Right there!" Jackie then said, "Don't you see it?"

Cuddy did. It appeared the Howsh spaceship had landed close to the house. His mind raced. Had the Howsh now taken Momma—in addition to Kyle? Or had they killed her? Killed them both? He looked at Jackie, his face registering indecision.

Jackie in turn looked first at the AI, then at Tow. "Is that orb thing capable of … doing more than hovering around? Can it fight?"

Tow said, "The AI orb can speak for itself, Jackie, and will do what is asked of it."

"Both my articulating arms are equipped with integrated plasma implements. Utilized mostly for close-range welding and cutting," the AI orb said.

"And they can be reconfigured?" Cuddy asked.

"Affirmative."

"As weapons?" Jackie asked.

"Affirmative."

"Then do it …" Cuddy ordered.

Jackie leaned in toward the *viewscape* display and made a face. "Shit, that looks like …"

"Police cruisers," Cuddy said, raising the crowbar grasped still in his right fist. "We need to get over there, Tow. I know that violence is not your thing, so maybe you could get started initializing the drives?'

"Yes … I will do that."

★ ★ ★

Cuddy and Jackie ran full out, skirting in-and-out between trees, as the hovering AI orb kept pace alongside them. Never before in his life had Cuddy been this scared. His newly intelligent, informed mind was useless dealing with the mental bombardment—the all-too-real possible scenarios of what might be going on now at the ranch.

He followed behind Jackie as she leapt over the brook, and they heard the *crack crack crack* of gunfire, coming from up ahead. Jackie quickly glanced back over her shoulder then slowed so he could catch up with her.

Cuddy shouldn't have been surprised. It was only a matter of time before the Howsh found the *Evermore*. But only one Howsh ship had appeared on the display. *Where were the others? Would they too be landing soon? Would the U.S. military start bombarding this area? Maybe with nuclear weapons?*

Cuddy, now taking the lead, ran out from the line of trees as gunfire continued to fire. Cuddy, Jackie, and the orb entered the barn, quickly slowing down their pace. Out of breath, Cuddy and Jackie leaned over and, with hands on knees, heaved in deep lungfuls of air. The AI orb continued forward, moving toward the open doorway then hovered there. Still out of breath, Cuddy joined the orb in the barn doorway and peered out toward the house. *Thank God, it's still stand-*

ing! Both the Maxima and VW bug were where they'd been parked. But near to the road was a landed spaceship, equal in size to the *Evermore.* It was supported above the ground by three landing struts. A gangway ramp extended out, beneath the ship's underside. Fifty yards further down the road were two police vehicles parked at angles on the road. Cuddy recognized the vehicles as the sheriff's and Officer Plumkin's. Both driver-side doors were open—used for cover—as the officers periodically fired toward the spaceship. The sheriff was firing a rifle while Plumkin used his side arm.

Cuddy felt Jackie move up to stand close by his side. Placing a hand on his arm, she asked, "What's going on?"

"Sheriff and Plumkin are shooting."

"So do you see them ... what are they called, the Howsh?" Jackie asked.

"No, not yet. Wait ... there ... there's one of them."

They watched as a tall, furry creature came around the corner at the far side of the house, holding a weapon—a rifle of some sort. Then Cuddy noticed the front screen door of the house was partially open, hanging loosely on a single hinge. *Momma!*

Chapter 25

Standing outside on the porch—Rufus barked continuously. The dog was obviously highly agitated at what was going on inside. It took all Cuddy's willpower not to charge forward—run full out toward the house. He didn't know if Momma was still safe inside or if she'd already been taken. *Was she even alive?*

The alien beast, lurking by the side of the house, fired back toward the sheriff's police cruiser. Bright red bolts of energy hit the open car door, leaving in their wake several charred—glowing hot—craters. A second, nearly identical Howsh joined the one at the side of the house. He too held an energy weapon, which he raised and began firing toward the second police SUV, parked farther back down the road. Cuddy heard Officer Plumkin make a yelping sound, then quickly duck his head back behind the open car door.

Cuddy could see someone else, sitting inside the sheriff's cruiser. Seated in the passenger seat, peering out over the dashboard, were, unmistakably, the two white strips of adhesive tape across Tony Bone's nose. The sheriff's son.

Three more sets of furry legs were descending the gangway, which made at least five Howsh that needed to be dealt with—*somehow*. Even one was a problem. Cuddy wondered how many more were still on board the spaceship.

Crack! Startled, Cuddy and Jackie flinched as a loud rifle report resounded out from within the house. He turned in time, hearing a second loud *crack*, to catch a bright muzzle flash through the kitchen window.

Cuddy threw caution to the wind and sprinted out the barn door, hearing Jackie's desperate plea behind him: *"No ... Cuddy ... wait!"* But he couldn't let them take Momma—or worse, hurt her.

In one long stride, he leapt up onto the porch. Crossing his forearms in front of his face, he plowed his two hundred pounds into the off-kilter, hanging screen door, which crumbled and splintered into kindling on impact. Cuddy ran past the foyer and into the kitchen, nearly tripping over a Howsh body, lying, its furry limbs askew, on the floor. Cuddy noticed a good portion of his head had been blown away—a splattering of skull shards, fur, and brain matter, covered the adjacent wall.

Hearing a choking, gurgling sound, he ran down the hallway on the other side of the kitchen and found another Howsh. Momma's shotgun—its breach open—was lying on the carpet. The Howsh had one arm raised high—a ginormous fist wrapped around Momma's neck, pinning her high up on the wall. Her legs thrashed as she desperately tried to kick out and free herself. One shoe had fallen to the floor. What came next was both terrifying and comforting. *It was a voice*. Cuddy knew it was the AI orb, somehow speaking out to him. *Use your mind ... use your will to prevail.*

Crazed with fury, Cuddy's hands balled into white-knuckled fists. Yet he did as the unseen voice suggested and constructively applied both his anger and will power and watched as the alien's hand and fingers, so tightly gripped around Momma's neck, suddenly burst into a splattered cloud. A blood-red mist filled the hallway. Cuddy reached Momma's side as she fell to the floor. Desperately gasping—her hands clawed at her throat. The Howsh wailed—a high-pitched, blood curdling, otherworldly sound. Blood rhythmically spurted out from his lower arm—now with no hand. The alien beast, bent over in pain, used his other hand to tug his ruined appendage—its matted fur now slick with blood—into himself. His anger had only increased—stepping in closer, Cuddy ratcheted his right arm backward, simultaneously twisting—torquing—his upper body around. The ensuing, spring-action release—like a human pile-driver—drove Cuddy's right fist into the back of the alien's head with enough force to shatter his skull into hundreds of pieces. The alien died right where it stood, teetering for only a moment. Cuddy shoved the lifeless body away from Momma as it crumpled and fell to the floor in a heap.

Cuddy knelt down next to her, still having trouble breathing, but he could see by her expression she was okay. She swallowed hard and tried to speak. "How did you …?"

"Don't try to talk, Momma."

She swallowed again, this time croaking out the words, "There are others …"

"I know. Hold on …" Hurrying into the kitchen, he returned moments later with a glass of water. "Drink this." He waited for her to take several sips. "I need to get back out there. Will you be all right?"

She nodded. "How did you do that … his hand …"

"I don't know … not really."

"I got one of them, too … did you see?"

"I saw, Momma. Guess they picked the wrong humans to mess with."

Cuddy heard the same inner voice—the AI orb again communicating with him. He didn't understand how that was possible.

I still await your orders, Cuddy Perkins.

Orders? Where are you?

I am where you left me … at the barn.

Cuddy made his way through the kitchen, then onto the porch. Jackie and the orb were still where he left them, hiding in the barn doorway. Off to his left, more Howsh were milling around. Seeing both the sheriff's and Officer Plumkin's police vehicles on fire he wondered if they'd died in the flames. Turning to face the barn, he made eye contact with Jackie, who looked nervous. She mouthed the words: *What should we do?*

Cuddy, telecasting mentally, which had become a surprisingly natural talent, said, *Orb … I want you to protect us. Go destroy the Howsh … all of them … if you can.*

Cuddy then turned around, reentering the house, as he recalled what was lying on the kitchen floor. Just around the corner, he saw the dead Howsh his mother had shot. Extending out from beneath his legs was the muzzle of a weapon. Cuddy used his foot to roll the body over and snatched the strange-looking rifle up from the floor. Holding it in his hands, he found it heavy, and also strange, to grasp such a thing. Yet, upon looking it over, it didn't appear particularly difficult to use. He had no experience with guns, but it had a trigger and he knew which end to point at the enemy.

More plasma fire erupted outside, but sounding somewhat different than what he heard before. Making his way through the kitchen and onto the porch, he used extra care not to be spotted. Jackie, he noted, still huddled in the barn, though the AI orb was not there. Jackie pointed toward the spacecraft and shrugged.

He saw the orb momentarily hover beneath the ship. Its quick movements were a blur. He noticed two Howsh bodies, lying prone on the ground near the gangway, and briefly wondered if that was the police officers' handiwork or the AI orb's.

The two Howsh he'd spotted earlier, lurking around the

side of the house, began firing their weapons toward the road—in the orb's direction.

How many are there? he wondered. He watched the AI orb stop long enough to fire off more bright blue energy bolts from its two outstretched articulating arms.

Cuddy brought his attention back to the weapon he held in his hands. Lifting it up, he placed the stock firmly against his shoulder—just like he'd seen done in so many movies. He stared down the muzzle, noting three sets of sights, then lined up all three with the Howsh alien, standing by the corner of the house—some thirty or forty feet away. He pulled the trigger. A bright-red plasma bolt hit the side of the house, missing the target by several feet. He fired again, this time missing by only a foot. Unfortunately, he had gotten the alien's attention, who was now bringing his weapon around toward Cuddy's direction. Cuddy fired again, this time taking little aim, and it was a direct hit onto the alien's chest. He watched the alien drop to the ground. He'd never purposely harmed another living thing—never in his life—and now he'd killed two beings in a matter of minutes. He didn't want to dwell on that.

Cuddy noticed the second Howsh had moved forward, had assumed the position held by his dead comrade. When the alien looked across, from around the corner of the house, they made eye contact. Raising weapons at the same time, they fired simultaneously.

Chapter 26

Cuddy was hit hard by something coming in low—in from his right side. The momentum lifted him off his feet and jammed him up against the house. A series of plasma bolts sizzled past him in the air and undoubtedly would have killed him, except for Jackie, who had careened into him. Still stunned, he watched her grab the alien's rifle from his clutches, then spin around and fire the weapon. Cuddy hadn't been aware the Howsh alien had steadily advanced on them—was less than twenty feet away. Jackie continued to pull the trigger, though the Howsh alien was obviously on the ground dead. Dead, and on fire, from more plasma fire than necessary.

"I think that'll do it, Jackie," Cuddy said, stepping away from the wall.

"You're welcome," she said.

"I guess I'm not a very good shot," he said

"Good thing I am … thanks to my dad." Staring down at the weapon in her hands, she added, "This is beyond cool. I'm keeping it."

"Fine with me—keep it. Come on, let's go see how the AI orb is doing." He headed toward the alien spacecraft, stopping only long enough to pick up another plasma weapon that had been dropped next to the corner of the house.

"Want me to show you how to use that?" Jackie asked, still three strides back.

Cuddy didn't bother to answer. Reaching the top of the drive, he now had a far better vantage point. Of the Howsh invasion, the first word that came to mind was *battlefield.* No less than eight Howsh fur-balls lay sprawled on the road, at various locations. Adding also to the body count were those slain in and around the house—tallying up to an even dozen. With still no sign of the AI orb, Cuddy ran to the first smoldering police vehicle. Black smoke still spiraled into the air from the four charred tires. Peering into the glassless window frame, there was little left to see—both bucket-seat frames, with their blackened coil springs, showed no signs of incinerated bodies. But Cuddy wasn't sure if even skeletal remains could endure the kind of blaze that took place here. He next moved on to inspect the SUV, Officer Plumkin's vehicle, and found the same thing. Nothing in the car's ruins—no skeletal body in the driver's seat.

He looked back to see Jackie collecting Howsh weapons. She'd mounted them into a pile by the side of the road and was adding another to the top.

Cuddy asked, "Any sign of the AI orb?" After first doing a cursory glance around, she replied, "Nope."

He could see she was feeling pretty pleased with herself. *Cocky*, while he was still dealing with feelings of some remorse and guilt. He knew it was illogical. The aliens came here to kill Tow—as well as them. He stared up at the top of the gangway.

"Cuddy!" Momma shouted, heading their way. She'd changed her clothes and was wearing tennis shoes. Meeting her halfway, he could see she was upset. "What is it? What happened?"

"On TV … we're being attacked!" She looked at Cuddy

and then Jackie. What she had learned was reflected by the shock on her face.

Cuddy gestured toward the spacecraft. "By them?"

"Yes by them … Washington, D.C. … New York. And other places I don't remember, all over the world. Two alien ships are firing their weapons … turning cities into rubble. Many thousands have been killed so far. It's horrible …" she sobbed, wiping away the tears on her cheeks with her fingers. Jackie put her arms around her, pulling her close for a hug.

Maybe that explains why the military didn't show up here, Cuddy mused. *The whole world was on the brink of disaster.* For the first time, Momma noticed the carnage around them. She looked over at Cuddy. She looked impressed.

"This wasn't me, Momma. I found out soon enough I'm a terrible shot."

She turned to Jackie. "You did …"

"No … well, just those two, lying outside by the house. But hey, you killed one too …"

Momma shrugged and nodded.

"Look, Momma … best you go back to the house now, okay?" Taking another quick look around, Momma headed back down the drive. Cuddy waited until she disappeared into the house.

"So, are we going to go in there?" Jackie asked.

"Yeah … I have to, my brother might be in there. You don't have to come …"

"No … I'll be right behind you," she said, raising the plasma rifle to emphasize the point.

Cuddy headed up the ramp—his weapon poised to shoot anything with fur. Entering the quasi-circular compartment, he started to gag.

"Ugh … it's so foul! This area reeks … smells like shit," Jackie said, expressing the obvious.

While his eyes adjusted to the dimness, he slowed his pace. Jackie, right behind him added, "It's like a damn cave in here."

His brow now furrowing, Cuddy glanced back at her and whispered, *"Shhhhh!"*

They followed a narrow, but tall-ceilinged passageway. On either side, the bulkheads were covered with what looked like streaks of grease. Cuddy thought of the contrast between this filthy environment and the meticulously clean *Evermore*. Noises were heard ahead when they reached a stairway with four, wide open grated treads. "Watch your step … something brown's on that bottom one."

Jackie mumbled something undecipherable.

Reaching the top step, Cuddy was presented with three options—three different corridors—and he chose the one on the right. They passed a series of closed hatchways—three on one side, two on the other. The noises were getting louder, coming from the same direction they were headed. Cuddy raised the barrel of his weapon, prepared to shoot if necessary, then stood still to listen. The noises were actually voices—and he understood what was being said.

"Screw you, Perkins … if I wanted advice, it wouldn't be from a lowlife, redneck hillbilly like you…"

Cuddly glanced back at Jackie. She said, "I think I know that voice. That's Tony Bone." They slowly approached what he figured was the ship's primary corridor. Twice as wide as the one they were now in, it formed a T-junction. He peered around the corner, to the left. *All clear.* Then, looking to the right, his breath caught in his chest. The AI orb was lying down on the deck. Several blackened scorch marks made it clear what had happened. One of the orb's articulating arms was outstretched, while its other one was awkwardly curled underneath. As quietly as possible, Cuddy stepped closer and, kneeling next to it, found several tiny lights still blinking. Carefully, he took hold of the extended arm and lifted the orb up from the deck. Rising up, he held the orb an arm's length away.

"Is it … dead?" Jackie asked.

All of a sudden, Cuddy's mind was filled with a slew of bright flashes—incongruent images. Unbalanced, he swayed back and forth, as Jackie helped to steady him, looking concerned. It was as if his mind had been hijacked. He realized he was seeing through the eyes … *eye* … of the AI orb! He watched its two articulating arms—both extended out in front—fire continuous, bright-blue energy bolts. And he realized he was viewing earlier events that transpired outside on the road, when the orb was beneath the ship. Cuddy inwardly watched the orb's battle with the Howsh. The speed in which the orb maneuvered—dodging this way and that—was breathtaking. He felt nauseous trying to track the course of those events. One by one enemy Howsh were vanquished. Cuddy watched as the orb moved up the ramp and into the bowels of the ship. Unknowingly, he and Jackie had followed the same route inside as the orb. And then, apparently, the orb met its match. Cuddy watched as a Howsh alien came into view, wearing a red sash. Worn on a diagonal, the sash crossed from shoulder to the opposite hip. The alien didn't move like the others. He was fast; seemed to instinctively know where and how to move to avoid the orb's plasma fire. He fired his weapon at the orb only once. And then, just as suddenly, Cuddy's inner visions ceased and he found himself gazing into Jackie's concerned eyes.

"Where did you go?" she asked.

Chapter 27

Cuddy still had ahold of the orb's outstretched articulating arm. He lifted it higher and noticed, at the sphere's apex—within the concave circular section—the aperture still emanated faint blue light. He held it up like a dead chicken, letting it sway back and forth under its own weight.

Jackie said, "Come on, maybe you can bring it with us."

Cuddy lowered his arm. He had no intention of leaving the orb behind. Squabbling voices could be heard ahead as he and Jackie hurried across the wide, perpendicular corridor to the other side. Continuing on, and noting an open entrance on the right, Cuddy edged up to the corner and peered in. He quickly pulled back, wide-eyed and disgusted, staring blankly at the opposing bulkhead.

"What is it? Let me see!" He moved aside so she could take his vacated spot, closer to the entrance. Looking in, Cuddy heard her quick inhalation of breath. When she pulled back, turning toward him, in barely controlled hushed tones she exclaimed, "That's horrible! They're just hanging there … like sides of beef!"

The vivid mental image of the havoc in the adjacent

compartment was all too prominent in Cuddy's mind. No less than twenty people, almost half of them naked, were strung up, hanging by their feet, their bodies swaying back and forth. Among them were Sheriff Bone, shirtless Officer Plumkin, Tony Bone, and—closest to the entrance—his brother Kyle. Also others, who were dead. Their blackened, malformed corpses showed they'd been terribly beaten, beyond anything he could imagine.

He wanted to rescue Kyle. Rush in there and help them all. But if he and Jackie weren't extremely careful, they too could end up in there, hanging upside-down, like the others. Cuddy was having a hard time controlling his breathing. He didn't think he'd ever been this scared. Too scared to move, like he was again seven years old.

"Hey … are you doing okay? We just need to stay calm … at least try," Jackie whispered.

He shook his head. *No, he wasn't okay* and wondered how she could even ask such a question.

"Well, stay here. Keep guard and let me know if anyone's coming."

"What are you doing? We shouldn't separate," he said, aware desperation was in his voice.

"Just stay here." Raising her weapon, she then slipped around the corner.

Standing alone in the passageway, Cuddy looked left and then right and saw a lone figure approaching from the distance; one clearly armed with a rifle. He wore a narrow band of red—a diagonally draped sash. A Howsh, he was casually walking forward as if he hadn't a care in the world. Cuddy felt a vibration in his right hand and, glancing down at the orb, noticed it was moving, trying to release itself from his grasp.

The Howsh walked right up to Cuddy, appraising him from head to toe. He was taller than he was by half a foot. Close to seven feet tall.

The orb was frantically jerking around in Cuddy's hand

so he let it drop to the deck. Paralyzed with fear, he wanted to yell out and warn Jackie, but he couldn't speak.

A dank odor wafted around them as the alien pivoted his head about, as though trying to figure something out, then spoke in a mixture of a growl and a language Cuddy didn't understand. The Howsh bared his teeth and raised the muzzle of his weapon and then there was searing pain in his chest—everything went black.

★ ★ ★

Cuddy awoke with an upside-down view of the same horrific compartment he'd earlier glimpsed. He was less than five feet away from his brother.

Kyle, now looking back at him, said, "Hey there, little brother."

"Hey Kyle."

"So … you two were what? Trying to rescue us … huh?"

Cuddy found it hard to think, even harder to speak, with so much blood throbbing in his head. "It gets a bit easier … in time," Kyle told him.

Cuddy heard another voice, nearby him but out of sight, ask, "Who sends the village idiot to attempt a rescue, anyway?"

"Shut up, Tony!" Kyle barked.

"Are you okay, Cuddy?" Jackie asked. Hearing the concern in her voice, he tried to jostle his body around to see her but couldn't make it happen.

Cuddy asked, "What is this place? What's happening …"

"Just look around, dip-weed," Tony said. "We're in some kind of alien laboratory. Look up … they have all kinds of nasty equipment to fuck us up with."

"I told you, Tony, knock it off!" Kyle said.

Cuddy, struggling, looked up toward his tightly bound feet. Separated into stand-alone stations were all sorts of hanging metallic devices, along with a variety of attached hoses. He didn't want to think about their uses.

"*Shit* … he's coming back," Tony said.

Moments later, Cuddy sensed the evil presence of the Howsh within the compartment—somewhere behind him.

"Don't touch me!" Jackie yelled.

Cuddy jerked and squirmed until his body, pendulum-like, finally spun around. The Howsh, he noted in alarm, was touching Jackie's hair—leaning into her and inhaling, while making a sniffing noise. He could see Jackie's anger turn to fear, and he shouted, "Hey! Leave her alone … get away from her!"

"You don't want to say that, Cuddy," Kyle said, in a lowered tone. "He'll punish you."

"Yeah, he'll hurt you something bad, boy," said Officer Plumkin.

Cuddy focused his attention beyond Jackie, then toward a swaying, shirtless figure whose big belly hung down onto his chest. His face was bruised and one eye swollen shut. He noticed the sheriff was hanging next to Plumkin. "Is the sheriff all right?"

Tony, Kyle, and Plumkin answered at the same time, "No, he's not."

Kyle watched as the Howsh continued to focus his attention on Jackie. He groped her breasts and snorted. She screamed, "Stop! Get the fuck away from me!"

Cuddy felt useless—*pathetic*—then remembered what he'd done to the Howsh who was attacking Momma. *How do I do that again? How do I use my mind that way?* He'd had the help of the AI orb and wondered where the orb was now. Cuddy mentally called out to it and listened for a response. *Nothing*. Swaying his body back and forth, he craned his neck around until he could see the entrance into the compartment. Something shiny lay on the deck—one of the AI orb's clawed arms—and the rest lay hidden in the passageway. *Has the orb been completely destroyed?* Cuddy wondered.

Suddenly, Cuddy's body was swung back in the opposite direction and the alien's face was mere inches from his own. His rank breath made Cuddy want to throw up. The snarl was back as he looked into Cuddy's eyes, then asked him in broken English, "Where is *Pashier* ship?"

Cuddy stared back at the angry furry face. "Um ... who are you?" Cuddy asked.

Growling in annoyance, he answered, "I am captain of ship. I am Holg. Now tell ... where is *Pashier* ship?"

Cuddy stared back at him, confused. *How could he not know?* The *Evermore* was less than a mile's distance away. Then he thought of something Tow had mentioned—that once both drives were operational, well synchronized, he could turn on some kind of additional shielding device, camouflaging the *Evermore* from being spotted from above or picked up by their sensors. *Is that what happened? Had the Howsh gotten so close then lost track of the* Evermore *at the last moment?*

"Tell him what he wants to know, Cuddy," Tony said. "He's asked that same question over and over again ... He beats us. He'll kill us, like he did the others here."

Cuddy heard his brother ask, "Do you even know where it is?"

Holg, listening intently to their conversation, was watching his face so perhaps he should just tell him. He didn't want anyone to die because of him. Especially Kyle and Jackie. But then he thought of Tow and his promise to him. Thought of the heritage pod. That no one would be left to return it to Primara. Cuddy didn't know what to do. He'd been so concerned with Tow and his incredible mission to save his kind that he'd almost lost track of the fact that his own kind ... his own family may pay the price. Maybe he should tell this foul-smelling best what he wants to know ... and just maybe he would let them all go.

Jackie said, "Don't you do it, Cuddy. The only reason we're

still breathing is because he doesn't have what he's looking for yet."

The alien's eyes flared with anger. He bared his teeth and roared over his shoulder in Jackie's direction, then spun back again. "You are called Cuddy … tell me, Cuddy, do you not want to go free? All go free? Do you, Cuddy?" Then, using a clawed furry hand, he scratched himself on the neck and Cuddy momentarily caught movement that looked like small insects scurrying around in the matted fur.

Holg then brought the same extended claw forward to rest on Cuddy's cheek, and as he applied increased downward pressure, Cuddy felt his face begin to bleed.

Chapter 28

The orb arrived outside the ship ten minutes earlier. Apparently, one of its articulating arms was still *somewhat* operational. Enough so, that it was capable of dragging itself around. The *Evermore*'s proximity alarm *twirped* twice—letting Tow know that there was outer movement, of some sort, approaching. Checking the bridge viewscape display, he saw the AI orb, lying outside the ship.

Opening the hatch and finding the orb there, obviously struggling, Tow felt both relief and deep concern. He hurried. Lifting the orb into his arms, he carried it back inside the ship. Earlier, he had feared the worst, witnessing the dreaded arrival of the Howsh spaceship. Soon after that, he lost mental contact with the orb and had to struggle with the prospect that the AI orb had been destroyed. Also, more than likely, the human, Cuddy, had been killed as well. And with that, all hope for his kind—the *Pashier*—would be forever gone. In the end, Tow's presence on Earth had only brought catastrophe.

Now, with a glimmer of hope rekindled, Tow carried the AI orb directly to a small, lower deck workshop, setting it down carefully on the bench. As much as the orb had become an annoyance over past months—years—he was surprised at the sadness he felt. For such a long time now, there'd only been the two of them, and he instinctively knew he wouldn't have made it this far all alone.

Tow took in the orb's multiple blackened scorch marks, resulting from Howsh plasma fire. Opening the small access panel on the underside of the orb, Tow noted there was little he'd be able to do since it was clearly evident much of the orb's mechanical functionality was severely damaged. Damaged, he could see, beyond repair. He exhaled a long breath. Moving slowly, and coughing continuously, Tow—leaving the orb lying on the bench—left the small workshop area. He moved aft and entered the second of two hold compartments. He knew exactly where to go; knew where everything on the ship could be found. His eyes scanned the many rows of deck-to-ceiling shelving, before he turned down and walked between the sixth and seventh set of shelves. Halfway down the row on the left, at eye level, he found exactly what he was seeking—twelve new, pristine, AI orb units. Each had two articulating arms—folded up and strapped down for optimal storage. Tow arbitrarily selected one. Pulling it off the shelf, he studied the inanimate object now lying in his hands.

* * *

Back again in his small workshop, Tow set the new AI orb unit next to the battered older one. He was somewhat familiar with the mechanics of transferring one orb's set of *dynamic-gel-tabs*—brains and memory plus a complete set of system interface components—into another unit. Typically, that type of technical work would be assigned to an orb to perform, but that was no longer an option. The trick was to ensure that the old *gel-tabs* didn't get compromised during the procedure's transfer. Gel-tabs, highly sensitive, were, in a sense, living organisms, possessing trillions upon trillions of firing synapses and active neurotransmitters. Much like those found in an actual organic brain—but with far more speed and capacity. It also explained why these hovering AI units took on, to some degree, a personality of their own. Tow wasn't at all sure that was a good thing. He briefly wondered if the older unit's gel-tabs were still salvageable … worth the trouble. There were new, unused ones, still back in the storage hold. No … he would try to salvage these.

He clipped off the shipping straps and unbound the AI orb's folded-in arms. He then flipped the orb over and opened its access panel. He knew already that new units were stored *brainless*, without functioning, *dynamic gel-tabs.*

Tow looked for, then found, *zero-sensory calipers* mounted up on the wall between numerous other complex tools and devices. He placed his thumb and forefinger into the end with two scissor-like openings then watched as the other end—which had a set of three, independent prongs—came alive. They were now in search mode—*looking … searching.* Tow, shifting his position before the bench, brought the calipers down—close to the damaged orb's access panel. As he lowered the calipers, the prongs continued to both move and work together, like animated worms. They constantly readjusted, in respect to the other, and to what lay within the open panel. Tow steadily lowered the prongs deeper and deeper into the AI orb's center cavity. They intrinsically knew what to look for. The same procedure could not be done by hand, as gel-tabs were far too sensitive to be touched by an organic being.

A series of tiny lights began to blink on and off, indicating the calipers had found, and were secured onto, the targeted gel-tabs. Now came the tricky part. Gently, Tow pulled up on the calipers. At the slightest resistance, he would need to stop. Either that, or risk damaging the living gel-tab's ultra-thin surrounding membrane. Feeling another series of racking coughs coming on, he steadied his hand, keeping the pressure of his fingers constant and consistent, while attempting also to clear his throat. But the coughs came on anyway. Tow's eyes filled with moisture and his chest burned as the hacking episode relentlessly persisted. All the while, he watched the set of tiny caliper indicator lights that continued to remain lit.

Tow's fit of coughing finally relented and he found he could breathe more easily again. Slowly, he continued raising his hand up until the prongs of the clippers came back into view, along with what they now held. Tow stared at the three glowing, bright blue, odd-shaped gel-taps. Not wanting to chance another coughing fit coming on, he quickly repositioned the calipers above the new AI orb unit. Then, lowering his hand, he felt the caliper device gently guiding his fingers to where the device needed to go. The same series of lights were blinking on and off in a new pattern now—confirmation the gel-tabs were seated properly. Tow removed the calipers, then returned them to the open slot on the tool board. After closing the access panel, he flipped the new AI orb over, and waited. Nothing happened.

Tow's mind suddenly became flooded with new imagery. He saw the interior of the Howsh ship but didn't understand what he was viewing. Not at first. There were numerous swaying forms—hung from somewhere high above. *Humans*. Both Cuddy and Jackie were among the prisoners.

So captivated by the horrific visions he was witnessing, Tow didn't at first notice that the AI orb had reinitialized and was hovering six feet off the deck. The orb said, "I shall return now … to assist Cuddy Perkins."

Tow said, "Welcome back, orb!" The orb hovered silently nearby.

"How many Howsh are on board the Howsh vessel?" Tow asked.

"Only one. Captain Holg."

After three years of relentless pursuit across the cosmos, Tow felt like he personally knew Holg. There'd been a few brief communications. Holg, offering Tow his life in exchange for destruction of the heritage pod, would be satisfied knowing Tow would die alone in space—his race of people eviscerated for all eternity.

Over time, Tow spent many hours doing in-depth research on his adversary, looking for areas of weakness. Perhaps some psychotic malady that would give Tow an upper hand. But he never found one. Holg was a warrior, through and through. Even among his own kind, he was considered ruthless. Ruthless and unyielding, he never ceased his aggression. Giving up was as foreign a concept to Holg as committing violence was to Tow.

Focusing his attention again on the AI orb, he wondered if that lone, small drone-like device could actually make a difference. Planet Earth was in the midst of something heinous. Those other two Howsh ships were repeating the same systematic, city-by-city annihilation they'd committed on Mahli. *It needed to stop.* They'd already won.

"I will go with you, orb. It's time I personally speak with Captain Holg."

★ ★ ★

As Tow descended the gangway, he spotted his favorite walking stick, lying nearby on the ground. As he'd done so many times before, he attempted, using his mind, to retrieve it, but soon found he was far too weak to elevate it off the ground. Instead, he walked the short distance, bent over, and picked it up one-handed. Then, after walking around for a while, he turned back and faced the *Evermore*, wondering if he would ever see his ship again. He pictured the heritage pod, entombed within the lower deck, and thought of Soweng. His heart ached. *I'm so very sorry, my love.*

He was weaker now and walking was difficult. As Tow and the orb moved farther into the trees, he queried the AI orb about any recently transpired events that he was unaware of. Then Tow said, "You can hurry ahead, orb. I will catch up."

Chapter 29

His face hurt where Holg, the Howsh with the red sash, clawed him. When a loud tone blared out somewhere above them the alien rushed off.

Now, with so much time to think—and little else to do—Cuddy wondered how the Howsh accomplished the arduous task of chaining up, feet first, all the prisoners. But he soon realized two large robots were also moving about. They didn't look anything like the AI orb on the *Evermore*. These robots were similar in size and girth to the Howsh themselves. Peculiar looking, they also were covered with fur—similar to that on the Howsh.

Cuddy watched the two robots silently work together, removing one of the dead bodies from the compartment. That was a good thing—the smell had gone way beyond toxic. Efficient in their movements, one robot raised itself high off the deck. Reaching out with a clawed mechanical arm, it opened a clasp attached to the chain above. The lifeless body of a large woman dropped to the deck, making an awful-sounding *thud*. Effortlessly, the second robot lifted her up off the deck and carried her from the compartment. The first robot then turned its attention on the next corpse—again, lifting itself up high in order to release the clasp. Another body, an old man this time, dropped below with a loud *thud*. It too was carted off.

The two robots next moved toward Sheriff Bone's hanging body. As one robot began to rise, the sheriff yelled, "Get away from me! I'm not dead yet! Get away!"

Cuddy knew that the sheriff was still alive, seeing him every so often twitch or move. But he understood how the robots could make that mistake. The older man, black and blue everywhere, looked to be in pretty bad shape. He had been terribly beaten.

Cuddy estimated it took the robots about ten minutes before the compartment was completely cleared, free of dead bodies. They left then, not returning. His eyes nervously glanced toward the entrance. Though trying hard not to think about it, he found it nearly impossible not to, praying he wouldn't see the robots again—carrying in Momma. Prayed they wouldn't find her back in the house and grab her, then return and hang her up as they had all the others.

Cuddy by now had become fairly proficient at moving his hips—pivoting his body around either left or right—so he could see the others. They all seemed to be asleep. He stared at Jackie for a while. Her long straw-colored hair hung down, swaying back and forth like she was underwater, moved by invisible currents.

Reluctantly, he turned his thoughts back to the strange *incident* that occurred at the house. When somehow he'd made that alien's hand … *vaporize*, using only the sheer force of his mind. Suddenly it went … *Poof!* For sure, the AI orb assisted him in some way. Could he now, mentally, do a similar thing on his own? The same way Tow so easily could? His sessions in the wellness chamber, he knew, did more than just fix his brain.

Off and on, Cuddy tried to manipulate things in his surroundings. Currently, he was attempting to make a distant and stationary hanging chain move about. But nothing seemed to be happening. What did the orb say to him? *Use your mind … your will to prevail.* Well … wasn't that exactly what he was struggling to do? Cuddy thought about that for a while. Perhaps, it wasn't so much *what* he was attempting to do, but *how he felt* while doing it. The orb's presence in his head at that time had made him feel safe. Safe and confident. He certainly didn't feel that way now. How could he, hanging upside down, along with Kyle and Jackie, when they all were in so much danger?

He noticed Jackie was now awake, looking at him. "What are you doing?" she asked.

"Trying to move that chain, on the other side of the room, with my mind."

"Seriously? Why would you want to do that?"

"Because of something I did … back in the house. It's hard to explain. Can you do something for me?"

Jackie almost smiled. "There's not much I can do for you, or anyone, in my current predicament."

"Can you … kinda just talk to me? Um … like tell me I can do it? That you believe in me. Or something like that?"

"I guess … sure, why not!"

Cuddy, focusing, brought his full attention back to the hanging chain and waited. "Okay … go ahead."

"You can do this, Cuddy. You can do anything you set your mind to. I believe in you, Cuddy."

Cuddy liked the sound of her voice. That she no longer spoke to him like he was plain stupid. As his mind began to wander a bit, he quickly reined his thoughts back in, concentrating on the distant, four-to-five-foot-long chain. Then, as if he were extending an invisible hand across space, he gave it a little push. The chain visibly began to sway back and forth. It wasn't as dramatic as making an alien's hand burst into a mist of blood and gore, but still, it was *something. Yes, I can do it!*

"Look Cuddy! Do you see that? The chain … it's moving," Jackie exclaimed excitedly.

"Oh for fuck's sake … they're all moving. Get real, retard," Tony Bone said.

The truth was, all the chains seemed to be swaying somewhat. Perhaps Tony was right. That it was simply wishful thinking on his part.

"Don't call him that, Tony!" Kyle ordered.

Cuddy noticed that those hanging were all wide-awake now, except for Officer Plumkin, who was snoring loudly. A large wet spot darkened his crotch area where he'd peed himself. Soon Cuddy felt he would do the same, as he needed to urinate pretty badly. Not something he would want Jackie to ever witness.

Holg, the Howsh captain, still wearing the red sash, entered the compartment and headed directly for Cuddy, his teeth bared. Evidently, something unlikely had occurred since he was last pulled away. The painful claw marks on Cuddy's cheek began to burn in anticipation of what he knew was coming.

Holg came to a stop directly in front of Cuddy. Pent up anger permeated the air around him like a bad smell. Cuddy hadn't noticed, until they were practically on top of him, that the two furry robots were there as well. Then two mechanical arms came around him and gripped him tight, below his shoulders and around his chest, in a vise-like hold that made it nearly impossible to breathe. The second robot released Cuddy's bound hands from behind his back, but the relief he suddenly felt was short-lived.

"Let him go! He doesn't know anything!" Kyle yelled.

Cuddy then felt his arm grasped in two places—above the wrist and just below the elbow.

Jackie said, "Stop! I know where it is. I've been to the ship. I'll tell you if you stop!"

The tension on Cuddy's arm grew steadily—its radius

and ulna bones beginning to bow and flex. Cuddy screamed out in agony.

Captain Holg, his interest now piqued, turned his head back toward Jackie, silently waiting for her to continue. But with the passing of every second—every microsecond—Cuddy's pain level steadily multiplied. His screams filled the compartment, his arm on the verge of breaking in two. Through Cuddy's tear-filled eyes, Captain Holg's furry form was barely a blur, as was the hovering black object that suddenly appeared next to his head. Cuddy, fast blinking away tears, could now see the glowing blue light at the object's center. Its two clawed, articulating arms, on either side of the large football-shaped construction, left little doubt that the AI orb had indeed returned.

Mere inches away, the orb's point-blank firing of its arms' plasma weapons eviscerated the Howsh captain's head. Even before his lifeless body dropped to the deck, the orb was moving about, firing on the two robots.

While the tension and pain in Cuddy's arm abated some, the orb and both robots battled on. Though they'd previously seemed somewhat meandering and clumsy in their movements, the robots now moved with the same lightning speed as the orb. Armed with their own integrated plasma weaponry, they were firing indiscriminately—red energy bolts coursed through the air. Cuddy heard Jackie scream out something. She was no longer in his field of vision, but he knew she'd been hit. He flinched as a series of plasma fire whizzed by him, inches from his own face.

The two robots, effectively working together, maneuvered the AI orb into the far back corner of the compartment. Managing as well as it could—dodging this way and that—the orb was clearly losing the battle. Never designed or intended for war, it was clearly outmatched.

In the short period of time Cuddy and the orb had interacted, he'd formed a bond of sorts with it. Now, for the second time, he helplessly watched as the orb selflessly fought on in his, and the others', behalf. It wouldn't be long now.

Chapter 30

The AI orb had been driven down—now hovering close to the deck. Less and less it was firing back and the two Howsh robots moved in closer for the kill.

Cuddy wanted to look away. Didn't want to watch as the inevitable ensued.

When Tow entered the compartment, it took Cuddy several moments for the realization to set in that he was actually there. He moved slowly but with purpose. For a moment Cuddy wondered if being a pacifist carried over to such things as fighting robots. But the question was quickly moot.

Tow used his two hands to direct his kinetic energy. Still firing, one of the robots rose up from the deck and hovered there a moment—then it was careening across the compartment while picking up more and more speed along its trajectory. By the time it careened into the farthest bulkhead, it was a blur of motion. It hit with enough force to shake the entire ship—enough inertia for the robot's mechanical limbs to separate from its torso. For all of its intelligent processes to forever be quelled.

Tow brought his attention back to the other robot who,

seeming distracted by the demise of his brethren bot, had stopped firing on the AI orb. With his hands raised higher now—fingers outstretched—Tow quickly pulled his arms apart in separate directions. The robot dismantled into a thousand pieces—like junkyard scrap metal—components pulled away—to eventually fall harmlessly to the deck.

Tow slumped down to one knee, clearly drained to the point of exhaustion.

"What the hell did I just see?" Tony Bone said.

Cuddy continued to stare at Tow. Miraculously, he'd rescued them. Saved their lives. But now he was terribly weak—was struggling. He tried to reach for him to somehow comfort his ailing friend. He felt so useless. Cuddy's thoughts turned to Jackie … He'd heard her scream. Desperately, now able to use his arms, he swung his body around until her hanging form came into view. She was alive. Alive and rubbing a blackened scorch mark on her upper shoulder. With a furrowed brow, she gave an *I'll live* … smile.

★ ★ ★

Surprisingly, the AI orb, with the exception of numerous plasma blast marks, was still fully operational. Cuddy had been the first to be freed. He made the process go faster with the others by lifting them up and relieving the tension of the chain so the orb could undo the attaching clasps.

Jackie was attending Tow. He hadn't gotten up from where he'd faced off with the two Howsh robots. He looked up as Cuddy approached.

"Please … help me to return to the *Evermore*. You and I have much to accomplish in a short amount of time."

"Accomplish?"

"I had wondered about it … hoped for it … with the introduction of Pashier genetics into your physiology. That you'd posses kinetic abilities."

Cuddy still didn't know what Tow was talking about.

"I am aware of what you did to the Howsh … to the one who was attacking your mother. Cuddy … your mind … it can be trained."

"Is it important … now?"

"How do you think I made it this far … on a spacecraft without weapons? The power of the mind is formidable … but it must be properly trained."

Cuddy shook his head. "Only if there is time."

Tow continued to stare blank-faced up at him. Cuddy saw that his body had nearly lost all of its glow.

The others moved in around them—Jackie and Kyle—and Tony Bone, who was doing his best to support the weight of his father, the sheriff—and Officer Plumkin, with his stained trousers.

Cuddy felt the weight of what he said next. "That will have to wait, Tow. I'm sorry." Cuddy gestured to the surrounding space with his hands. "We have this ship. A ship with weapons. It can be used to fend of the other two Howsh vessels … the ones currently attacking Earth … yes?"

Tow, obviously not used to thinking in terms of inflicting violence onto others, slowly nodded. He said, "But I cannot be the one to …"

"You can show me … show us all?"

Tow said, "I do not have much time … I'm sorry, Cuddy … but yes, I will do what I can."

Cuddy turned to the others. "I don't know if we are the best ones to do this … especially me. But we're here, now."

"What are you talking about?" Tony said. "And why are you suddenly talking like you have a brain?"

Jackie said, "He's talking about us taking this ship to fight the other two … the ones destroying cities all around the globe. And maybe it's just you're getting stupider."

"Us? Are you crazy? That's a job for the fricken military … or NASA or anyone else that knows a hell of a lot more about that sort of stuff."

Jackie said, "In the time that it would take to get them here … the agencies you just spoke of … how many more thousands of people will die? And what about Tow here? What do you think they'll do to him? And remember … he's the one who just saved all of our lives."

The sheriff cleared his throat and tried to say something. He tried again, his voice barely audible. "She's right. We're here …" he looked over to Tow still crouched on the deck. "If he and the flying robot can show us … we can fight." The sheriff looked at his son. "Stop being such a pansy … stop complaining so much and help." He coughed and dropped his head. His eyes shut and fluttered.

Tony staggered on the dead weight of his unconscious father. Cuddy saw that the sheriff's chest continued to expand and contract with slow, shallow, breaths.

"I still think it's crazy," Tony said. "But I guess so is me standing here looking at a naked alien."

★ ★ ★

With the help of Officer Plumkin and Tony, the sheriff was escorted to the lower deck and then outside. Tow was fairly certain the older human would perish soon if not given the proper medical attention. The plan was for them to borrow Momma's automobile and drive to the hospital after Kyle first checked on his mother.

En route to the alien bridge, Tow, who'd often wondered before what the interior of the Howsh vessels looked like, was appalled. The foul space was an appropriate match for these barbaric aliens. He gazed at his surroundings, at the greasy bulkheads around them. Tuffs of errant strands of fur clung to them, as if somehow they were alive. Beneath his feet, the widely spaced grate decking had been used for bodily waste, even though more conventional waste facilities were provided on each deck. The humans had eagerly made use of those.

At present, Cuddy walked beside Tow, his arm around him adding support. "You're going to have to tell me where to head next, Tow. So many passageways … I'm already getting lost."

Tow knew the Howsh ship's layout almost as well as he did the *Evermore*'s, since her sensors provided him with a schematic layout on the bridge viewscape display. He knew they were approaching another stairway and wondered if he had the strength to climb them. He said, "Keep going the way we're going, Cuddy. We need to climb those stairs up ahead."

Jackie, closely following them, was never more than several paces behind. She asked, "Are you up to piloting this ship … well enough for that, Tow?"

Tow, musing on that same issue himself, knew the answer was *no*. He belonged on the *Evermore,* along with the heritage pod. "I will show you and Cuddy the basics. Just know … even on board the *Evermore* … the AI orb does most of the piloting. You will have the orb with you … to assist you."

On the landing below the stairway, Cuddy gathered Tow into his arms. Tow felt grateful to the young human that he didn't have to ask him for help. Halfway up the stairway, Tow heard the sound of running footsteps coming from below. Kyle and Tony had returned. Cuddy, pleasantly surprised, found Rufus again at his side. He probably came back with Kyle. A moment later, the AI orb hovered near the group, then continued moving past.

Cuddy asked over his shoulder, "Kyle … how's Momma?"

"She was struggling with one of the dead Howsh … trying to drag it outside. Tony and I helped her. Then we threw both Howsh bodies into the barn. To answer your question, she's fine. Carries one of those alien rifles around with her … never lets go of it."

Tow, listening to the conversation, was amazed that violence came so easily to their species. He then pointed to the right. "Turn here, Cuddy. We're almost there."

Jackie said, "Tony, you didn't want to go with your father … to the hospital."

"I thought about it. Then thought maybe I'd be of more use here … with you guys. Plus, he's got Plumkin with him."

Tow, only half-listening to them, strove to make a mental connection with the AI orb, something that once had been second nature. He was disheartened. His battle with the two robots had so thoroughly drained him he now, apparently, had lost that ability.

★ ★ ★

Cuddy gazed down at the frail alien in his arms, a shell of the being he'd encountered only days before. How quickly his health was declining. They climbed two more sets of stairs.

"We have reached the top level," Tow said.

Cuddy had already come to that same conclusion.

The AI orb, hovering by the wide entrance into the compartment, said, "Cuddy Perkins, you have arrived at the bridge."

Cuddy entered the bridge and took it all in. Somewhat larger than the bridge on the *Evermore*, it too seemed, like the rest of the ship, to smell awful—beyond disgusting. The overall seating was metal and the technology appeared archaic.

Tony Bone said, "So Tow, those alien assholes defeated you, huh? No offense, but nothing here looks, um, all that sophisticated."

Tow said, "Whatever technology there is on board was pilfered from other races … other worlds. What the Howsh are most proficient at is the destruction of other civilizations. Killing off divergent life forms. For the Howsh, the mere existence of other species within the universe is an insult to their God …"

Cuddy set Tow down on one of the metal seats at the most prominent set of consoles.

"Permission, Cuddy Perkins, to activate the ship's core systems," the AI orb then requested.

Tony, giving Cuddy a sideways glance, queried, "Why ask him for permission?"

Jackie answered, "Because Tow is sick, as you can see. He's handed the command of the AI orb over to Cuddy. And before you make another smartass remark, know that Cuddy's been ... transformed. He's probably smarter than all of us, at this point."

Cuddy wasn't at all sure he'd agree with that assessment, though over the last few hours he was conscious of experiencing improved mental acuity. He looked warily across at Tony, still wearing two, quite dirty, white strips of tape across his damaged nose.

"Thank you, Jackie ... let's all take a seat. Tow is very tired so we only get this one chance to listen to his instructions regarding the piloting of this ship. So let's listen up. Tow ...?"

★ ★ ★

It took Tow a full hour to explain the five major systems aboard the Howsh vessel: Navigation, Environmental, Propulsion, Tactical/Weaponry, and Intelligence. In that regard, Cuddy knew their systems were similar to the *Evermore*, although weaponry was not part of the mix on the other ship. Quickly tiring, Tow had referred to the hovering AI orb to provide most of the more in-depth explanations, only adding a few pertinent details along the way.

Reviewing first the overwhelming amount of information thus far provided, the orb next took and answered questions. Cuddy gestured toward the various consoles around the compartment, then toward the strange-looking colorless screens. He asked, "Is there a way to change all the screen prompts over to English? And also for the ship's AI to speak in English?"

"That has already been addressed, Cuddy Perkins."

Tony asked, "Is there a way for you to stop saying both his first and last name every time you speak to him? I mean, if he's now the captain … call him that. Just saying …"

"How about you just call me Cuddy, orb. You can call me captain when I've earned it."

Jackie said, "Shouldn't we go. Every minute we waste … the destruction—"

"I am sorry, but it is now time for me to leave," Tow said. "I will need some help returning to the *Evermore*."

"I'll help you, Tow," Cuddy said, and looking at the AI orb, added, "Do what needs to be done to ready this ship, then come join us on the *Evermore*."

Chapter 31

Cuddy again picked up Tow, carrying him in his arms as they made their way back to the *Evermore*. Few words were spoken along the way. The wind had picked up as they left the ranch and entered the wooded pine forest. The tall evergreens violently shook and rustled around them, as if in the midst of throwing a rebellious tantrum.

The others elected to follow along, not wishing to breathe the rank air in the Howsh spacecraft any longer than necessary. Out of consideration to Tow, his failing health, they kept well back, fully aware his time was short and inappropriate for idle conversation. As they approached the *Evermore*, the AI orb, now joining them, drew close. Cuddy nodded to it in the direction of the ship. Immediately, the hatchway began to open, the gangway to descend.

Halfway up the ramp, Cuddy felt Tow's gentle touch on his face. He looked down, surprised to see Tow's arms hadn't moved—were still down at his side.

"Thank you for this … Cuddy. You can take me below."

"Below?" Cuddy looked at his friend and noticed he was smiling.

"It is time now … you too possess the knowledge. Knowledge that Soweng passed on to you."

"But why now?" Cuddy asked. "Please … not quite yet, Tow, I'm not ready for you to go …"

"Now is a good time, Cuddy."

"I've forgotten what to do! No … it's best you wait."

"Do not worry, all you need to know will come to you when the time is right. All *Pashier* instinctively know the *Shain* ritual of the *rejoining*."

Cuddy hesitated at the open hatch and looked back as Jackie, Kyle and Tony entered the clearing. "Would it be all right if Jackie came with us?"

"Yes. That would be fine. They all should come …"

★ ★ ★

Jackie wasn't really sure what to expect. And, if she was honest with herself, she was more than a little freaked out. What she did know was Cuddy wanted her there and for now that would be enough. The last one to climb down to the sub-level of the *Evermore*, she waited for her eyes to adjust to the near-darkness. After several moments, she recognized the dark silhouettes of the others nearby. Cuddy—tall and broad—was walking toward her, with Rufus close by his side.

He said, "I'm glad you're here, Jackie. For you to see this … be a part of it."

When she heard the emotion in his voice, it made her want to reach out, but she held back and instead hugged herself. Cuddy, now at her side, turned to face the center of the room and gestured toward a hovering blue light in the near distance. Jackie realized it was the AI orb. Tow now lay flat on the deck and the two were conversing in low tones.

"I'm sorry … Cuddy. I don't really know what's going on, but I can tell you're hurting deep inside."

He shook his head. "I just wish I'd had more time with

him. Maybe … someday."

Now Jackie was totally confused, but she held her tongue. She reached a tentative hand out and placed it on his upper arm. He didn't acknowledge it—his eyes steadily locked on Tow and the orb. Then, taking in a deep breath, he sighed, "It's time."

Jackie watched Cuddy slowly walk in the direction of the AI orb and the still faintly glowing alien. She moved closer to Kyle and Tony, and even though she couldn't quite make out their faces in the dark, she could faintly see the two bands of white over Tony's healing nose.

When Tony leaned in to ask Kyle, "What's with this crazy shit?" he answered back, "Maybe if you keep quiet long enough, you'll find out." Jackie, thinking somewhat along Tony's line of thought, suddenly felt it—a soft breeze lightly stirring within the space. A series of sounds—pretty musical tones—suddenly became audible around them. Placing her palms over her heart, she felt its beat—so emotionally charged that it just might burst within her chest. Then, a large, organic object appeared in the middle of the compartment, becoming fully visible. *So that's the heritage pod*, she thought in solemn awe.

Jackie gasped aloud as spectacular, sparkling white lights began fountaining upward in the air. Slowly, opening from the pod's top, one by one large leaves curled backward and then, one after another, slowly extended outward, eventually coming to rest on the lower deck. So many leaf layers she lost count. By now, the soft breeze had turned into a steady cool wind.

Jackie smiled and then laughed at the spectacular beauty. She spun her body around and around—taking in the moving, sparkling, lights encircling them—so many dazzling lights. And then they became conscious of being present within a spectacular spiraling galaxy—of countless slow-moving stars within a universe of unimaginable depth.

Jackie's eyes then caught sight of Tow, now standing. He was gazing at something deep within the distant swirling stars. Cuddy, next to him, seemed to glow even brighter than Tow. Beautiful subtle hues—pinks and blues and greens—emanated from him.

Jackie then could see what Tow was so enthralled with. A star was moving—getting closer—growing larger. As the glittering light took on form, the shape of an actual being, Jackie *knew* it was a Pashier. One like Tow … but instead, a beautiful female. Her features were small—her expression full of anticipation. Holding her hand out, she beckoned Tow toward her.

Together, Tow and Cuddy walked forward—deeper and deeper into that starlit brightness that increased with their every step. Squinting now—the light becoming too bright to see into—brighter than the Sun—Jackie was forced to hold a hand before her eyes. And then, just as suddenly, the blinding light was gone, the musical tones quieted. The swirling stars were now moving in the opposite direction—returning back to the pod. The heritage pod's giant leaves began to rise off the deck and reform into their original pod-like shape. Jackie's eyes roamed the space—searching for Tow and Cuddy. They weren't there. They were gone. Her mind raced … *had Cuddy delivered Tow into that incredible afterlife realm … never to return? Without so much as saying a goodbye*? Suddenly, her sense of loss was profound, but then, all too quickly, her sadness turned to anger. Her hands tightened into fists, her breath quickening with the passage of every progressive second. *How could he … just leave us here?* Leave *me* here?

The glittering lights were all but gone now, hastening their rate as they funneled into the top of the heritage pod. All but one.

Jackie took a hesitant step forward, her eyes not wavering from the barely perceptive, yet increasing in size, light. Cuddy's form soon took shape and she saw him walking toward her—crossing from that ethereal realm of glittering stars, an infinite universe—back to the everyday reality of the here and now.

Running toward him before she realized it, her arms open, she pulled Cuddy to her with desperation—with hunger for closeness she was unaware she felt. Burying her face into his chest, she sobbed uncontrollably as his strong arms enveloped her. Then she heard his voice by her ear. "It was so beautiful there, Jackie, like nothing you could possibly imagine. But it wasn't my time to stay. And I felt you … felt you pulling me back here."

Suddenly embarrassed, Jackie pushed herself away. Briefly looking up, without making eye contact, she noted the tears on his cheeks.

He said, "I wish … I wish he didn't have to leave. I already miss him."

"You said something … before. You said, maybe someday?"

Cuddy didn't reply, instead stared across at the lone body, lying on the deck. "I now must bury my friend."

Jackie watched Cuddy move away and head toward Tow's body. She hadn't realized it until that very moment, but what she'd earlier witnessed was something else … perhaps Tow's essence—rising up, departing. What remained here was simply his discarded form.

Gently, Cuddy picked up Tow's body. The AI orb, hovering mere feet away, stayed close by them. As Cuddy passed Jackie, he requested, "In the hold … can you find me something to dig with."

★ ★ ★

Dusk had now turned into night and a waxing moon was providing just enough light to see by. Deep in the woods, they discovered seven elongated mounds of soil. Cuddy had found the burial site of Tow's deceased crewmembers. Although

Kyle offered, Cuddy insisted that he, himself, should dig Tow's grave, and then made it as deep and symmetrical a rectangle as he could manage.

Perspiration and dirt covered Cuddy from head to toe. Now, standing within the six-foot-deep hole, he reached up a hand. Tony and Kyle pulled him up and out, and then—with their help—lowered Tow's body into the grave. Taking turns, they refilled the hole, shoveling in the piled up soil around it.

Cuddy spent several minutes looking for eight round rocks—each approximately the same size—and set them in a pile. When the last one dropped onto the pile, Cuddy turned to the AI orb, hovering nearby. He gestured toward the rocks then toward the elongated mound of soil. The orb moved with silent efficiency—taking ahold, one by one, one rock after another, delivering each to the head of the mound of Tow's grave, then placed them around the top of the gravesite forming a perfect circle.

Jackie questioned, "Eight … the number of crewmembers on the *Evermore*?"

Cuddy nodded and attempted a smile. She smiled back, though she still hadn't made eye contact with him since their embrace. He didn't fully understand the whole situation.

Tony Bone asked, "What now?" turning toward Kyle, who was patting dust and dirt from his jeans. Kyle shrugged and looked at Jackie, then at Cuddy.

"Now … we take back our planet," Cuddy told them.

Chapter 32

They were running now—Cuddy, Jackie, Kyle and Tony. They leapt over the babbling brook, heading toward the edge of the forest where it met the Perkins' property-line boundary. Rufus and the AI orb easily kept pace as the four hurried around the corral, into the barn, then out the other side. The horse was in the pasture, eating hay.

Cuddy yelled to the orb, "Get to the ship … I'll be there in a few minutes."

The AI orb did as it was instructed, while the others detoured left—toward the house. Cuddy, first to reach the porch, noted the battered screen door and that the front door was both closed and locked. Pounding on it with a clenched fist, he yelled, "Momma?"

He knocked again, then looked back at Kyle. Shrugging, his brother leapt from the porch and moved around to the large front-facing kitchen window. He brought his face close to the glass and peered in. "It's dark … can't see a thing inside."

"There!" Jackie said. "My car."

Cuddy watched her quickly stride across the old wooden planks, hop off the porch, and then hurry over to her car. In the dark, he'd missed it—a piece of white notebook paper lay pinned beneath one of the windshield wipers.

Jackie pulled it free and began to read. After several beats she looked up and, cocking her head to one side, smiling, said, "She's gone."

"Momma?"

"I guess Officer Plumkin brought her car back. She left right after that … says she's at the hospital. Got freaked out being all alone here, with those dead aliens lying around."

"Can't really blame her," Tony said. "I'm a little creeped out myself."

All eyes went to Cuddy. "We can't wait," he said, looking at Kyle. "Are you coming with me?"

The question took Kyle off guard. "You need to ask? Yeah … I'm coming!"

"I'm coming too!" Jackie said.

Cuddy stared back at her for a long moment. "You can't … you can't come with us."

"Why not! What are you talking about?"

"It's something Tow told me before … before he left. He told me you were to stay here when we took off in the Howsh ship, along with some other things as well. He was very clear … you were not to travel with us."

"Well, too bad, I'm going anyway."

"If we survive … we'll be back for the *Evermore*, and the other thing I will then need to do."

"Other thing?" Kyle asked.

Jackie answered the question first, clearly angry. "Take the *Evermore*—the heritage pod—to some *flippin'* world on the other side of the galaxy. That's all … no big deal. But first, he has to run off and fight two alien spacecraft. Hey, it's all in a day's work, right? You don't need me …"

"I'm sorry, Jackie. Please tell Momma, well … just tell her goodbye for me … for us, okay?"

Tony broke the tension: "Hey, maybe I should stay here,

too. Go with Jackie back to the hospital."

Fuming, Jackie still continued to glare at Cuddy. "No … go with them, Tony," she said firmly, bringing her attention to him. "They'll need your help."

"One more thing," Cuddy said.

"Uh huh … what's that?" Jackie asked, already walking toward her car.

"Could you take Rufus with you?"

The question somewhat softened her stony expression. "*Whatever.* Rufus, come on …"

They watched Jackie climb into her car, then reach across and open the passenger-side door. She called for the dog.

"Go on, boy," Cuddy said.

Jackie called again and the old yellow lab jumped into the passenger seat of the VW. The door closed as the engine sprang to life. Revving up the engine, she put the car in reverse then backed out. After completing a three-point turn, she sped up the drive. At the top of the driveway she drove beneath the Howsh spacecraft, maneuvering around several dead Howsh bodies, and then she was gone—speeding away. Cuddy watched until the VW's taillights disappeared into the oncoming darkness.

★ ★ ★

Cuddy led the way up the gangway into the Howsh ship. Knowing Tow was no longer there—he felt alone. *Almost disconnected.*

"Isn't there a way to like … open a window in here, or something?" Tony asked, adding, "That smell … it's like a combination of shit, a wet blanket, and Rudy Myers' body odor, in 6th grade gym class. Remember Rudy Myers, Kyle?"

Kyle said, "Yeah, he was younger than me … few grades lower, but I remember Rudy. I then discovered he was a fellow inmate when at Whiteville. No surprise … he still had that outrageous BO."

Climbing the last set of stairs, Cuddy listened to them talk. For the first time, he felt slighted—like he'd missed out on some part of life most boys took for granted.

Reaching the bridge, they could see the AI orb hovering low in front of the primary forward console. "Everything ready to go?" Cuddy asked, taking a seat. Kyle and Tony sat down too, both seeming rather nervous. Cuddy knew that he, more than likely, looked equally uneasy.

"Yes, Cuddy … the spacecraft is nearly ready. I have retracted the gangway. The *Arm of Lia* is ready to lift off."

"Wait … that's what this ship's called? The *Arm of Lia*? That's the stupidest name for a ship I've ever heard," Kyle barked out.

"Yeah," Tony said, "we need something bad-ass. Like the *Enforcer* or *Doomsday*."

"Can we change the ship's name, AI orb? Is there some way to do that?" Cuddy asked.

"Yes … it is a simple procedure."

Cuddy thought about name-switching for a moment, then said, "Change it to … the *Revenge*."

Both Kyle and Tony nodded appreciatively.

Tony said, "Um … while we're at it, that orb thingy has a lame name too. How about we rename it?"

Cuddy was well aware they were stalling—doing everything possible to avoid the inevitable battle ahead. He studied the AI orb, then said, "Naw … the orb is what Tow referred to it as, so we'll just keep it."

"Plain old orb it is then," Tony said, going along with his decision.

"I have reconfigured the ship's name," the AI orb said.

"I guess we should get going, orb. Where are the two Howsh vessels now?"

"They are together, above the central Asian nation of Uzbekistan. Their current course is northwest, possibly en route to Moscow."

"Where were they before that?" Cuddy asked.

"Bangladesh … it has since been destroyed."

"That's crazy, how is that even possible?" Cuddy said, now watching Tony peer around. "What are you after?" Cuddy asked.

"Looking for seat belts. Doesn't this smelly heap have seatbelts?"

The orb answered, "No, on board there are sufficient G-force compensators. So strapping oneself down will not be necessary."

"Let's just get going, orb. We've avoided taking off long enough."

The deck beneath their feet began to vibrate and multiple displays sprang to life around the compartment. The elongated observation window, which once held a nighttime view of the house and barn at the bottom of the drive, now showed a sea of black. Cuddy felt a strange uneasiness in the pit of his stomach. He'd never flown before, never been in a plane, so this new sensation of movement—both vertical and horizontal—was disconcerting.

All three stood, then moved across to various windows on either side of the craft. As the details of the landscape below quickly contracted, like a camera's zooming out effect, Cuddy could now see the entire town of Woodbury. His eyes found and focused on one of the larger buildings, Stone River Hospital. He thought of Momma, wondering if she was all right. He'd never been this far away from her … not ever. Then he thought of Jackie and found himself smiling, though she'd still be mad at him for quite a while.

Woodbury now was only a dot in the distance. The *Revenge* was moving at incredible speed and, true to what the orb had said, there was no sense of movement at all.

"How long before we reach the other …"

"Five minutes, Cuddy," the orb replied.

Chapter 33

Kyle was the first to stand, quickly followed by Tony and Cuddy. Bright strobes of red light reflected in through the forward observation window. *Plasma strikes*. From his vantage point, Cuddy could see fantastic, billowing eruptions of fire within the sprawling devastated city below.

"That's what's left of St. Basil's Cathedral, and there's Red Square next to it …" Cuddy said, pointing.

Both Tony and Kyle glanced over to Cuddy.

"I remember somehow … must have seen it on TV … maybe National Geographic or something."

"Whatever … it's pretty much rubble now," Kyle said.

"Do they know we're here?" Cuddy asked.

The orb said, "Yes, of course. They have been tracking our position since we left the ranch. On an ongoing basis, the two ships have been hailing us."

"So, they don't know their sister ship has been seized?" Tony asked.

"I do not believe so," the orb replied. "The assumption would be a communications malfunction."

"Good … can we get in closer?" Cuddy asked.

The orb shifted position from one console to another, its articulating arms constantly moving—its mechanical four-fingered hands making new adjustments.

"Yes, but in monitoring their communications … the captains of both of these Howsh vessels are becoming suspicious. Their guard is up."

Cuddy asked, "Where are spaceships, like this one, the weakest … uh, what's the word?"

"You mean most vulnerable?" Kyle asked.

"Aft. The propulsion system," the orb replied.

"Up the old tailpipe … huh?" Tony threw in.

"Let's do that! Can you find a way to sneak up from behind? Then fire on both ships at the same time?" Cuddy asked, as he watched the orientation of the landscape outside suddenly pivot around. The orb had altered their course. Also, the *Revenge*'s speed had increased.

Tony sat back down, reaching out for something to hold on to. As the orb piloted the ship, with what seemed phenomenal skill, Kyle and Cuddy exchanged a quick look. They were moving in fast. Directly ahead of them, Cuddy spotted the enemy ship's aft thrusters—two on the left and two further away, on the right.

"Shall I fire the *Revenge*'s plasma weapons?" the orb asked.

Tony and Kyle looked at Cuddy. Hesitating, he was reminded that Tow had placed the orb under his direction.

"Yes! Blow them out of the fucking sky," Tony interjected.

The orb waited.

Cuddy hesitated. Just days ago, he had the mind of a seven-year-old boy; his biggest responsibility was feeding Rufus. And, truthfully, he often was not good remembering to do that. How was it that he, of all people everywhere, was now ready to perform something of such unfathomable importance?

"Yes, do what he said! Fire … fire!" Cuddy yelled.

As the orb went on the offensive, Cuddy did his best to take in everything around him: The action outside the observation window; the moving icon representations on the mounted display screens; as well as the orb's various setting changes and button presses. Somehow, he was tracking it all—actually comprehending complex data he'd never before understood. *So this is what it feels like to be smart!* It seemed the faster events occurred around him, the more he was able, somehow, *to slow things down*. As his eyes took in the two Howsh ships out the forward observation window, they appeared to be unmoving, and the orb hovered in slow motion. *How am I doing that?* Then suddenly the world around him was moving fast—back in real time again. Plasma fire erupted from the *Revenge*'s port and starboard wing tips. Bright bolts of red coursed through the air—separately tracking the two spacecraft targets.

"Direct hits on both Howsh ships. They are now taking evasive action," the orb said.

"Yes! We got 'em! Did you see that?" Tony yelled, punching the air with a fist.

Cuddy was well aware both ships were simultaneously hit. Each had lost a drive, resulting in right thrusters flaring out. He watched as the Howsh ships accelerated off in opposite directions—arcing around, while firing off their own plasma weapons. The orb began a series of evasive maneuvers that went well beyond the capabilities of the inertia stabilizers. Grabbing ahold of the console supports and seat backs, all three were violently jerked left and right and up and down. Suddenly, Tony lost his grip and was thrown across the compartment—face first—into a bulkhead. Blood erupted from his already damaged nose and he fell to the deck, unconscious.

"A ship!" Kyle yelled, pointing out the starboard window. He instinctively ducked as enemy plasma fire flashed past by what looked like mere inches.

Cuddy watched the display, noting the second Howsh ship was approaching them from their underside. He was tempted to tell the orb, but he was certain the hovering AI was tracking everything now happening.

Cuddy briefly wondered if the enemy ships were piloted by Howsh crewmembers or by the furry-looking robots? The answer came to him in the blink of an eye—*the robots*! For the first time since the Howsh alien attacked Momma back at the house, he once again felt the orb's presence within his consciousness.

When the deck suddenly dropped away beneath Cuddy's feet, as the *Revenge* took multiple hard-hitting plasma strikes, he fell hard to the deck, next to Tony's inert body. An overhead klaxon alarm began to wail and a growly voice repeated an alien phrase over and over again.

Kyle, remarkably, had remained on his feet and was asking the orb questions. But with the loud klaxon blaring and the growly warnings overhead, Cuddy couldn't hear what the orb said back.

Three more powerful strikes hit the *Revenge*, one after another, and Cuddy felt the ship's speed suddenly decline. One of their drives had been struck. Suddenly, the *Revenge* banked left, then abruptly right. Cuddy found a chair support to grab on to, as Tony's body slid further away. At least he wasn't conscious now to feel anything.

Using both hands, Cuddy rose to his feet and stood next to his brother. When he looked out the window, he saw they were up in space. *When did that happen?* He felt his heart rate increase. *We're in space … does this make us astronauts?*

Kyle leaned in closer and said, "Hey … snap out of it! If you haven't noticed, we're up shit creek, little brother. Orb's not sounding too confident we're going to pull this endeavor off."

Cuddy noticed more trails of bright red plasma fire crisscrossing the blackness of space. *For us to survive this, Cuddy, you will need to assist me.*

Cuddy stared at Kyle, then the orb. The request had not been a verbal one … it was instructing his mind. He knew what the orb was asking, but he'd been unable to conjure up those mental powers—whatever they were—ever since the alien altercation with Momma at the ranch.

How?

I will bring the enemy into your field of vision.

Sluggish in its response, Cuddy felt the *Revenge* change course. It took several moments before a Howsh ship came back into view.

I am here with you, so calm your mind, Cuddy … do not question your capabilities … do what must be done to save those you care about … to save your world …

Cuddy liked the tone of the orb's mental voice, found it comforting. He concentrated on the fast-moving enemy vessel visible out the forward window. Nothing seemed to happen for several long moments when, all at once, one of the stubby wings on the other spacecraft began to glow. As the wing disintegrated, red hot embers trailed away into space. Next, the back of the fuselage began to glow—first yellow, then red—and then, here too, red hot embers erupted like a Fourth of July sparkler. The Howsh ship was adrift in space.

"Are they … dead?"

"Yes, the hull has been breached. I am not detecting any signs of life," the orb said.

Beyond exhausted, Cuddy wavered on his feet. It reminded him of being underwater, when he and Kyle were swimming down at Long Pond as kids. Submerged beneath the surface, where it was so quiet only the faintest of sounds made their way into the watery depth.

Cuddy was aware of the other enemy ship, now approaching from directly ahead. He saw that the orb was bringing the *Revenge* back down into the atmosphere. Red plasma fire filled his field of view, but darkness was closing in around him.

"What are you doing? Do something, Cuddy!" Kyle yelled.

Cuddy fought to stay awake—needed to stay awake. But

he was tired and so very weak. Cuddy drifted into unconscious just prior to his body hitting the deck.

Chapter 34

Jackie was still fuming. Who did Cuddy think he was? Who all of a sudden made him the boss? It wasn't so long ago he had trouble counting to twenty. Now he's dictating where she can and cannot go!

She arrived at the hospital only to find the parking lot was a total madhouse of activity. Hordes of people coming and going. A hell of a lot more people than lived in the little town of Woodbury. She glanced over to Rufus sitting in the passenger seat. "This is crazy, huh Rufus?"

Having given up, she was now looking for a place to park several blocks out on a side street. She was surprised to see her father was there—slowly walking—arm-in-arm with Momma Perkins. She spotted the old Maxima up ahead. Jackie lowered her passenger side window and pulled up alongside them.

"Dad … Mrs. Perkins … what are you doing here?"

Momma gave a little wave. Her father glanced over to her with a surprised expression. She saw him remove his arm from hers—obviously using her for support. She saw him attempt to stand a little taller.

"What's it look like we're doing?" he said. "Are you daft? We're walking to Dotty's car."

"I can see that, Dad … but why are you out of the hospital? You just had surgery … not to mention a heart attack."

Her father stopped and looked at her. "I'm well aware of what I've been through. Heart attacks aren't something one easily forgets. Dotty's taking me home. It seems my daughter has been too busy to make time for such trivialities."

Jackie rolled her eyes. Then saw that there were two cars now waiting behind her—wanting to pass but the opposing traffic was pretty much non-stop. "Any word on Sheriff Bone's condition, Mrs. Perkins?" Jackie asked.

"Oh, he's got a few broken bones. Two ribs and he has a cast on his left arm. His wrist I think. Also has a concussion. Other than that, he'll live. Already making a fuss about getting back to work." Looking concerned, Momma asked, "Any word about my boys?"

Jackie shook her head. "No. Sorry."

The two of them had arrived at the Maxima. Momma used a key fob to unlock the passenger door. She opened it and held it wide for her father to lower himself into.

Jackie felt guilty. She should be the one driving him home. The car behind her honked—then the one behind that and the one behind that one all honked their horns. She held her left hand out the driver-side window and flipped the lot of them the bird.

Momma was making her way around her car.

"Well, I guess I'll see you back at Dad's farm."

"Okay, dear … we'll see you there."

★ ★ ★

She spun the dial determining only two local radio stations were still broadcasting—both so filled with static, it was nearly impossible to hear what was being said. She glanced in her rearview mirror and saw the Maxima was there, three cars back. She spun the dial again and hit pay dirt. She recognized the announcer's voice as that from the local CBS affiliate all-news station.

"… the amount of damage … the devastation along the eastern seaboard is nothing short of catastrophic. Death tolls are estimated into the millions. With that said, there are population pockets … even within Manhattan itself … that were, miraculously, bypassed. Moving on to Washington D.C. … there too has sustained much damage. But I'm reporting that the White House still stands … I repeat … the White House still stands. As does the Capitol Building. The President of the United States is said to be safe and conducting business from an undisclosed safe bunker location. The Naval Station at Norfolk, in nearby Virginia, has been completely destroyed. As were the bases at Newport, Annapolis, Charleston, Kings Bay, and Jacksonville. It is apparent that the alien attackers' primary targets were … and still are … primary U.S. and worldwide military installations. Let's quickly turn our attention to the events going on over Europe and Russia. We go now to Peter Colten … our on-the-ground correspondent in St. Petersburg, Russia. Peter … what can you tell us?"

"Yeah, Simon, what we're getting, and this is from multiple eye witness accounts … is that two alien crafts had entered the Russian airspace. The Russians were ready for them … deploying a substantial number of their MiG29k jet fighters. All of which were quickly destroyed. Then came what seemed to be an almost endless rampage of Russian surface to air and sea to air missiles … unfortunately, these too had zero effect on the alien crafts. The aliens began strafing the ground with their energy weapons … just as they had done along the eastern seaboard in the U.S. and then to other countries in Europe and China. As the attack ensued, much of Moscow has been turned to rubble. But here's the really bizarre part, Simon … reportedly a third spaceship engaged the enemy, identical looking to the other two alien crafts … From which point an aerial battle ensued. Eventually, the battle continued up in space."

"So how do things stand now, Peter?"

"Simon … one alien spacecraft has definitely been destroyed. That has been verified. The other one was either destroyed or at the very least incapacitated in high orbit over Earth."

"And what has happened to the other spacecraft … our apparent savior … or was that the craft which was destroyed?"

"There's no way to know, at this point, there's still much more to come, Simon …"

Jackie had reached her father's farm. She turned off the engine and continued to stare at the car radio. There was a good chance, Cuddy and Kyle … as well as Tony Bone were dead. Killed by the alien craft. She didn't want to think about it. She couldn't think about it.

She watched as Mrs. Perkins and her father extricated themselves from the Maxima. Momma helped her father walk toward the house. *It should be me helping him,* she thought—but, surprisingly, she was fine with Mrs. Perkins taking on that responsibility.

Jackie got out of her car and slowly followed behind them. Then, snapping out of her funk, she hurried forward and opened the front door for them. It was unlocked—always unlocked—she didn't remember, even as a child, the door ever being locked.

Momma gently guided her father toward the back of the house where the master bedroom was located. Jackie felt numb. So much had happened—all starting days before, with the frantic call informing her that her father had had a massive heart attack. Hell … in a normal world, that would have been terrifying enough. But it had only been the beginning of a string of implausible events that were … well … beyond incredible. *But was all of it a nightmare?* Certainly not Cuddy's mental transformation. Now that presented its own unique set of problems for her.

She noticed a red light was blinking on her dad's old fashioned answering machine on the kitchen counter. She pressed play and listened to a series of well-wishers for her father's quick recovery. There was a message from the pharmacist about new prescriptions being ready for pickup, and then there was a message for her. It was Brian. He was worried sick about her. Couldn't understand why she wasn't picking up on her cell phone. She tried to remember where she'd left it—then remembered she'd last had it in her pocket when she'd been taken aboard the Howsh ship. She brought her attention back to Brian's voice

"Babe … if you get this message, please call … day or night … Jackie, let me know you're all right."

She listened to the phone machine say, "End of messages."

She looked up to see Momma was coming down the hallway.

"He okay?"

"Yes … wants to rest for a while."

"I can't thank you enough for helping with Dad … It should have been me—"

Momma waved her words away. "It's a welcome distraction with everything going on. The attacks around the world … Cuddy and Kyle gone." Momma gestured toward something undefined above.

Jackie said, "I found a radio station … while in the car. Reports about the attacks on the other side of the world."

Momma's attention was piqued, "Well? Anything about … the boys … what they were trying to do?"

Jackie nodded. "There was a third ship … it must have been them … the report said it attacked the other two ships … up in space. One was definitely destroyed … not sure about the other one … it may have reentered the atmosphere."

Momma stared back at her, waiting for Jackie to continue.

"I don't know, Mrs. Perkins … there's no way to know. I guess all we can do is wait."

Chapter 35

Cuddy awoke to the loud, grating voice of Tony Bone. Clearly upset, he was complaining about his nose.

" … of all the places on my body I could have been smacked … an arm … an ear … hell, my nuts, but no … I get hit again, right in the nose!"

Cuddy slowly sat up, realizing Kyle was crouched down next to him.

"Easy there, little brother, you hit your head pretty hard."

Cuddy thought back to the last thing he'd seen—the Howsh spacecraft coming right at them, from out the observation window. "We're … still alive!"

"Thanks to you. You and the orb. How you did what you did, making that ship disintegrate, like that …"

Cuddy's vision was only now clearing—capable of focusing on his surroundings. The AI orb still hovered in front of the forward console and Cuddy noted they were again up in space. He glanced over at Tony, now seated with his back up against the opposite bulkhead. Dried blood covered much of his lower face along with practically all his T-shirt.

"Sorry about your nose, Tony."

"It's not your fault, Cuddy. It was already reinjured." Tony gave Kyle a mean look.

"Can you help me up, Kyle?" Cuddy asked. With the help of his brother, he climbed to his feet. He wavered then steadied himself. "Orb … where are we? What are we doing back in space?"

"On three occasions I attempted to return to Earth's atmosphere. Of those still functioning sufficiently, Earth's strategic defenses—primarily ballistic missile systems—are all on high alert. The *Revenge* has taken numerous direct hits and our ability to cloak our presence is no longer possible. Added to that, our protective shields are ineffectual."

Tony, sounding nasally, asked, "Can't we just tell them who we are … that we're the good guys?"

Cuddy and Kyle looked at each other. Kyle shrugged and asked, "Is that possible?"

The orb stopped what it was doing—as if momentarily considering the question—then replied, "This vessel has a variety of communication capabilities, including radio frequency transmission."

"Who would we talk to?" Tony asked. "I mean, who would believe us? We'd sound like prankster ass-clowns …"

Kyle nodded and pointed a finger at Tony. "That's why you're going to contact your father … the sheriff. Who else do we know who has any clout? Since he's been on this ship, it won't be all that far-fetched." Tony gave back a pained expression.

"What's the big deal?" Kyle asked.

"I don't know if he's even out of the hospital yet. And I don't get along very well with him, anyway."

"Tough. Would you rather die up here? Be atomized by a fucking missile from Iran, or maybe Poland? You want to die from a Polish missile, Tony? Would that make you happy?" Kyle asked.

Tony started to laugh at that. "Fine … um … you, orb, do

you know how to connect to, communicate with, the Woodbury Police Dispatch? That's always the best way to get ahold of my father."

"Stand by … I will attempt to make the necessary connections."

"Whatever," Tony said, rising to his feet. "He still may not believe me."

Cuddy wasn't sure Tony was right about that, since the sheriff had been taken prisoner too—had been a prisoner on this same alien ship. It wouldn't be that much of a stretch to realize his son was still on board.

They were startled by the sound of loud static, then Sheriff Bone's craggy voice, blaring into the bridge compartment: "Who is this …? This is a police emergency frequency."

Tony looked around the compartment, like he didn't know in which direction to address his words.

"Just start talking, Tony!" Kyle said, annoyed.

"Dad? Um … it's Tony …"

There was a long static pause before the sheriff spoke again. "Tony?"

"Yes … like … your son."

"Where the hell are you? I've been looking for you, damn it. What are you doing on this frequency?"

"Just listen, Dad … I want you to know I'm not fooling around here. This is for real, okay?"

"I'm extremely busy, son. I've just gotten back from the hospital … what is it?"

"I'm up in space. I'm still in the Howsh ship. This is the spacecraft that just destroyed the other two spaceships … like over Russia." Tony shook his head and stared over at Kyle then Cuddy. He mouthed the words, *He thinks I'm pulling his chain*.

"That was you? How …?"

"Well, I'm not flying it … that's the orb's doing. Anyway, it's a long story, but it's all very true. Even I couldn't make shit up this crazy."

"Watch your language on an open channel, son. Are you coming home now?"

"Yeah … just as soon as Poland stops firing missiles at us."

"Poland?"

"Look, Dad, the rest of the world has no idea what's really happened. They don't know we're the good guys up here. You need to call … I don't know … like NASA or the President or someone. We need to be able to land. Dad, weren't you in the Navy? Can't you call someone?"

"You're really up in space? I've been listening to the news … that was you?"

"I already told you, it wasn't just me. Truth is, I'm really more of an observer, though it's too hard to explain right now. Just get the military to stop firing on us … can you do that?"

"Guess I can try. How can I contact you?" Tony looked over to the orb for guidance.

The orb said, "I will continue to monitor this police band. If your father speaks, I will hear him."

"Did you hear that? Did you hear what the orb said?"

"I heard it. Okay, let me get to it. Take care of yourself, son."

"Thanks, Dad … you too." Their connection ended.

Cuddy said, "There's still the issue of keeping this ship … us too … out of the hands of the government. We need to avoid capture."

"Why do we care?" Tony asked. "I just want to get home. Let them take the damn ship."

Cuddy felt his anger rise up, "No … that can't happen. I made a promise. I'm going to Primara. This ship, and the *Evermore*, cannot be taken. I … cannot be taken." But clearly, by their expression, neither Kyle nor Tony fully understood why.

★ ★ ★

Over the next two hours, Cuddy had time to think. And he did so with a level of laser-sharp clarity that, even with everything else that had changed within him, was still surprising. His brain—his consciousness—had continued to evolve. He anticipated that when the sheriff came back online, he would be handing off all further communications to some authority figure in the military—maybe a general, or someone else high up—who would demand the ship land at some pre-designated location. But that wouldn't work with what Cuddy planned to do.

"Orb … when we reenter the Earth's atmosphere, can the *Revenge* be tracked?"

"Yes, primarily by various types of commercial and military radar. And the *Revenge* is no longer invisible. What did you call it—stealth?"

"I may be able to repair that functionality."

"Why didn't you mention that earlier?" Kyle asked.

"I was unfamiliar with the characteristics of this vessel. Since then, I have completed an in-depth evaluation of each of the ship's systems. The stealth mode generators, which are part of the Tactical system, do have a certain amount of redundancy built in. I can make the necessary repairs … make use of the redundant system on board. It will take me another hour."

"So you're saying the *Revenge* will, in fact, be able to avoid detection? We're not going to be blown out of the sky by some missile?" Cuddy asked.

"That is correct. At least, for Earth-based technology, I am confident the *Revenge* cannot be tracked."

"What other technology would we have to worry about?" Kyle asked. "We destroyed the other two Howsh ships."

The orb, hovering close to one of the larger display screens, replied, "I've detected this …"

At first, Cuddy didn't understand what he was seeing on the screen. It just looked like a lot of slow-moving icons.

"What you now are viewing are ten Howsh Marauder-Class star fighters. Individually, they are highly capable crafts. Together, they become a powerful force."

"What is the *Revenge* like in comparison?" Kyle asked.

"The *Revenge* is referred to as a Scout-Class vessel."

"Scout?" Tony queried. "That doesn't sound very good. Scout sounds nothing like Marauder-Class star fighters. We're fucked."

"How far away are they, and how long before they reach Earth?" Cuddy asked.

"They are not headed for Earth; I believe they are destined for Primara."

Chapter 36

It was a good two hours before the orb alerted Cuddy that Sheriff Bone's voice had again been detected on the Woodbury police emergency band. And, as anticipated, the sheriff said he had a General Hastings, of the U.S. Air Force, standing by to work out the logistics.

Hastings' voice sounded younger than Cuddy envisioned a general would sound like.

"Who is it that I am addressing on the alien vessel?" he asked. Kyle and Tony looked to Cuddy.

"I am Cuddy Perkins, sir."

"Okay, Mr. Perkins … who is there with you?"

"Tony Bone, the sheriff's son, and my brother, Kyle. Oh … and the AI orb, who I think you've already been speaking with."

"You're saying that was an artificial intelligence previously on the line?"

"Yes, sir, that's what I'm saying." Cuddy glanced at his brother and shook his head. With so much weird stuff going on, he was surprised the general picked up on the AI being the most bizarre aspect.

"Look, Mr. Perkins, the U.S. military has substantial resources. Within minutes of being contacted by Sheriff Bone, our people were digging into who exactly you were. Who all of you were."

"Okay, that's good … I guess," Cuddy said, wanting to move things along.

"No … not so good, Mr. Perkins. Because our intel resources came back with conflicting information. For one thing, the only Cuddy Perkins we have on record, son of one Dorothy, *or Dotty*, Perkins, is nineteen years of age, with a mental I.Q. of sixty-three. Severely mentally disabled. Functionally, a five-year-old."

"You'll have to take my word for it, sir … I've gotten a lot smarter. Do you think we can we move this along … there's—"

Hastings continued right over Cuddy's words, "Next we have one Kyle Perkins, your brother, who is twenty-two. He was released from West Tennessee State Penitentiary—the Whiteville Correctional Facility—only last week. Seems he has an aptitude for stealing cars … as well as getting caught. And finally we have Mr. Tony Bone. Out of respect for Mr. Dale Bone, the Sheriff of Woodbury … I won't go into the colorful past of this twenty-two-year-old hoodlum. Just leave it to say, the Three Stooges would make a far more likely crew for what Sheriff Bone tells me transpired today. But he insisted you three—along with the artificial intelligence—are responsible for the destruction of the two other alien craft and the aliens responsible for the mass-destruction on Earth—the loss of millions of lives across our planet. But I am at a loss to provide an alternative explanation. My technical personnel tell me that you are, in fact, up there in space. And each still-operating news agency has been broadcasting the footage of a third alien ship, battling two others over Eastern Europe and Russia. So I am in the awkward position of having to offer humble gratitude to you, and the others with you, on behalf of the entire planet."

"Oh … well, okay! You're welcome, General," Cuddy said.

"Yeah … no biggie," Tony added.

"With that said, I'm sure you'll understand that we must conduct what follows with all due diligence … with extreme caution. I will be providing you with very specific low-orbit reentry coordinates. In exactly one hour, you will start your descent. Once you level off at an altitude of 35,000 feet, a squadron of U.S. F35A Lightning fighter jets will be ready to escort you down to Nellis Air Force Base, in Nevada. There can be no deviation from these directives. These highly trained airmen have orders to shoot you down at the slightest divergence of our instructions …"

Cuddy, by now, was only half-listening to the general. His mind was still on the band of Howsh ships headed for Primara. That they intended to destroy that planet he had little doubt. He needed to quickly get back to Woodbury—back to the *Evermore.*

"Is everything I've said clearly understood, Mr. Perkins? Do you have any questions?" General Hastings asked.

The orb turned its attention toward Cuddy.

Cuddy said, "No, General … no questions. We understand and thank you for helping us. Um, we're ready for those reentry coordinates when you are … sir."

As much as the general's directives made perfect sense, Cuddy was becoming more and more impatient. He was reminded once again that his emotional evolution hadn't progressed yet to the same level as his cognitive side. He really wanted to move things along. *Jeez … waiting another full hour would be like waiting an eternity.*

The orb then took over, having a back-and-forth conversation with the general, getting more landing specifics ironed out.

Tony, keeping his voice low, asked. "If the orb's got the stealth thing working again, why don't we just blow him off and leave now? Why are we even waiting to be escorted to … where the hell was it? Arizona?"

"Nevada," Cuddy said, noting the orb had disconnected from General Hastings. Cuddy continued, "The orb has the stealth functionality working, Tony, but not the shields … remember? If, by chance, we're spotted … like a line-of-sight-type thing … we can be locked on to. Isn't that right, orb?"

"Correct, but there is only a small chance of that."

"So what's the plan?" Kyle asked.

"I've been thinking about that. Orb, if we wait until the designated time, when the U.S. military, and probably other world militaries too, are tracking that specified reentry location, what if it's not us entering the atmosphere? What if, instead, it's what's left of the other Howsh ship?"

"You're talking about having a distraction," Kyle said.

"Genius! Our village idiot is a total *friggin'* genius," Tony exclaimed, impressed.

The orb said, "I believe I can trigger the other Howsh ship to explode soon after entering the atmosphere. Would that be of benefit?"

"That would be a huge benefit," Cuddy said. "They'd think all three Howsh ships were destroyed and they'd no longer be looking for us."

"Um, not to be a total downer here …" Tony said, "but that other Howsh ship, I saw what you did to it. It's pretty much toast. How do we get what's left of it to enter the atmosphere?" He looked over at the orb and asked, "Does this ship have some kind of tractor beam … like in the movies?"

"No," the orb answered. Then, continuing in a matter-of-fact tone, said, "Cuddy will have to manage that aspect. He has already demonstrated he has, at least to some degree, the same mental kinetic capabilities as the Pashier."

Cuddy, still not fully recovered from his last use of those newly acquired abilities, unconsciously placed a hand on his unsettled stomach. He thought about the plan and liked it.

With that said, once in Woodbury, landing back at the ranch, they'd have to move fast. The *Revenge* still might be spotted—perhaps overheard by the military. By a jet or even a satellite.

"Okay … I guess we have a plan," Cuddy said. He looked over to Tony. "When we land, it will take us some time to get the *Evermore* back up into space. Can you hold off contacting your father—"

"Wait! You think I'm going back home? Seriously?"

Cuddy shrugged, not knowing what to think.

"No … I'm going with you guys. I'm on your team."

Cuddy and Kyle stared at each other. They hadn't had time to discuss whether Kyle even wanted to go. Events were happening too fast.

"I don't know, Cuddy. I mean … who would take care of Momma? Plus, I just got released from a two-year stint inside a prison cell …"

"I get it, more confined spaces. That's okay, Kyle," Cuddy said.

Tony looked disappointed at Kyle's decision. "Hey, then it's you and me, Cuddy … we'll take on the Howsh. We'll kick their furry asses."

Cuddy honestly didn't know if Tony would be of help, or be a hindrance—but he appreciated the support, just the same. He asked, "Orb, how soon before we're supposed to reenter the atmosphere?"

"Fifty-three minutes."

"How will I know what to do?"

"I will assist you, like I have done on two previous occasions. It should be less taxing. Moving an object in space is far easier than making an object disintegrate."

* * *

Slowly the orb navigated the *Revenge*, bringing it close to the other Howsh ship. Cuddy watched through the forward observation window as they came right beside it—approaching from its stern. At this close distance, he got a good look at the damage he'd inflicted, using only mind projection. The whole tail end of the spacecraft was scorched black, and he could see several breached open patches where it was possible to actually see into the ship. It was then that it struck him—the loss of life he'd caused.

"How many were on board?" Cuddy quietly asked the AI orb.

"Crew of twenty-seven Howsh."

Cuddy knew any sadness he felt was unjustified. They would have destroyed the *Revenge*, and everyone aboard, without a second thought. He well understood that, on an analytical level, but he wasn't feeling analytical right then—simply guilty.

Kyle broke the silence. "So what now? How do we work this?"

Cuddy said, "We need the *Revenge* to disappear from view. Orb … can you turn on that stealth mode?"

"They're not stupid … aren't they going to see … detect … that there were two ships up here, then, all of a sudden there's just one?" Kyle asked.

"They may not fully understand it, but they'll continue tracking the one ship that they do see. We're only looking to buy ourselves a little extra time."

Chapter 37

Jackie had hung around the house just long enough to start feeling uncomfortable. Her father was obviously convalescing, but the sparks going off between Mrs. Perkins and her old man—well, it was embarrassing to be around them. She'd heard that high-stress situations can bring people together, and this—what was going on—most certainly, qualified as a high-stress situation.

It was Jackie's suggestion that she drive back to the Perkins' ranch and see to Ellie. To get her into her stall within the barn. Speeding along the country roads, Rufus, there beside her on the passenger seat, was good company—content just hanging his head out the side passenger window—and letting his ears flap in the wind. Halfway there, she remembered all the dead Howsh bodies, lying on the property. *Shit.* There must be ten of the weird aliens—piled up, one atop another, like big, hairy cords of wood. She'd just have to deal with it. After all, she was pre-med … not like she'd never been around dead bodies before.

She was startled from her reverie as the local CBS station was blaring out news over the car radio:

"... this really is an amazing turn of events, Simon. Inside sources tell us the interchange can take place at any time now. Obviously, exact coordinates and timeframes are classified, but I've been told the alien craft, which has been designated the *Revenge* by its present human crew, is currently on the move."

Jackie had followed the ongoing events occurring in space back at her dad's house. She'd learned that Kyle, Tony, and Cuddy were now acclaimed heroes—the men of the hour—hell, of the century! But instead of being grateful they were alive—that the world had been saved from certain destruction—she was angry. Just hearing of their actions in space made her blood boil. She should have been up there with them. Cuddy had no right to tell her not to come. Once again, being a female meant being short-changed in life. *Screw him … screw them all.* She had her own life to lead; important things of her own to accomplish.

As if on cue, her father's cell phone began to ring. He'd offered it to her before she left his house. The smart phone, a gift from her to him the year before, was almost never used. He didn't understand all the icons and buttons.

She looked at the screen, noting Brian was on the line, and answered the call. *Why wouldn't she?* She had a life of her own that extended *far* beyond Cuddy …

"Hello?"

"Jackie? Finally, where the hell have you been? Do you know how long I've been trying to get in touch with you?'

"I know … and I'm sorry. It's just been crazy. More than you could possibly realize, actually."

"I think I have a good idea what you've been going through," he said.

"What?"

"I'm here … at your dad's place. Must have just missed

you. Been getting the skinny on—"

"Wait! You're … here?" she asked.

"Yes, and I want to see you. As soon as possible."

"Well, I'm … I have to do some things, Brian. Maybe later we can connect."

"Connect? You make it sound like a business transaction. I'm your boyfriend and I'm worried about you. I love you!"

"Sorry, bad choice of words. Not connect … connect is a stupid word. We'll meet … meet up, okay? Just not right now. Later on."

"You're acting strange. What's going on with you? Is it us? Are you having second—"

"No! Of course not! Well … not exactly," she said, annoying even herself with her vague responses. "Hold on, Brian … I want to hear this news report."

"Okay … I've got confirmation; the alien craft is on the move.

"Peter, tell our listeners what's happening."

"Simon … I'm told the alien ship is proceeding slowly, just now leaving Earth's low orbit … entering what is called the Exosphere … where space and the atmosphere merge. From there, the ship will descend to the Thermosphere, and then to the Mesosphere. This will take approximately five minutes."

"Very exciting news, Peter. And where, exactly, will the U.S. squadron of F35A Lightning fighters be waiting?"

"That will be at the Stratosphere level, Simon. The same altitude where most military and commercial flights take place; where there's enough oxygen. Oh my God!"

"Peter?"

"I'm sorry, Simon, but new reports are now coming in regarding a catastrophic explosion. Hold on … yes, it is confirmed … the alien spacecraft has exploded. I repeat, the alien craft, designated the *Revenge*, has exploded in midair. This is truly awful … a terrible … "

Their voices turned to static as the radio lost its signal. Jackie stared at the car radio in stunned silence. The Howsh ship had exploded! Oh God … *Cuddy*.

She pulled to the side of the road, letting the engine idle while she stared out the windshield, feeling numb within. In the distance, she saw the tall roofline of the Perkins's barn. Hearing a distant voice speaking, she realized Brian was still on the phone and brought it up to her ear.

"Damn it, Jackie! Are you there?"

"Please stop screaming into the phone, Brian."

"Tell me where you are. I'm coming to you …"

Without even looking at the phone, Jackie disconnected, letting her hand fall limply to her lap. She continued to stare blankly at the Perkins' dilapidated old ranch house in the distance. *They were all dead—she would never see them again.* She would never see Cuddy again. Everything he was trying to do—for Tow—for a race of people, called the Pashier, was never going to happen. A single tear, rolling unconsciously down her cheek, led to uncontrollable sobbing. Unbuckling her seatbelt, she wrapped her arms around the old yellow Lab. Rufus licked her face—the tears on her cheeks.

A thunderous sound suddenly roared just above her. Jackie jolted upright and Rufus barked. What she saw out the windshield didn't make sense. Powerful thrusters were churning up dust all around. *The Howsh spaceship!* The *Revenge* was landing on the same exact spot it had taken off from. She quickly wiped her cheeks and studied her shocked reflection in the rearview mirror. *Assholes.*

Jackie waited for the dust to settle a bit before climbing out from her car, then held the door open for Rufus to jump out. The now-landed alien ship rested twenty yards farther down the road, its gangway already descending. She leaned back against the car's hood and waited, her arms crossed defiantly over her chest.

The first one down the ramp was Tony Bone. He spotted her and confidently nodded. He wore a pompous expression that only made her want to slap it off his pimply face. Next, came Kyle, then Cuddy. Both looked most surprised to see her.

"Jackie … what are you doing here?" Cuddy asked. "How did you know …"

"You don't think I fell for that obvious ruse about your ship disintegrating in space, do you? I knew you'd be coming back here, so Rufus and I cruised on over. And guess what, here you are." Jackie avoided making eye contact—afraid Cuddy would pick up on her load of bullshit.

She watched the AI orb emerge from the ship as the gangway began to retract upward, back into the ship. The three guys, looking highly satisfied with themselves, approached her.

"So what now?" she asked. "It won't be long before you have a combination of U.S. military forces here … and they're not going to be happy."

Cuddy said, "That is why we have to go … take the *Evermore* back into space."

"We? Who's we?" she asked, gazing from Cuddy to the other two.

Tony said, "Me and Cuddy. Kyle's a pussy and wants to stay home with his momma."

"Screw you, Bone," Kyle said back.

"No!" she said vehemently, as the three squinted at her in confusion.

Cuddy asked, "No? What do you mean *no*?"

"I mean not this time … you're not leaving without me."

"We talked about that, Jackie. I'm sorry, but—"

"But nothing! I'm part of this too and there's nothing you, or anyone else, can say that's going to make me change my mind. The sooner you three get that through your heads the better. And as far as your momma is concerned, Kyle, it seems she's got herself a new boyfriend."

"What are you talking about? What new boyfriend?" Kyle asked, looking hostile.

Cuddy, too, looked ready to pounce.

"It's my father. They've been making goo-goo eyes at each other ever since she collected him from the hospital and took him home."

"Really?" Cuddy exclaimed.

"Your dad? I thought he died in the hospital … a heart attack, or something," Tony said.

"Believe me, he's still very much alive," Jackie said, glaring at Tony, who was really starting to annoy her big time.

Both Jackie and Cuddy turned to Kyle, who seemed to be mulling the news about his mother over in his mind. He suddenly smiled. "Then there's no reason for me to stay behind. I'm in."

"And I'm going too … right?" she asked.

Cuddy smiled, then winked over at her. Jackie had never seen him do that—wink at her like that. It was so out of character, she laughed out loud.

The hovering AI orb approached them then stopped. "There are vehicles approaching at a high rate of speed."

"From the sky?" Cuddy asked.

"No, on this same road."

Then Jackie heard it, a car coming fast. She recognized it—it belonged to Dr. Horowitz. Dr. Brian Horowitz. Driving his pride and joy, a brand new red Mercedes 500 SL convertible, Brian was leaving a rooster tail of dust behind him as he sped toward them.

"Oh crap!" she said.

Chapter 38

"Who's that coming?" Tony asked.

"That's Brian," Jackie said.

Cuddy looked from the fast-approaching convertible over to Jackie, who seemed highly agitated. He heard her cursing under her breath. "Why's he coming here?" he asked.

Jackie shrugged, keeping her eyes on the car as it skidded to a stop behind her VW bug. Cuddy could see that Brian was older than the rest of them—*maybe in his thirties*—though he wasn't all that good at guessing ages. He had curly black hair—probably longish—and it was bound up in some kind of a bun near the crown of his head. Wearing sunglasses, he sported a perfectly trimmed goatee. He exited his car, never taking his eyes off the spacecraft that loomed above them.

"What are you doing here?" Jackie asked. "You can't be here, Brian …"

He continued to stare at the ship in awe, then said, "I had to see you … find you."

"Well, you've found me. But you have to go. Now!"

Cuddy, deciding to introduce himself, held a hand out for Brian to shake, but he either didn't see it or chose to ignore it. Cuddy wasn't sure which one.

"This is the spaceship the military think exploded on entering the atmosphere. Why is it here … What have you done?" Brian asked in an accusatory tone.

"You mean beyond saving the planet, along with your sorry ass?" Tony threw in.

For the first time, Cuddy watched Brian acknowledge Jackie, looking her over, from head to toe. Cuddy had silently been admiring the same spectacular vision. Wearing a yellow and black plaid shirt, and faded blue jeans that seemed to be painted onto her long slender legs, she wore only the slightest hint of makeup. Highlights in her long, straw-colored hair shimmered in the light as she moved. Cuddy was totally mesmerized by the sight of her, ever since walking down the ramp. He again questioned himself: *Why hadn't he truly appreciated her beauty long before now?*

"So what's this guy to you anyway, Jackie? Is he like a boyfriend or something?" Kyle asked.

Suddenly flustered, she snapped back, "What does it matter to you?" But her worried eyes defied her feigned anger. She glanced toward Cuddy, who only now was processing the deeper implications of her relationship with Brian.

Could Jackie belong to someone else? Cuddy wondered. That hadn't been something he'd considered before, but now it made complete sense. What had he ever been to her, but a pathetic man-boy? A simpleton—one who'd never leave the safety of his Momma's ranch.

The orb, which Cuddy had noticed was good at going undetected, if it chose to, was now rising higher into the air and hovering in place. "There are other vehicles approaching. We should hurry, Cuddy."

As much as the spaceship, then Jackie, captivated Brian's attention, the orb's sudden appearance did more so. "What … is … that?"

Cuddy ignored him. "What other vehicles are coming, orb?"

The orb, rising higher, reported after several moments, "Military vehicles … three … approaching fast."

Jackie spun on Brian, shouting, "What have you done?"

"I did what was necessary … what was right. With much reluctance, your mother told me what happened here. About the spaceship, and the battle with the aliens. I thought you might come back here."

"So … what … you called out the Army?"

He nodded. "I thought you were in danger. Your little gang of misfits is in way over your heads. You have to know that, Jackie. You do have an education beyond the third grade. But these guys …"

"Bite me, boy bun," Tony said.

Cuddy could now see the three olive-green Army trucks en-route to their location. One truck had a soldier seated up high behind a weapon.

"Run!" Cuddy said. "Everyone get to the *Evermore*!" While they all rushed, including Brian, down the Perkins's driveway, Cuddy suddenly halted, noticing the orb was unmoving where it hovered.

"Cuddy, I must pilot the *Revenge*. The *Evermore* will be incapable of fending off the Howsh in space."

"Who will pilot the …"

"You will, Cuddy. I will assist you," the orb replied. "Now go … get to the *Evermore*'s cockpit."

Cuddy ran down the drive, Rufus loping along at his side. By the time he reached the barn, he heard the *Revenge*'s remaining drive power up and then its thrusters engage. Cuddy glanced back just in time to see the Howsh ship steadily rising into the air. He also noted the three military vehicles were maneuvering around the red sports car and also the VW bug. They were turning down the driveway as he sprinted into the barn.

★ ★ ★

Gasping for breath, Cuddy ran out of the woods and into the open clearing. The others were waiting for him next to the *Evermore*. He stared frantically at the closed hatchway and wondered how they would get inside?

I am here with you, Cuddy. I will instruct you in how to open the hatchway, as well as accomplish other functions, simply through the employment of your mind.

Cuddy was instantly relieved, feeling the orb's presence within his consciousness. He mentally spotted the controls, situated right inside the hatchway on the bulkhead.

"Use the Pashier part of your mind, Cuddy. Open the hatch now and extend the gangway."

The others stood by, staring up at him, waiting for him to do *something*. He mentally envisioned activating the controls and the *Evermore*'s hatch began to slide open and the gangway to descend. Tony Bone was the first to run up the ramp and into the ship, with Kyle quickly following on his heels.

Jackie gestured for Cuddy to go past her, saying, "Go on … I need to talk to Brian for a minute."

Cuddy said, "Okay, but we have to leave … immediately." Brian gave him a less than friendly look as he ran past them and up the gangway. Inside, Kyle and Tony were nervously waiting for him.

"What's happening with Jackie? Is she coming or not?" Tony asked.

"Not sure. I need to get to the bridge." Cuddy hurried forward, feeling strange being inside without Tow, or even the orb—almost like trespassing. Reaching the bridge, he took a seat at the forward console. The displays around him came alive and he caught the unique outline of the *Revenge* nearby—hovering just above the treetops.

You must start the propulsion system, Cuddy. The two drives can be initialized via the controls, located on the far right of the panel.

Cuddy's eyes scanned the myriad of touch controls—all

the strange symbols—and he felt an overwhelming urge to flee. Get off the ship and run as fast as his feet could take him—he was incapable of doing what the orb now told him to do.

Then his worried gaze settled on the two elongated levers. But what was even stranger, he could now read the series of exotic symbols printed beneath them:

Emersion Drive 1 | Emersion Drive 2

Cuddy flipped the levers and immediately felt the vibration of the big drives coming up beneath his feet.

Very good; now you need to secure the ship, Cuddy.

Cuddy then remembered the hatch was open to the outside and the gangway still extended. Lifting off his console seat, he peered out the bridge starboard-side window. Jackie and Brian were still in the clearing, engaged in a heated discussion.

You need to get the Evermore *into space, Cuddy. Look at the Viewscape display … as you can see, the military forces—twelve humans, holding automatic weapons … have entered the woods and are headed your way. It is time to leave.*

Tony and Kyle entered the bridge, sitting nosily down in open seats.

"What the hell are we waiting for?" Tony asked, his eyes locked onto the Viewscape display. "Are those soldiers the ones the orb mentioned?"

Kyle said, "We're going to have to leave her. I'm sorry, little brother, but—"

"You were going to leave without me?"

Hearing Jackie's scolding voice, all three spun around to see her, standing at the entrance to the bridge. One hand rested on her hip, and she wore a defiant expression that flustered Cuddy. He looked out the window but could no longer see Brian.

"Is he out there?" Kyle asked.

Cuddy, resuming his seat, shook his head. "He's gone."

"Actually … he's not," Jackie said. "He's decided to come with us. Wants to stay with me. I couldn't talk him out of it."

Cuddy looked past Jackie and saw the somewhat older man, now standing close behind her, his hand resting on her shoulder.

"Shit!" Kyle yelled, pointing toward the tree line. "Troops!"

Cuddy saw them too. The Army guys had arrived—some moving right, some left—as if to surround the ship. Three soldiers were moving forward—toward the still open hatch.

Chapter 39

Gunfire erupted from all around the ship. Cuddy was well aware the *Evermore* was practically impregnable—bullets would have zero effect. Then he stopped to listen to the sounds that were not gunfire. Barking. Rufus was barking. Cuddy hurried to the side window and peered out. He saw the end of the gangway below and Rufus there—noisily holding his ground against the approaching soldiers. Paralyzed with fear, Cuddy was unable to speak or move—he simply watched in horror as the old dog was getting more and more riled up.

Cuddy heard both Kyle and Jackie screaming for Rufus to come back inside. Only then did Cuddy pull himself free from his frozen stupor. He ran out of the bridge and into the main open cabin. He pushed Tony and then Brian out of the way. Reaching the open hatch, he wedged himself between Jackie and Kyle standing there—where he saw three helmeted men closing in—all dressed in black with protective combat vests. All three had their automatic weapons raised. Instinctively, Cuddy flung his hands out toward them—while dispatching a tremendous wave of energy. All three attackers were sent up and backwards—as if an invisible cord had yanked each of them away—out of sight, deep into the trees.

Only then did Cuddy see Rufus. He was lying on the gangway. There was blood at his midsection—obviously he'd been shot. No longer concerned with the other soldiers and sound of increased gunfire, he hurried down the ramp—slid his two arms beneath the injured dog and lifted him up. Turning back to the ship, bullets raked the gangway—he heard the *zing* of a supersonic round passing within an inch of his left ear.

Even before clearing the hatch, Cuddy used his unique mental abilities to initiate closing it and to retract the gangway. As the hatch slid into place he heard multiple rounds colliding with the outer hull. He looked down at Rufus. His eyes were open and watery. He stood there for a moment not knowing what to do. He looked up to the see the shocked faces of the others. Mentally, he reached out to the orb. *What do I do now? He's dying … please help me.*

Jackie took a tentative step forward. "Cuddy … I'm so sorry."

Cuddy looked down at Rufus and saw what she saw. He was gone. Rufus was gone.

He heard the orb's words in his head.

Cuddy … you need to get the Evermore *into the air. Hurry now. Have someone put the dog down below … he'll be safe and secure there. I'm very sorry.*

Cuddy found Kyle's eyes. "Take him to the lower subdeck." He carefully transferred the dog into Kyle's now open arms.

"Okay, Cuddy … I'll take him right now."

Cuddy saw the tears in Kyle's eyes and briefly wondered why he himself felt nothing but anger … an internal rage building to an almost uncontrollable level.

He hurried forward—back to the bridge. Tony, right behind him, moved to the side windows. He said, "Sorry man … about Rufus." He glanced out the window. "Um … those guys out there don't look happy."

Cuddy listened to the orb in his head.

Cuddy, you must energize the Evermore*'s thrusters. Using the three, in-line slide controls, slowly bring the thrust levels up, in equal amounts, to the mid-way point. Do so now!*

Cuddy found the three sliders off to the left and quickly did as told, repositioning the controls at the mid-point. The *Evermore* lurched, both up and forward, throwing Kyle and Tony to the deck. Cuddy grabbed on to the console for support. Hearing someone else curse from the main cabin, Cuddy figured it must be Brian.

Not only had he brought the thrust levels up too fast, he hadn't done so evenly. As Cuddy readjusted the controls, equally lining them up at the mid-point, the ship leveled out and continued to ascend into air space above. He pushed any thoughts about Rufus aside. This was not the time to grieve.

A flood of visual images suddenly filled Cuddy's consciousness—vectors, coordinates, and calculations of spatial distances. He bent over, as if he'd been gut punched, feeling dizzy. His head hurt. *Orb … stop! That's too much information … I can't process it all … I don't understand everything …*

You will, Cuddy … the information is now there for you … and you will remember when the time is right.

But how …

Human DNA … 5.5 petabits of data … around 700 terabytes … in a single gram of DNA. The human brain has a remarkable untapped memory storage capacity. Where others, those who have not had multiple sessions within a wellness chamber, do not have the capability to sequence the DNA to retrieve this information … you do.

"Hey, you okay, Cuddy?" Kyle asked, looking concerned. He'd returned from the sub-deck and, like Cuddy, his arms were stained with Rufus's blood.

Almost as quickly as the pain had struck—it vanished. Cuddy stood up and took in a deep breath. "I'm fine, Kyle." The spaceship had already reached an altitude of several thousand feet.

"Wicked! I can see the whole town below us,"Tony said.

Kyle threw in, "I'm only sorry we didn't tell Momma … didn't say goodbye to her." Cuddy, glancing over at him, said, "We'll be back."

"We'd better come back. I didn't sign up for any one-way trip," Brian said, still standing at the entrance to the bridge.

No one replied to his comment.

Cuddy only knew he was mentally directed to perform the job at hand—getting the *Evermore* ever deeper into space. Now, as he became more and more familiar with the board—the controls, the information dump he'd last received from the orb not only became crucial—but relevant. As if inwardly glancing, not dissimilar to looking at a computer's hard drive file system—Cuddy saw the type of information that had been transmitted in to his brain … into his very DNA. Certainly every aspect of how to pilot this ship as well as what would be required for its maintenance—it was all there.

The others had now moved away from the windows and were staring at the Viewscape display. Looking over his shoulder, he saw them studying both him and the display. He leaned over and pulled on the diagonal ends—increasing the virtual display size—making it easier for them to view. The nearly transparent outline of the *Revenge* let them know that it too was ascending, and was close by.

"So why don't you tell us what you're doing … what's going on?" Jackie asked.

He wasn't aware she'd moved, was now standing so close to him. He smelled the faint scent of strawberries—probably from the shampoo she used.

"I'm being guided by the orb, doing what it instructs me to do."

"You mean … like mentally … psychically?" Brian sneered cynically. He stepped up close behind Jackie, cupping his hands on her shoulders. A possessive gesture that didn't go unnoticed by Cuddy.

"Yes, the orb mentally … speaks to me; provides me with mental images. That sort of thing."

"That's impossible. Take it from me. I'm a doctor … a neurosurgeon, to be more specific. I'm sorry, big guy, but humans simply aren't capable of doing something like that."

Jackie shrugged Brian's hands away from her shoulders and glared up at him. "Well, maybe he's not entirely *just* human … did you ever consider that? There's a lot you don't know, Brian. Being a pompous ass is only going to alienate you more from everyone here."

Brian raised his hands in mock surrender. "Hey, easy does it, there … just getting the lay of the land around here."

Cuddy, scanning the Viewscape, noted multiple icons now making their way off the surface, heading toward the *Evermore*. "That's not good. Incoming missiles! Best everyone sit down and strap in." Cuddy then looked over to Kyle and said, "Um … can you get everyone out of the bridge … have them strap in out there? I need to concentrate."

"Sure." As Cuddy watched Kyle usher everyone off the bridge, he knew they weren't really interfering with his concentration—except for Brian, who was already getting under his skin. He really didn't like the guy.

The orb again was communicating within his mind.

Cuddy … I need to break away for a while. It seems my makeshift repairs to the cloaking system on the Revenge *have failed. Added to that, the one remaining functioning drive is becoming problematic, as well. My sensors tell me there are numerous incoming projectiles … missiles … coming from various strategic land, sea, and air locations around the planet. It's a full-on attack, Cuddy. They have locked on to this spacecraft. Unfortunately, without functioning shields, I now need to separate from the* Evermore *and fend off the attack on my own. Fortunately, the* Evermore *is fully functional; its shields and propulsion readings are optimal. Cuddy, you have everything you need to progress to the upper atmosphere then beyond into distant space. Increase your rate of ascent, Cuddy … do that now!*

Before Cuddy could object, the *Revenge* was banking away. He tried reaching out to the orb with his mind but knew the physical distance apart was already too great. He suddenly felt alone and vulnerable, but doing as the orb instructed, he increased their rate of ascent. His eyes stayed locked onto the Viewscape display, helplessly watching as numerous missiles approached the *Revenge*. The Howsh ship took decisive evasive action—spinning off to the right then reversing its direction—then going into a spiraling downward roll. The *Revenge* next fired off its plasma weapons and two missiles exploded simultaneously.

"There's … too many!"

Cuddy glanced back over his shoulder to see Kyle standing there. He'd come back in.

"Can't we do something? He's being overwhelmed," Kyle groaned.

"I don't think so. The *Evermore* doesn't have weapons on board … the Pashier were pacifists," Cuddy told him. Like his brother, he felt increasingly powerless.

Cuddy glanced out the window and noticed the surrounding darkening blue of the upper atmosphere. Soon they would be reaching outer space.

Now staring at the Viewscape with relief, they saw that the orb was getting the upper hand with the ongoing air battle. One after another, all of the incoming missiles were being destroyed.

"Get 'em … get 'em all!" Kyle cheered.

Cuddy smiled at his brother's enthusiasm and also began to breathe a little easier. Noting they'd now entered space, he brought the ship into a low orbit.

"Um … what's that, Cuddy?" Kyle asked.

Cuddy turned back to the Viewscape display—something was approaching the *Revenge*.

"Why doesn't the orb just get away from there?" Kyle questioned.

"That Howsh ship's got mechanical issues. The orb mentioned its one working drive was having problems," Cuddy said.

It was now apparent that the object approaching the *Revenge* was not a singular thing but a huge foray of multiple missiles—certainly no less than one hundred.

Cuddy's stomach sank. He whispered, "Come on, orb … just get away from them … do something!" He was aware the others had quietly crept back onto the bridge and were silently watching the *Revenge* too. No longer maneuvering this way and that, the ship no longer deployed countless plasma bolts to protect itself either. As the first incoming missiles descended upon their intended target, a bright flash at the center of the display indicated a tremendous explosion had occurred. And then nothing could be seen on the display. No missiles … and no Howsh spacecraft. The *Revenge* had been destroyed, *the orb now … gone.*

Cuddy slowly turned and stared at all the other stunned faces. No one spoke.

Finally, Brian broke the silence. "The flying robot thing … it's destroyed, right?"

Cuddy nodded.

"And it was the intelligence behind everything, what you were trying to do … right?"

When no one uttered a word, Brian added, "You need to turn back. You do know that, don't you? Take us back to the ranch and, with luck, nobody's jacked with my car yet."

"You're a major tool, do you know that?" Tony said, leering at him.

"Look … you may not like what I'm saying, but at some level you know it's true. I'm the oldest one here and have the most real-life experience. I make life-altering decisions on a daily basis, so it's time now you let a grownup make the big decisions. I'm telling you, take us back to Earth."

Cuddy shifted his eyes toward Jackie. Still focused on Brain, she seemed to be considering what he was saying, and he could see indecision in her eyes.

When Cuddy spoke, his words were barely audible. "I'm taking this ship to Primara. Neither you, nor anyone else, will get in my way of doing that. You chose to come along so you're going to have to deal with it. Now get off my bridge … all of you!" Cuddy turned his back on Jackie and studied the console. He wondered if the orb was right—that possibly he already knew what was necessary for them to reach Primara. He honestly didn't know. What he did know was that he already felt the orb's loss. His thoughts turned to another … *how can I do this alone, Tow?*

Chapter 40

His official title was Lorgue Prime Eminence Norsh—but the standard, less formal way to address him was simply Lorgue Norsh. Currently, he was making his way forward, toward the *Pintial*'s command center. Normally, he'd stop and converse with officers and crewmembers along the way, but not today. Norsh was in a hurry, and also in a foul mood. He fumed thinking about the news he'd received only that morning—an interstellar dispatch, coming from a distant quadrant that typically was of little concern to the Howsh.

Lorgue Norsh entered the Howsh Marauder-Class star fighter's command center. Like the spacecraft itself, the command center was voluminous. Norsh strode toward the principal dais—a raised section at the center of the command center—where only the most senior officers were permitted to enter. Norsh spotted the officer he was looking for off to the right of the dais—Sub-Forgue Molth, his second-in-command.

There were nearly sixty command-center deck officers present, and they nervously watched their principal commander make his way toward his first officer. Lorgue Norsh was an impressive sight. Like all those on board this Marauder-Class vessel, he appeared well manicured. His golden-colored body fur was trimmed down to a quarter of an inch in length. He wore a smart white uniform with an angled crimson sash that had row after row of ornate metals and ribbons—each symbolic of some past act of either valor or bravery in battle. Although Lorgue Norsh's bearlike snout had turned silver, it was the only evidence of his advancing years. There was none other on board the *Pintial*, young or old, who could match the commanding officer's capacity for close-quarter combat.

"Sub-Forgue Molth!" he said.

The first officer turned as the Howsh commander strode toward him. "Yes, Lorgue Norsh." The lowly deck officer who had been conversing with Sub-Forgue Molth, lowered his head in submission and backed away.

Norsh towered over the smaller, slighter, Molth. Staring down at him, Norsh tried not to stare at a pinkish, mole-like growth between the Howsh officer's eyes. Like a third unblinking eye, it had been growing—its overall mass ever-expanding over the past year. He was ready to order Molth to deal with it; get it removed or die trying. It was that distracting. That revolting.

"Who ordered the three scout ships into the Sol System? More importantly, who gave them permission to enter a primitive's world's atmosphere? To actually land there?" Norsh asked.

Sub-Forgue Molth exhibited the appropriate expression of confusion, mixed with dismay, and replied, "Scout vessels are intended for pursuit only … certainly not engagement."

Molth was spouting the obvious and Norsh didn't buy his act. He already knew that Molth had given the interstellar order. The real question was why? Crews manning the many thousands of Scout-Class vessels, dispatched throughout the galaxy, were one step above barbarians. Norsh had determined earlier that the filthy, ghastly beasts weren't actually Howsh, but more like the cave dwellers seen on many of the worlds he'd come across over the decades. The ingrates defecated indiscriminately—anytime—anywhere! No, they didn't have the necessary genetic makeup to string two thoughts together, let alone make war with other life forms. Clearly, Howsh Scout-Class vessels were good for one thing only—menial pursuit duties, and they were required to report back. Scout ships and their crews were disposable—trash.

"Unfortunately, their action will reflect poorly on my jurisdictional command. Something our High Eminence will have little tolerance for."

Sub-Forgue Molth said, "I am immensely sorry, Lorgue Norsh … but there may be a silver lining to this turn of events."

Norsh grunted, waiting for him to continue.

"We are already en-route to Primara. Destruction of that foul world is a forgone conclusion. What we do know is that the elusive Pashier spacecraft, the *Evermore*, has returned to space—is back on course, heading toward Primara. We will easily accomplish what three ineffectual Scout ships could not. Primara and the *Evermore* will soon come to their appropriate inevitable end—two problems solved."

Lorgue Norsh thought about that. Sub-Forgue Molth was conveniently omitting the fact that the small fleet of Howsh Scouts, over the span of several years, had been decimated by an equal-sized fleet of fleeing Pashier ships, ones that were, for the most part, defenseless. Decimated not by reciprocal acts of violence, but by other means—most of which seemed to have stemmed from telekinetic acts—resulting in mechanical sabotage, often leaving Howsh ships adrift in space. The last Pashier—the one called Tow—had been far more resourceful than ever thought possible. Especially being the product of an inferior race. It was generally assumed that the heritage pod too had survived, which was unacceptable. Admirable as it was that Tow managed to evade the Scout ships over vast distances of the cosmos. Yes, Tow was certainly worthy of admiration, but it didn't change the fact that his destiny would follow that of his world, Mahli, and his fellow Pashier compatriots, in destruction and death.

Lorgue Norsh and Sub-Forgue Molth walked together toward available officer seating in the principal dais area. Norsh sat down first and surveyed the surrounding *Pintial*'s command center.

Irritably, he gestured for Molth to sit. "There can be no more losses. Our High Eminence has little tolerance for ineptitude. We can only hope he has not learned of the latest series of blunders. Being in his good favor is not a given."

"Lorgue Norsh, you command the most powerful warships within known space. Ten Marauder-Class fighters are a far cry from fifteen inconsequential little Scouts. I will not displease you again, Lorgue—"

"Fine. We will split the fleet. Five stealth Marauders will stay back and await the *Evermore*, traveling along its current course. You will command those ships, Sub-Forgue Molth. Perhaps an opportunity for redemption, yes?"

"Thank you, Lorgue. Yes ... the *Evermore* will finally be destroyed. Once and for all we will finally put an end to the Pashier."

Norsh, glancing again at his subordinate, caught him nervously picking at his disgusting growth. Grimacing, he looked away and said, "Go now and make the preparations for what I have outlined. We will reunite the fleet at Primara."

Norsh watched as his second-in-command quickly headed for the Command center's exit. As revolting as the Howsh first officer was in person, one-on-one, he was an adequate commander, both driven and ruthless. Two admirable qualities.

Chapter 41

Cuddy sat at the console, scanning the myriad of buttons and switches across the board. He knew what each was used for—its purpose—as well as how to configure it. Apparently, the orb's final mental download still had a far-reaching effect on him.

He entered in the navigational coordinates to their final destination—Primara—knowing much work would need doing over subsequent weeks. Requirements that went far beyond what Cuddy felt capable of completing on his own. The *Evermore*'s five independent systems were autonomous to a certain degree, but the vessel was designed to operate best with a supervising AI interface—an AI orb. As part of his mental download, Cuddy now possessed the basic knowledge of where to find the necessary parts within the hold and how to initialize a new AI orb. He was excited to get started on the project. To have something creative to do—to think about—other than of Rufus and the orb, now gone, or how much he was missing Momma. Or how annoying Brian was steadily becoming, by the minute.

Cuddy heard Brian's grating voice within the main cabin, complaining again about one thing or another. Cuddy rose from his seat to stare outside into the darkness before him. Space seemed so cold and impersonal. Several hours had passed since they'd left Earth, and they were quickly making their way through the solar system.

"Hey … how you holding up?"

Cuddy spun around. Jackie, standing at the entrance to the bridge, then asked him, "You get us on course, and all that?"

"I think so. Best I can figure out, anyway. I need to assemble another AI orb. That'll give me a bit more reassurance."

"I think I saw the parts for them down in the first hold … when we were working on the propulsion system."

Cuddy nodded.

"So … you up for giving everyone a quick tour? I'd do it, but I'm not as familiar with the ship as you are," Jackie said, smiling.

Cuddy was pretty sure the request had come from Brian. "Yeah … sure, I can do that." As he approached her, she leaned in and gave him a quick kiss on the cheek.

"What was that for?"

"Rufus … mostly, I guess."

He stepped past her and entered the main cabin, where Kyle and Tony were seated. Their feet were up, and they were talking and laughing about something. Cuddy didn't see Brian, at first, then saw him aft, coming up the passageway.

"Well … okay … I guess you figured out this is the *Evermore*'s main cabin." Cuddy said, inwardly checking his memories to see if there was anything to add concerning this section of the ship. *There was*! "There's seating in here for about ten people and an entertainment feature too." He strode over to a round, padded thing that looked somewhat like a big donut, which Kyle and Tony were using to prop their feet up on. He gestured for them to remove their feet and placed an open palm on its top surface. A holographic-type display suddenly appeared, emanating from the *donut*'s open area.

"As you can see, you can view the display from anywhere in the compartment. What you're looking at now is the main menu. I don't really know much about what's available to watch, or see, so you'll have to play with it. It will respond to your voice prompts although that's not how the Pashier typically used it."

"No, I'm sure *they* used their superior, kinetic, mindset to handle that sort of thing," Brian said, an edge to his voice.

Cuddy shrugged and nodded. "Guess so."

Both Tony and Kyle were already immersed in checking out what they later dubbed *the big whoopee cushion.*

"Look … Pashier movies!" Tony said excitedly, digging into sub menus, which displayed even more entertainment options.

"Come on, guys, we're taking a tour of the ship right now," Jackie said. Cuddy led the way down the aft passageway, informing them, "And here we're passing berth port and starboard sleeping compartments." He opened the hatch into the ones portside, stepping aside so they could all move past him into the narrow space. Three bunk-bed-style sets of two bunks each were crammed in, with a single stand-alone bunk at the far end.

"Great … communal living … just like summer camp," Brian sneered. "So where does one drain the snake in the middle of the night?"

Jackie made a face. "There's a door … hatch … right there. See for yourself."

Brian did, discovering a communal bathroom that facilitated up to four crew at a time.

"You'll have to figure out how to use the shower and toilet system on your own. They're nothing like anything we have back on Earth," Jackie added.

Brian exited the head, looking unimpressed. Then, with his hands on his hips, he surveyed the bunks. "Well, enjoy the

… what did you call them, the portside berth compartment? Jackie and I will be crashing on the starboard-side bunk compartment. That only makes sense, since we're a couple."

Cuddy, noticing Kyle and Jackie were both about to speak, interjected—raising a hand. "That sounds like a good idea, Brian. Just know the area is somewhat smaller than this one."

Brian said, "That's fine. It'll just be the two of us." He winked at Jackie, who looked away—her cheeks reddening. He strode from the compartment and moved across the passageway to an identical, opposite hatch and opened it.

Tow must have repaired the hatch door, enough so it could now be opened. But little had been done about the festering lingering smell. The crushed-in space, to Cuddy, looked like how a tin can of soda would appear from the inside—after being stepped on first. There was no way to enter the compartment, let alone sleep there.

Brian held the back of his hand over his nose. "What the hell is that smell? And what happened in there?"

Jackie said, "That is what happens when there's a hull breach." She looked at Cuddy with a questioning expression, unsure of her choice of words. He nodded back to her.

"Hull breach? How often does that happen?" Brian asked, still staring into the decimated compartment.

"I don't know," Cuddy said flatly. "Part of the risk one takes, living in space, Brian."

"Dude … close that hatch," Tony said.

Cuddy led them further down the passageway, which had several more hatch doors on either side.

"What's in them?" Brian asked.

"Don't be concerned with those areas, they are kept locked. There's nothing for you to see in those compartments." Cuddy then turned around, before entering the larger hatch door at the end of the passageway, to inform them, "In here is the *Evermore*'s propulsion system … Engineering. Go in and take a fast look around, but know there's probably no reason for anyone to ever go in there, so this area will remain locked."

Again, Cuddy stood aside, permitting the group to pass by him and enter the compartment.

Brian stepped in, seeming disinterested, and asked, "And what … you're the gatekeeper to all these off-limits areas?"

Cuddy followed into Engineering with the others. It was louder in here. Cuddy felt the constant vibration beneath his feet. "Safer for everyone that way."

Kyle stood at the large portside drive unit, and queried, "What if one, or both, of these babies goes down? Do you know how any of this works, Cuddy?"

Brian sneered at the prospect of Cuddy actually answering him.

"With emersion drives, such as these, simply put … antiprotons are used to heat a solid, high-atomic weight refractory metal core. Reusable propellant is pumped into the hot core and expanded through the aft nozzles to generate regulated thrust."

They all stared at Cuddy in astonishment for a long moment.

Kyle asked, "How do you know that, little brother? How could you possibly know that?"

"The orb, before it … left … transferred a ton of information to me. Truth is, I didn't even know I knew that until you asked."

Jackie, looking impressed, then focused past Cuddy. "Where is Brian?"

Cuddy, noting he was halfway down the passageway and moving forward, pointed, "He's out there."

The group, catching up to Brian, one by one took the spiral staircase down to the second level, where Cuddy spent extra time describing the operation of the food replicators, the various dispensers for H^2O, plus another liquid, called xicachan. Then they all, including Cuddy, opened and closed cabinets and inspected various, appliance-like, units. Some were easily figured out, while others remained a total mystery.

They moved into two, identically sized, ship holds, strolling through aisles of tall shelves. It became apparent that much of the stores there were now depleted. Not unexpected, since the *Evermore* had been in space for more than three years now.

"Oh, here are other orb bodies, Cuddy," Jackie said, pointing to a collection of AI orb parts, neatly stored on several shelves. Cuddy eyed the spheres, with their folded up appendages, and the assortment of gel-tabs close by.

They then moved into the second hold area, which seemed nearly identical to the first. Everyone was pretty much wandering around on his or her own, by this point. Cuddy slowed down when he heard hushed voices, coming from the next aisle over. He heard Brian's voice, then Jackie's, then the almost imperceptible sound of two people kissing. Cuddy's heart ached, thinking of the two of them together—becoming intimate.

Cuddy hurried down the aisle and caught sight of Kyle, walking toward the exit.

"Ship seems a lot bigger from the inside. Seems almost roomy in here," Tony said.

Cuddy nodded and grumbled something imperceptible—he wanted to leave the hold before Brian and Jackie caught up to them.

Chapter 42

As Brian and Jackie rejoined the group, she seemed to be avoiding eye contact with everyone, though Brian, in turn, smugly stared back at Cuddy.

"Where to now? You going to show us where the toilets empty out?" Brian snickered at his own humor. "Lead on kemosabe …"

Next, Cuddy showed the group the wellness chamber. He stood at the entrance, while the others took seats within the sterile circular compartment.

"So, this place is what made you … like super human?" Tony asked.

Cuddy shrugged, uncomfortable talking about his private sessions here. Eventually, everyone cleared out of the chamber, except for Brian. He was taking in every detail—spending the most amount of time staring at the blinking, multi-colored lights on the control panel, positioned midway up and to the right of the entrance hatch.

"What can you tell me about this panel?"

"Why do you want to know?" Cuddy asked, more defensively than he intended.

"Look … in case you've forgotten, I'm a physician. A surgeon. Don't you think a sophisticated wellness chamber would be of interest to me? Don't you think here is where I could do the most good, on our journey to God knows where … wherever it is we're going?"

"Maybe, but nobody's sick. And this chamber was designed for the Pashier, not humans. It could be dangerous," Cuddy said.

Brian scoffed at that. "Uh huh. So says the one who's benefitted most. Heightened intelligence, not to mention kinetic and psychic capabilities, which no human has ever possessed."

"That's the thing, Brian. I am no longer human. Not completely. Are you willing to give that up … your humanity? To become a living mutation … one not wholly of a particular species?"

"Sure … why not? I could care less what species I'm called. No, I need to know everything about this chamber."

"Well … sorry, but I don't know how to configure that panel. That was not part of the information download I received from the orb," Cuddy lied. "Best you don't mess with it. Sorry."

Brian eyed Cuddy, clearly not buying it.

"You guys coming? I found another cool compartment," Jackie said, looking out from a hatchway ten feet further down the corridor. Again, she avoided making eye contact with Cuddy, and he wondered, *Have I lost her … my best friend?*

He followed Brian into the next hatchway and peered curiously around, never having been inside before.

"I think it's a Pashier chapel, or a church," Jackie said.

A large compartment, with soft lighting, there was an overall tranquil feeling to the space. Its original metal decking had been replaced with a more organic-type of flooring, not wood—but something similar. Comfortable-looking seating was arranged in a circular fashion. Kyle tapped Cuddy's upper arm, gesturing him to look upward, where a suspended galaxy of tiny lights hung. He wasn't sure if they were some kind of projection, or something else. They certainly looked real—three-dimensional. Although he had no memory of ever visiting this compartment before, he only knew he liked it—the way it made him feel. Cuddy knew he would be returning soon.

"It's a sanctuary. It's so beautiful," Jackie said. "It makes sense … the Pashier were kind, spiritual beings." As she and the others started to file out, she said, "Other than the bridge, which we've already seen, and a few bathrooms, I mean *heads*, scattered about … that's the complete fifty-cent tour, folks."

Brian waited for Cuddy, the last one to leave the sanctuary. "How about you show me that sub-level compartment, bro. I hear it's really some—"

Cuddy moved fast, before he knew what he was doing. "Never go down there! Ever!" With his left hand, he grabbed a fistful of Brian's shirt and lifted him two feet off the deck. Then, taking a step forward, he slammed him up against the closest bulkhead. He brought back his other clenched fist, ready to unload his 6'3", two hundred pounds of body mass, into one killing blow. Wide-eyed, Brian squirmed and tried to free himself. Cuddy's tight grip on his throat made it impossible for him to utter more than a few whimpering squeals.

"Stop! Cuddy … stop! Please put him down."

Cuddy ignored Jackie's request, though he felt her presence behind him in the corridor. Felt her eyes boring into his back.

"He's an ass … that's no secret. But killing him would hurt you too, Cuddy. That's not you; not the person you are."

Cuddy released his death grip on Brian's throat—he was now gasping for air. Cuddy took a step away from him. Cuddy's mental power kept Brian pinned, high up on the bulkhead—his legs flailing. His voice, little more than a croak, screamed out, "Let me down you … you fucking freak!"

Cuddy brushed past Jackie without slowing down. He

was halfway up the winding staircase before he inwardly relaxed his invisible hold on Brian. He heard Brian hit the floor with a clamoring thud. Smiling, because Jackie was wrong. She didn't know who he was—not now—not anymore.

★ ★ ★

Later, after everyone retreated to a personal berth to get some sleep, Cuddy left the bridge and returned to the lower level. He followed the aft passageway into Hold #1 and made his way over to the shelving that contained all the various AI orb parts. He lifted the inert sphere unit off the shelf then moved to where the boxes of gel-tabs were located, and grabbed one. After a final scan of the shelf, checking to see if there was anything else he was supposed to get, he left the hold and headed forward, toward Tow's small hidden workshop.

It took Cuddy four and a half hours to complete a job he figured Tow would be able to do in a matter of minutes. But his fingers were thick and clumsy, and he only discovered the necessary calipers tool, with its wiggly, life-like prongs, after a frustrating hour of no progress. To accomplish the essential task of bringing a new AI to life, Cuddy drew on memories furnished by the new orb's predecessor. Now more accustomed to drawing on thoughts that weren't his own, he wondered at what point he might fully discern everything that the AI had downloaded into his mind—though perhaps never.

After making the final settings configuration, he next ensured that the orb was indeed powered on. He knew the AI was going through a series of self-tests, doing millions, if not billions, of assessments—determinations.

Startled by the orb's rapid ascent into the air—where it quietly hovered—he said, "Hello … I am Cuddy Perkins."

Yes, hello, Cuddy Perkins … I now must address several pressing issues on the Evermore*: Environmental filters need swapping …*

there is a slight alignment issue with the second emersion drive. Cuddy watched as the sphere sped away. Only then did he realize the orb had spoken to him telepathically.

Suddenly, Cuddy felt very tired, needing sleep. He left the little workshop and found his way to the upper-deck berths. He tried to be quiet as everyone was sound asleep. He stopped and looked down at Jackie's sleeping face—*so beautiful*—and wondered if she was angry at him for the altercation with Brian? *Of course she was.*

In the dim light, he made his way to his berth then crawled into it, too tired to undress. He just needed sleep. His mind drifted into the murky state between consciousness and sleep, and he felt himself drifting off, going deeper and deeper. Then suddenly his eyes opened wide and he sat up. He remembered something. Something that wasn't there. In the semi-darkness, he found Brian's berth, the one atop Jackie's—it was empty.

Chapter 43

Cuddy crept past the sleeping passengers, out the berth compartment, and headed forward. Reaching the bridge, he saw that it was empty. The orb should have been here. Thinking about it, he had a pretty good idea where both Brian, and the orb, had gone. It also suddenly occurred to him that he hadn't taken the time to set up a command structure for the orb. He cursed himself, this was something he'd been reminded to do by the other AI. He hurried aft, crossed through the main cabin and took the circular staircase down, taking three steps at a time. Reaching level two, he hit the deck running. Halfway down the aft passageway, he noticed the hatchway to the wellness chamber was closed. Symbols on the small access panel told him the chamber was in use—the hatch locked. He banged on the hatch with a closed fist several times, and then brought his head closer to it to listen. He definitely heard Brian's voice within. Frustrated, Cuddy banged again, followed with several strong kicks.

Use your mind! Cuddy remembered and reached out to the orb:

Yes, Cuddy Perkins … can I assist you?

Relieved that he hadn't been completely locked out from contacting the AI, he proceeded to handle the most important business first.

I would like to set up the Evermore*'s hierarchical command structure.*

Yes, Cuddy Perkins … you may proceed.

Captain is Cuddy Perkins. First Officer is … Cuddy had to think about that for a few heartbeats … *Kyle Perkins. Third officer is … Jackie?*

And the other two on board this ship, Captain Perkins?

Tony Bone … leave him undesignated at this time. Brian Horowitz, though, is not part of the Evermore*'s crew and you are not permitted to follow any of his orders, or directives, without the Captain's, or First Officer's, prior sign-off. Is that understood?*

Understood and logged.

Now open the hatch!

The wellness chamber hatch slid to one side and Cuddy stared into the brightly lit compartment. Brian was seated in there, naked, directly before him. His hair bun was undone and a long ponytail hung down over one shoulder. His face—his entire body—looked strangely bloated, added to the fact he was glowing bright enough to still see, even in the highly illuminated chamber. To Cuddy, Brian looked like an oversized, glowing slug as he gazed back at him through half-lidded eyes.

"Orb, what's going on with Brian? What's wrong with him?" Cuddy asked out loud.

"Brian has completed his fifth wellness session, Captain Perkins."

Cuddy realized that this was the first time he was actually hearing the AI orb speaking vocally. Even more surprising, the voice sounded different than its predecessor. More friendly.

"Humans cannot withstand any more than two sessions within the chamber in so short a time span. Why did you let him do that?"

"At the time, there was no hierarchical command structure in place."

That was true and he should have anticipated Brian pulling something like this. Cuddy stepped into the wellness chamber and took a seat next to Brian.

"Brian … can you hear me?"

Yeah … but can you dial it aback a little … so fucking loud.

Cuddy watched the slightly older man's face, noting he hadn't moved his lips. *He, like Cuddy, was now part Pashier.*

"Are you in pain?" Cuddy asked, keeping his voice low.

Yes.

Cuddy looked up to the hovering orb. *What can we do for him?*

The wellness chamber was not designed with a human genome in mind. The effects from too many recurring sessions at one time cannot be undone. He may not survive the journey.

You're not sure?

No, Captain Perkins, as there are no previous records of any such occurrence. No case studies to which to refer.

Cuddy noticed Brian staring at him, only this time he spoke aloud: "You do know … I can hear what you're saying … your mental chit-chat?"

"Oh … all right. I don't know how to keep mental, telepathic conversations exclusive to only myself."

"I'm going to croak … I heard Bob."

"Bob?"

"That's what I've been calling the orb. Bob … because he's always bobbing up and down."

He was surprised to find he felt *somewhat* bad about what was happening to Brian. It was true, he detested the guy. There was no two ways about it. But seeing him like this, Cuddy actually felt a little sympathy for him. Truth was, this was partially Cuddy's own fault and now Brian might die because of his lack of forethought.

"I'm not ready to give up yet on getting you back to the

way you were, Brian."

"You sure you want to do that? I know you hated me … and I know why."

Cuddy waved off the comment, and added, "Oh come on, none of that matters now. You're part of the crew and we all need to stick together, right?"

"Do I look as bad as I think I do?" Brian asked. He seemed to have grown even more in girth over the last few minutes. Cuddy wasn't completely sure Brian was capable of studying his own body, due to his now fleshy, protruding neck.

"Well … you still have great looking hair," Cuddy said, smiling wryly.

That made Brian laugh out loud. He laughed until tears formed at the corners of his eyes. Then he was crying—quietly sobbing.

"Um … do you think you can walk?"

"I don't know. You and Bob … the orb … will need to help me, I think."

Cuddy stood in front of him, taking ahold of Brian's two hands. "When I lift him, get in behind him … okay, Bob?"

Cuddy inwardly heard its mental acknowledgement. "Here we go … one … two … three, stand up, Brian!"

Brian rose halfway up and stalled. But once Bob got hovered in the right position and pushed, Brian rose all the way up, into a wavering, standing position. He put his hands out to steady himself. Only then did Cuddy realize that Brian's bulbous belly flesh hung over, completely shrouding, his private parts.

"Okay … let's try to walk," Cuddy said. "I've got a good grip on your arm, so take one step at a time." Although clumsy and awkward, Brian was able to walk. At the end of the passageway, Cuddy steered him toward the stairway.

"I don't think …"

Cuddy cut him off mid-sentence. Brian had to climb up to the top level—where the sleeping berths were, and the kitchen—where he would be most comfortable. "We'll take it one step at a time, okay?"

In response, Brian gave him a weary look, coming to a standstill at the bottom of the stairway.

"You get in front of him, Bob, and I'll push from behind." Brian took his first step and then rested on the bottom tread. Cuddy heard his labored breathing.

"Okay ... next one, Brian."

Brian did as asked, but Cuddy, feeling increased bodily resistance, had to take on more of Brian's weight. *This isn't going to work.* Then a new inner nudge came to him:

Use your mind.

Cuddy, readying himself, did exactly that. He willed Brian's body to move several inches up off the stairs. A heavy strain, he wasn't sure how long he could hold on to him—even though it was only few inches. "Bob, pull him toward you ... up the stairs."

Brian said, "Uh huh ... this is kinda cool. I'm floating like a feather."

"In time, Brian, you'll be able to do this all by yourself—it's part of the package of becoming a Pashier. I can help you learn the kinetic basics tomorrow, if you like."

At the top of the stairs, Brian—again bearing his own weight—said, "Yes ... that would make things a lot easier. Right now, I couldn't take a crap by myself."

Between them, Cuddy and the orb managed to maneuver Brian's bulk around the kitchen and into the top-level passageway, then into the portside berth compartment. It was semi-dark and the others were still sound asleep. Cuddy did his best not to make any noise, though Brian was both huffing and puffing pretty loudly as he was moved to his berth, underneath Jackie's. Cuddy, judging the bunk to no longer be a good fit, far too restrictive, used mental persuasion to reach out to Brian.

Why don't you take my berth, Brian? It's more accessible ... a lot easier to get in and out of.

Really? I liked being under Jackie …

Cuddy, catching the slight smile on Brian's bloated face, thought at least he still has a sense of humor.

Bob and Cuddy together lowered Brian into the one singular berth by the bulkhead in an upright position, letting him then catch his breath. Next, Cuddy grabbed ahold of Brian's ankles and swung them up some, forcing Brian to lie flat on his back. Kneeling down on the deck, he leaned in close to Brian.

How's that? You'll be able to sleep okay like that?

Sure … I think so. Hey, thank you for all you've done. I'm sorry. This is my fault. I knew at the time I was taking a big risk. The orb … Bob … warned me.

Cuddy gave Brian a couple of pats on his chest. *We'll get it figured out, I promise.*

"Cuddy … is that you?"

Cuddy stood and moved over to Jackie's top berth. "Yeah … I'm only now going to bed. Goodnight."

"Goodnight, Cuddy," Jackie said sleepily and turned onto her side.

Chapter 44

Jackie woke, less than four hours later. The cabin was dark and she heard soft snores coming from either Tony or Kyle. She slowly sat up and stretched. She badly wanted a hot shower, but first she needed to pee. Throwing the covers aside she stood, somewhat surprised no one else was up yet. But that was probably a good thing, since she was only wearing panties and her oversized plaid shirt. She leaned over and searched the deck for her jeans, but found them instead tossed at the foot of her berth. Grabbing them up, she headed for the communal head then stopped mid-stride. Even in the dimly lit cabin, she could see something was terribly wrong. She leaned in closer and screamed.

"What! What is it!?" Kyle yelled out.

"What's going on?" Tony yelled.

"It's Cuddy. He's … he's transformed into … I don't know *what* he is," Jackie said, her hands covering her mouth in disbelief.

"No, I'm here, Jackie … that's Brian," Cuddy said, sounding groggy.

She spun around, finding Cuddy lying in Brian's berth,

and then swung back to check who was sleeping in Cuddy's berth. This time as she leaned in closer, she noticed Brian's long black ponytail. "What the hell happened to him? I don't even recognize him. He's all … bloated, or something."

"Good morning, Jackie."

"Brian? Are you … okay? Um … does it hurt?"

"No, I don't think so. I don't know. It feels weird, though. Like I'm living in someone else's body."

"More like five people's body," Tony added, now standing next to Jackie.

Angry, Jackie fumed, "Tell me what happened to you. How could something like that happen?"

"It's my fault. I messed with the wellness chamber," Brian told her. "I wanted to improve on the effects that Cuddy acquired in there … so I foolishly double-upped on the sessions."

Jackie stood still, staring down at him and shaking her head. "I have to pee … um … just stay there." She heard him mutter, "Yeah … I'll do that."

* * *

AI orb *Bob* was telepathically reaching out to him. *Captain Perkins … you are needed on the bridge.*

Cuddy said, "I'm on my way." Then, remembering, he spoke the words back telepathically.

"Huh?" Tony queried.

"Not you. I was talking to Bob … I'm needed on the bridge."

"Okay, but who's Bob?" Tony asked, though Cuddy was already running down the corridor. In less than two minutes he reached the bridge. The orb hovered there, at the forward console, and for the first time Cuddy noticed that this orb, *Bob*, was shaped slightly different than the first one. Perhaps more streamlined in its design.

"What's going on, Bob? Why do you need me here?"

Bob gestured with one of its articulating arms—*something else the first orb never did*—toward the Viewscape display.

"What am I looking at here?"

"Five Howsh, Marauder-Class, star fighters."

Cuddy sat down. "I thought there were ten of them? And that they were far off, not an imminent concern."

The orb hovered back to the board and made a few adjustments to what Cuddy recognized was the ship's cloaking. "Apparently, the fleet has split. These warships are now on an intersecting course with the *Evermore*."

Cuddy, afraid something like that would happen, asked, "How close?"

"Close, Captain. Keep in mind the *Evermore* has been continuously outpacing FTL speeds by a factor of seven, ever since leaving Sol System. I suspect the Howsh vessels, albeit not nearly as fast as the *Evermore*, are now traveling at their maximum capabilities as well. Currently, keeping those same joint rates of speed, we will intersect in five days, seven hours, and forty-three minutes."

"There has to be something we can do ... get away from them ... somehow?" Cuddy asked.

"The *Evermore*'s cloaking capability is far superior to that of the Howsh vessels. But enabling the ship with cloaking earlier would have slowed our progress by a factor of 4.3 percent. I thought it prudent to reinitialize the cloaking program now instead, noticing their relative proximity."

"Good! So we'll just speed right past them. They won't see us, right?"

"No, Captain. No cloaking system is perfect. Although an accurate lock on us would be nearly impossible, vessels as advanced as these Marauders will be able to track the spatial aberrations in our wake. Only when stationary will we become completely hidden from their sensor scans."

"What about the five other Howsh ships? Let me guess,

they're still headed for Primara."

"Correct. They will reach that planet within eight days."

★ ★ ★

Over the next hour, Cuddy tried to come up with some semblance of a battle strategy. The orb was helpful—answered all his questions, then provided just enough technical details to pretty much squash anything he came up with. Cuddy was becoming more and more cognizant of the fact he was not a tactician. He knew nothing of preparing for war; how to formulate a battle plan—and nothing in the old orb's info-dump-download pertained to the subject. He was reminded, for the umpteenth time, that the Pashier were pacifists. *Had they come this far on their journey, only to be crushed by five Howsh warships?*

Cuddy leaned back in his seat and exhaled a heavy breath—aware the orb was moving out through the exit hatch. He closed his eyes for a moment and thought of Momma, and his life before he became the being he now was. *What am I?*

He opened his eyes, realizing the overhead lighting had significantly dimmed. And then he saw him … Tow was aglow, like he'd never seen him before. He moved onto the bridge, his footfalls imperceptible, then sat down in the seat next to Cuddy's. His smiling face emanated forth both grace and humility.

Cuddy stared back at him. "How is this even possible?"

"You tell me, Cuddy. Tell me how *you* have come so very far?"

Suddenly, Cuddy felt ashamed—to the point he had to look away. "I have done nothing. I am lost here, Tow, and soon this space voyage will come to its sad, inevitable end."

"Do you remember, Cuddy, the last time we spoke? On the sub-level deck where you guided me into the heritage pod? Do you remember what we spoke about …?"

★ ★ ★

The overriding feeling Cuddy was experiencing was immense pride. He felt so honored to be the one to guide his new friend Tow into this swirling mist of glittering lights—into his next stage of existence—or *whatever this was all about.* Walking side by side, he felt the light touch of Tow's arm resting on his—light as a feather. He looked down, noting the smile on his friend's face, his look of anticipation. Of what was—*maybe amazing things*—surely coming. Tow wondered if, when the time was right, he too would be allowed to participate in this beautiful, otherworldly, ritual. He hoped so.

"Cuddy … listen to me carefully."

Tow slowed his pace—even as the swirling galaxy of lights glimmered brilliantly before him. More serious now, Tow looked up at him and said, "Cuddy, it will be easy to lose your way; easy to play by the rules of others—those driven by darker impulses. Those who only think short-term, willing to ignore what's truly there … hidden deep within their hearts."

Cuddy was reminded of the horrific turn of events Tow and his people were forced to endure over the years. And yet here he was now, the last one. The last Pashier, speaking only of kindness, not spite or revenge.

"But you didn't survive … none of you survived, Tow. Was it worth it? To be walking into … um … what's the word?"

"Extinction? Is that what you think, Cuddy?" Tow looked up and gestured to the magnificence around them. "Extinction is not possible … in fact, it's impossible. It is a term that corresponds only to forms of physicality, but does not exist on subliminal levels. Not really. Think about what truly endures forever. What can't be eviscerated—either by time or by acts of evil, ever."

Cuddy thought about that. *What could endure throughout time …?*

"When you figure that out, the problems, the distress … will disappear. Remember, hope is real when your intentions are in alignment with your true self. The answers will come to you, Cuddy. I promise you that."

Tow then picked up his pace and his smile returned. Anticipation of what was still to come emanated out from him with the brilliance of a hundred suns. "One more thing, Cuddy. You forget … I am not the last Pashier."

"Captain Perkins … did you hear me?" Cuddy blinked away the magnificent vision and looked around the bridge. The overhead lights were bright again. The orb still hovered above the forward console, and then it came to him … *what endures for all time*? Unconsciously, he placed his palm on his chest—over his heart.

Cuddy stood, then, studying the Viewscape display, said, "Bob … we've been going about this all wrong."

Chapter 45

Over the next five days, Cuddy, with Bob's invaluable assistance, immersed himself into the Howsh's long, pernicious history. Whatever was available on that ancient alien empire, and stored within the orb's memory banks, Cuddy needed to know about. All the while, the approaching fleet of five Howsh Marauders was a continual source of tension onboard the *Evermore*. Cuddy, Kyle, and Tony would periodically check their status on the Viewscape display.

Little had been seen of Jackie and Brian. With the help of Kyle and Tony, they'd moved his stand-alone sleeping berth into one of the less-crowded upper deck compartments. Brian had become increasingly self-conscious about his appearance—his total lack of mobility. Basically, Jackie had become his full-time on-call nurse, and for that Cuddy gave her all due credit—never hearing her complain, not even once.

Cuddy, currently seated in the rear of the bridge, where he'd set up a makeshift desk of sorts, had three separate query terminals positioned for easy access into the AI's extensive memory banks. He found it easier to write things down using pencil and paper. Bob had spent a significant amount of time providing him with a close facsimile of paper, and then a pencil—now stacks of notes were strewn all around the top of the desk.

Cuddy's thoughts, as they inevitably did, turned to Jackie. He did his best to bury his feelings—envious of the increasing amount of time Jackie spent alone with Brian. So when he heard her voice behind him, he was pleasantly surprised.

Jackie entered the bridge, looking rumpled and tired, then plunked down hard in the seat next to him, and stared over at the Viewscape display. "Bob, how much time do we have left … before the Howsh reach us?" she asked.

"Less than one hour, Jackie."

Cuddy watched her expression. She looked irritated and began to chew on the inside of her cheek. Something he knew she did when she was overly frustrated.

"You doing okay?" Cuddy asked.

She didn't look at him, at first. Didn't say anything, either. Cuddy shifted in his seat, not really knowing what to say next. *Did I do something wrong?*

Jackie glanced over to the AI orb and asked, "Bob … can you give us a little privacy? I need to speak with Cuddy alone."

"Of course. I will take care of some maintenance issues in Engineering."

"Oh, and close the bridge hatch as you go," she added.

Cuddy wasn't aware the bridge even had a closable hatch, but on hearing it slide closed, he realized it did.

"What did I do? Or forget to do? Go ahead and yell at me, Jackie. I've been so immersed here on the bridge …"

"Yell at you? What for?" she asked.

"I don't know … you don't look … all that happy."

"So I don't look happy, uh … I wonder why? I mean, according to AI Bob, we've probably got less than an hour to live. And let's pile on a little more shit. I've been playing nursemaid to an ungrateful, misogynistic ass for five days, and the one person I need attention from … is too daft to notice."

It was as if Cuddy had been shocked with a cattle prod. This was uncharted territory for him. No amount of information downloaded from the orb could prepare him for this conversation. "Well, I thought you and Brian were … still close. I heard you kissing in the hold, and …" he let his words hang.

Jackie closed her eyes and shook her head. "No, he kissed me, I didn't kiss him back. I'd just told him that he and I were over. That I didn't love him anymore … that maybe I never did."

Jackie leaned forward in her seat, her knees lightly touching his. Then, resting her hands on his upper thighs, Jackie stared into his eyes. "It took me a while to get over who you were *before* … and who you have become. You were a boy. Now you're not. Now you're a man, in every sense of the word. I see the way you look at me, Cuddy. I know you want me … in the ways a man wants a woman."

Cuddy began to squirm and looked off toward the Viewscape display as if distracted.

The corners of her lips turned up. With surprising agility, she scooted off her chair and onto Cuddy's lap. Then her voice, a mere whisper, murmured, "I know this is all new to you, Cuddy. Just relax … I won't bite."

He looked at her, now up so close, and saw things he'd never noticed before: The dusting of freckles on her upper nose—a tiny mole on her left cheek—how perfectly straight her teeth were. Without rushing, she took his face in her hands and looked at him. Then she kissed him—gently. Her lips were soft and wet and tasted salty. Both their eyes remained open as their kissing became more passionate. He noticed her cheeks had flushed and could feel her breath quickening. She turned her kisses onto his neck and, as her lips brushed lightly against his ear, she whispered, "I've wanted this for such a long time, Cuddy."

Then Cuddy felt her take his hand in hers and guide it into the fabric of her unbuttoned shirt. She cupped his hand into hers then guided it over her left breast. He felt her hard nipple tickle the inside of his palm, which she then gently squeezed. "Yes … gently … just like that." They kissed harder now—probing—exploring each other's mouths with their tongues. He was hard, under the fabric of his jeans, sitting beneath her. He felt Jackie pressing down onto him. Their rapid breaths escalated—now in perfect sync.

In the background, Cuddy heard a repeating chime—one that progressively got louder and louder. Then, just as quickly as she'd slipped onto his lap, Jackie was off, moving away. As the bridge hatch slid open, he heard her let out a long breathy sigh and laugh, saying, "Oh boy, oh boy …" Then she was gone.

The AI orb, now hovering in view, moved to the forward console. "The Howsh fleet has significantly increased speed. They will intersect with the *Evermore* within ten minutes."

"That's not possible! How did it go from an hour to only ten minutes?"

The orb did not answer.

Cuddy glanced over to the stacks of paper atop the desk and tried to recall all he'd learned over the course of five days; the many hours of practice he and Bob had endured. *Are we ready?* Then wondered, *is Bob ready?*

"Bob … can you open a communication channel to the commander of the approaching Howsh fleet?"

"Yes, I can open a channel, although it will be up to them whether they want to answer the hail or not."

"Remember, Bob, you cannot sound like a … an AI. You need to sound like an old Howsh supreme commander …"

★ ★ ★

Sub-Forgue Molth paced the circular raised dais while

keeping his eyes on the elevated screen. To him, there was no clear indication the *Evermore* was even out there, but the four bridge crewmen assigned to tactical assured him that indeed it was.

What he was now viewing was nothing more than a minuscule scattering of spatial artifacts that didn't look like much of anything. Molth was a nervous Howsh officer, told numerous times that he came across as trying too hard to please his superiors. Was too needy. But considering the fact that two previous first officers to Lorgue Prime Eminence Norsh had been demoted for incompetence, Molth was determined to make a far more positive, long-lasting impression.

He vigorously scratched the growth between his eyes then noticed it had started to bleed again. He casually glanced around the command center, checking to see if anyone had noticed him wiping his claws over the dark trousers of his uniform.

"Sub-Forgue Molth, there is an incoming hail coming from the *Evermore*, sir."

"Who is it?"

"It is not that foul Pashier, the one called Tow. He says he is Lorgue Supreme Eminence Calph, and he is ordering us to stand down."

"Preposterous!" Suddenly nervous, Molth raised a claw to scratch his face again, but caught himself, and lowered his arm back down. *Could that even be possible?* he pondered. Lorgue Supreme Eminence Calph, a Howsh legend, was reportedly lost in space some ten years earlier. Molth was fairly certain that Calph was Lorgue Prime Eminence Norsh's mentor. A hero—numerous monuments, on their home world, had been erected in Calph's honor. *How could this possibly be?*

"Very well, put him through."

"Lorgue Supreme Eminence Calph, this is Sub-Forgue Molth … commander of this Marauder fleet. Would you please make yourself visible … disengage from stealth mode, if you would be so kind?"

Molth listened to dead air for several moments. Distant background noise sounded like papers being shuffled.

"I knew your father, Parliamentary Head Molth. Is he still alive?" Eminence Calph asked.

Sub-Forgue Molth's heart rate increased exponentially. "Ah, no sir … he died, um, two years past." A pregnant pause then ensued, with more crinkling of paper.

"He was a true leader, within a difficult Howsh bureaucracy. He will be missed. Now listen to me carefully, Sub-Forgue Molth. I was marooned on planet Earth for over ten years and have commandeered the *Evermore*. The Pashier I believe you are seeking, Captain Tow, has died. But not before he destroyed three Howsh Scout ships. I witnessed their destruction myself. Tow was one clever Pashier, I have to give him that. One more thing … there is a foul heritage pod still on board this vessel. Unfortunately, I do not have the means to destroy it myself."

"I understand, Lorgue Supreme Eminence Calph. I will immediately make provisions for you on board the command ship. Once on board, we can destroy the *Evermore*—along with the pod."

"Unfortunately, I am suffering with *Paltrope*. Do you know of it?"

"Yes, Eminence Calph."

"Then tell me … has a cure been found for this foul disease? Perhaps one over the past few years?"

Molth reflexively made a bitter face. *Paltrope* was a highly contagious, disgusting disease that caused hundreds of oozing skin legions. He too had been tested for it recently. Luckily, his facial growth was nothing more than an out-of-control mole. What he did know was he didn't want to get anywhere near that very contagious high commander.

"Yes, Eminence Calph. Your particular … *ailment* will require Califer Ionization Therapy … *CIT.* Unfortunately, the treatment is only available back on Rianna 5."

"Well, then you must escort me there at once!"

"Rianna 5 is hundreds of light-years' distance from our current coordinates, Lorgue Supreme Eminence Calph. I am truly sorry, but I have direct orders, from Lorgue Prime Eminence Norsh, to reassemble our fleets at another planet, called Primara, once my mission here has been completed."

"Yes, yes, I'm familiar with Primara. It's located at the far end of the quadrant … in the opposite direction of Rianna 5!"

"Again, I apologize. A quick detour to Primara first, then we should be able to accommodate you, sir," Molth told him. "Again, it is an honor to speak with you. This … today … is an historic event!" Although Molth had little doubt he was speaking to the high commander, he still would feel more at ease if his eminence would remove the stealth mode cover on the *Evermore*—to personally ensure that Eminence Calph was indeed alone on the vessel.

Molth continued, "At this time, would it be possible for you to come out of stealth mode, Eminence Calph? It is protocol … as I'm sure you are—"

Eminence Calph cut him off. "Ask me that again and I'll have you transferred to a scout ship, scraping out shit from sub-deck collectors. Do you understand me?"

"Yes, I do apologize, Lorgue Supreme Eminence Calph."

Calph, now taking a more conciliatory tone, continued, "If you really knew what advanced *Paltrope* did to someone, you would understand why I do not want to be observed. Fortunately, the *Evermore*'s stealth mode prohibits prying, invasive optic feeds. It allows me some privacy."

"Yes, of course. I understand, Lorgue Supreme Eminence Calph." Molth let it go, having zero doubt, anyway, who he was conversing with.

"Good, stand by. I will be joining your fleet within minutes, then you will have visual sighting of the *Evermore*. Together, we shall move toward Primara in all due haste."

Chapter 46

With the exception of Brian, the entire *Evermore* crew—Cuddy, Kyle, Jackie, and Tony—huddled into the bridge to witness the historic, impending event. Cuddy doubted anything like this had ever occurred before, where a Howsh fleet would actually escort an enemy—Pashier—spacecraft.

"And what … they're just going to let us merge into their fleet, like we're one of their own?" Kyle asked skeptically.

Cuddy shrugged, not completely sure what to expect either.

"There they are," Tony said, pointing out the forward observation window. "Fuck … look at the size of those things!"

As they approached the Howsh fleet, five large warships changed their positions, reassembling into a horseshoe formation.

The orb said, "I am being directed to decrease speed and bring the *Evermore* into their awaiting formation cluster."

"Guess it's too late to back out now," Jackie said, glancing over to Cuddy.

"Like she said, it's too late to back out now. Go ahead and

merge us in, Bob."

"There is an incoming hail for Lorgue Supreme Eminence Calph, Captain Perkins. I have implemented a translation module so you can better understand what is being said."

Cuddy nodded, then glanced back at his desk, at the stacks of papers, and wondered if he would need to help Bob out again, like before. "Okay ... answer it." There was a definitive clicking sound, then Cuddy heard the same voice—it was Molth.

"Greetings, Lorgue Supreme Eminence Calph. I have forwarded our specific course parameters, as well as the FTL configuration settings your ship's AI will need in order to synchronize precisely to the rest to the fleet."

All eyes turned to Bob as he began to speak in a gruff, bear-like, voice. "That's fine. Can we move things along now, Sub-Forgue Molth? *Paltrope* is an impatient malady. If you want me to survive the journey, you'll keep your drives running hot. Blaze the fastest trail to Primara. We need to get moving."

"Yes ... Supreme Eminence Calph, we will be underway in just a few moments."

"The channel is closed now, Captain," the orb said.

Tony began to laugh out loud. "I can't believe that voice ... the words that came out of your mouth, or speaker, or whatever it is you have, orb. That was awesome, dude!"

The orb ignored the remark.

They all watched as Bob navigated the *Evermore* into position within the other larger vessels.

"We are underway, Captain. We will be reaching FTL in two minutes."

Cuddy felt the *Evermore*'s drives' vibration beneath his feet, then the inertia dampeners kicking in. "ETA for Primara, Bob?"

"Ten days, Captain. Less, if they do as instructed and increase their FTL speeds accordingly."

"So we have ten days to prepare for phase two," Cuddy remarked, to no one in particular.

"Phase two? So this is what … phase one?" Jackie asked.

"That's right."

"What's phase two, other than not getting ourselves killed?" Kyle asked.

"To convince the Howsh, as a species, that it is no longer in their best interest to destroy Primara, nor the remaining Pashier."

"I didn't know there were any Pashier left," Jackie said.

"Yes, there are a few," Cuddy said, not elaborating further.

★ ★ ★

By day eight, life aboard the *Evermore* had ripened into something cohesive—busily routine. Jackie spent more and more time in the galley. She somehow figured out what the unique appliances were used for. The result was an astonishing array of gourmet food—breakfasts, lunches, and dinners—from good ol' home-style southern cooking to inventive meals, originating from far away, in other star systems—on other planets.

To Cuddy's growing regret, there were no more intimate moments with Jackie like the one they had on the bridge. He shrugged it off, knowing they both were far too busy. Busy to the point lack of sleep was starting to take its toll on him. Yet, if he were honest with himself, there actually were some brief occasions when a few stolen moments might have been possible. *Did she regret what they'd done together,* he mused. *Had her feelings changed?* How could he blame her? He had no idea what he was doing—was way out of his comfort area.

Tony and Kyle, when they weren't planted in front of the entertainment system, watching Pashier thrillers, intergalactic nature films, or even an errant love story, were tasked with delivering to Brian—confined in his sole occupancy compartment—three square meals every day. Plus, help in the assembly of eleven additional AI orb units that Cuddy had recently discovered. Hold #2, he found, had its own stash of spare orb parts.

The grand plan was for the eleven orbs to become their dutiful army. Getting them to that point required assistance from both Tony and Kyle. Cuddy and Bob taught them how to do basic assembly work—mainly installing the gel-tabs—then configure each individual orb with capabilities not previously required by the Pashier.

Cuddy entered the bridge, finding Bob at the controls, and heard an unintelligible Howsh conversation in progress. As Cuddy approached, Bob made a settings change and suddenly the alien's words were translated into English.

Cuddy asked, "What are we listening to?"

"A deep-space channel has just been acquired. Eavesdropping into it, Sub-Forgue Molth is speaking with Lorgue Prime Eminence Norsh—currently in high orbit around Primara—who commands the other half of the Howsh fleet."

"Crap … I didn't anticipate that. At least, not yet." Cuddy listened to what they were discussing—Eminence Norsh sounded irritated.

"No! Your orders were to destroy the *Evermore,* destroying the heritage pod in the process. It was a simple directive. Any idiot could follow those orders," Norsh said.

Sub-Forgue Molth said, "I assure you, Your Eminence, we are escorting Lorgue Supreme Eminence Calph. He was marooned on Earth … for ten years. His knowledge of the Howsh …"

Norsh cut him off, "You truly are an idiot, Molth. Whoever is on board that vessel is no more Lorgue Prime Eminence Calph than I am. You think it's a coincidence you haven't been able to establish visual verification by scanning that vessel? Stupid fool … you've been duped. All you've accomplished is to provide an escort for our enemy!"

Cuddy cringed. He'd hoped for a bit more time—to be closer to Primara before the deception was discovered. He asked Bob, "How close are we?"

"Not far. We will reach Primara in several days, at our current FTL rate of speed, Captain."

Cuddy glanced over at the Viewscape display, showing the symbolic, V-formation view of the small Howsh fleet, with the *Evermore* sited in its center.

"It's game time, Bob. We need to disable all of those ships … and we need to hurry," Cuddy said. Although the timing was not perfect, he felt they were ready. Three hours earlier, the eleven newly constructed AI orbs were discreetly released, one at a time, through an underbelly airlock. Using their clawed articulating arms, they maneuvered themselves around the *Evermore*'s fuselage underbelly, where they now clung, awaiting orders.

"Deploy the orbs, Bob. And cross your fingers they go undetected."

"The orbs have been deployed … are en route to their intended targets."

Cuddy watched the display. The orbs, tiny blue icons, quickly went out into space, all except one, moving farther and farther away from the *Evermore*. The icons, then organizing into sets of two, reached their intended Marauder ship targets. Once there, they located some irregularity on the hull's surface—some external structure—significant enough to cling to.

"Two orbs have dislodged, Captain."

Cuddy, already noticing, thought it unfortunate that they both had come loose from the same Marauder. *Damn.* He watched the display as the two blue icons spun ineffectively off into space. Fortunately, they had anticipated the possibility of such a thing occurring.

"Deploy the backup orb," Cuddy said.

Bob did as ordered, and the last orb, still clinging to the

Evermore's underbelly, sped off into space toward its intended Marauder target. Cuddy watched as the blue icon descended upon the Howsh ship. Making contact, it seemed to have found a way to secure itself, but then, like the other two orbs, it too spun off into space.

"That is the command ship, Captain Perkins. I apologize I did not determine that earlier. Apparently, that one vessel is equipped with advanced security measures—energized hull plating. The orbs' electronics were *fried* as soon as they came in contact with that particular Marauder command ship."

Cuddy glanced around the bridge—no one had any answers.

"They are powering weapons, Captain Perkins!"

"Hurry … raise our shields! Drop us out of formation."

Cuddy felt G-forces pulling on him as the *Evermore* banked away from the Howsh fleet.

"Taking evasive action," Bob said.

Bright red energy bolts could be seen crisscrossing from out the forward and side observation windows.

"Go ahead and initialize the orbs … put them to work," Cuddy ordered, which was the key component of their phase two plan. *If that doesn't work, well …* Cuddy didn't want to think any further about it. It had taken Bob four days to determine the potential technological weakness on that specific Howsh star-fighter model—a nondescript maintenance access panel, located on each ship's underbelly, near the warship's stern. And, at that very moment, the other deployed pairs of orbs were making their way to that exact access panel.

"You said it would be possible to get feeds from each the orbs … right?"

The viewscape display split into eight squares—each displaying the POV of individual orbs.

Cuddy was suddenly thrown from his feet as three consecutive plasma strikes hammered into the *Evermore*. Flat on his back, he looked up at the Viewscape display. The orb icons were supposed to turn from blue to green, once even one in the pair managed to breach the maintenance access panel. But … thus far … none had turned green.

Chapter 47

Cuddy noticed the others, lying on the deck too, had also been thrown off their feet. Apparently, the G-force dampeners were down. Desk papers were scattered all about. Bob, still hovering at the console, was taking the *Evermore* through a fast series of evasive maneuvers, which didn't allow them to do anything more than find something to hold on to and wait it out. Cuddy peered around Tony, to his right, and saw Jackie's cheek bleeding. It didn't look too serious, but he wanted to reach out to her just the same.

Jackie, sitting up, pointed to the display. "Green! They are starting to turn green!"

Cuddy followed her pointing finger to the Viewscape display. Sure enough, one by one, the individual frames around the eight video feeds were changing from blue to green. He hauled his body across the deck to get a closer view of the one pair still showing blue. Working as a team, the orb pair was in the process of prying open the Maurader's access panels, using their powerfully clawed digits. One orb did manage to pry up a small corner of a panel, but as the panel began to curl back on itself, the orb very quickly managed to open it far enough for the second orb to extend its articulating arm deep inside the breached cavity. Although out of view, Cuddy knew the orb was probing the interior of the space, seeking a specific, thick conduit bundle that supplied power to each of the warship's major systems—including tactical/weaponry, navigation, and the propulsion drive regulators. The feed frame suddenly changed from blue to green as the orb withdrew its articulating arm. It had severed the conduit bundle successfully.

In a matter of seconds, all but one Howsh warship had been deactivated—each floundering uselessly about in space. That one command ship, though, was traversing through space with astonishing speed. With each pass, it fired off another volley of devastating plasma fire, causing the *Evermore* to violently shake.

"We're going to die … we're going to fucking die!" Tony yelled.

Cuddy could see the fear in Jackie's eyes, too. He knew the *Evermore* couldn't withstand another hit like the last one.

"Shields are decreasing with each strike, Captain. Down to thirty-two percent," the orb reported, which was Cuddy's cue—time to implement phase three. With difficulty, he pulled himself up to his feet and went over to the forward console. Standing beside the AI orb, he stared out the forward observation window. "Go ahead, Bob. Order the orbs still operational back to the *Evermore*."

Cuddy watched as the Howsh command ship swung around for another fly by, then closed his eyes. Inhaling a deep breath, he opened them, his mind concentrating on a singular component within the command ship. A few days earlier, Bob provided him with numerous diagrams of what the Marauder's forward emergency escape hatch looked like. Technical drawings—as well as a myriad of technical data Cuddy didn't completely understand. But what he did know was how to blow the hatch. While he didn't have the mental kinetic dexterity to do what the eleven orbs had been tasked with, he knew he could manhandle those three thick metal levers. Each one needed to be flipped over—one hundred eighty degrees—into its opposite seated position. A simple brute-force action that was easy to accomplish—if you were a Howsh standing within the ship.

"Do something!" Tony yelled.

Cuddy, aware the others were now rising to their feet, did his best to concentrate. Again, he mentally pictured the emergency hatch, situated in the forward section of the Marauder. He visualized it in his mind—all its detail. The approaching ship was mere seconds from firing at them again. Cuddy raised a hand, miming the action of someone grabbing on to the cold hard metal of the first lever, then swung his arm over in an arc, feeling the first of the three levers pivot around and slam into its opposing position. He then did the same with lever number two. It too slammed down into position.

The Howsh command ship decided, it seemed, to move in closer proximity before it fired its three powerful plasma cannons. Its purpose, undoubtedly, was to bring the battle to a quick, definitive conclusion. But those two seconds of added time cost them dearly.

Cuddy mentally gripped the last metal lever. With another swing of his arm, the lever pivoted around, and he felt it too slam home.

By this point, the Howsh command ship was close enough for Cuddy to view a remarkable level of detail: the wear and tear on the warship's hull from three-plus years traversing the cosmos. Also, the forward starboard emergency escape hatch, which never was to be opened without first closing every internal adjacent hatchway.

A small explosion erupted near the bow of the approaching command ship. Fairly insignificant, compared to their blazingly bright plasma bolts that had been coursing through space only moments before—but effective nevertheless.

The Howsh command ship did not return fire but passed right under the nose of the *Evermore*. Cuddy tracked the ship's passing with his eyes as long as he could, before it too became nothing more than a white speck in distant space—like so many others.

"What's happening … why did it leave?" Jackie asked.

Bob said, "That Howsh command ship has currently lost atmospheric integrity. The vacuum of space is pulling all breathable air out through the blown hatch."

"So they're all dead?" Jackie asked.

"No …" the orb told her, "but crewmembers are certainly scurrying around trying to save themselves. Environmental suits have been deployed, their hatchways secured, as damage repair teams assemble. The Howsh command ship is now out of commission, at least for a while."

Kyle asked, "So what's been accomplished then, since all their ships can be repaired? They're still a threat. Maybe not right now … but eventually. Soon."

Cuddy smiled. "True. But we've done something else."

"What's that?"

"Kept in alignment with the way of the Pashier," Jackie said, answering before Cuddy could respond.

Cuddy said, "Look, for the Pashier all life is deemed sacred. If they are to make it safely to their new *home* world … Primara … it cannot be at the expense of others' lives."

"Not even the Howsh's?" Tony asked.

Kyle's expression changed. "Actually … especially not the Howsh."

"That's ridiculous," Tony replied back. "We killed a bunch of those fur balls back on Earth."

Cuddy and Kyle exchanged a knowing look.

★ ★ ★

Late on the previous night, Cuddy, feeling exhausted, left

the bridge and made his way into the main cabin where he found Kyle, sitting alone, watching something on the holographic display. "Where's Tony?" he asked.

"Asleep … everyone's in their bunks." He'd replied without looking up.

"What is that?" Cuddy asked, surprised to see Tow speaking into the camera. "Can you make it so it's understandable?"

"Yeah … wait … there's a million damn menu settings with this thing." Leaning forward, Kyle began tracing his finger along the top of the donut-shaped *whoopie* cushion—like using a giant mouse pad, much to Cuddy's surprise. Suddenly, Tow's words were now understandable.

"It just popped on the screen about ten minutes ago … that's Tow talking, isn't it?" Kyle asked.

Cuddy sat down next to his brother. "It sure is. He looks a bit younger there, but it's definitely him."

"Wait … I'll restart it for you. I think you're going to find this interesting." Kyle quickly restarted the film.

Watching the three-dimensional image of his recently departed friend, Cuddy felt that Tow was looking right at him. As he walked about speaking, Tow smiled and said, "As we discussed in the three previous segments, the Pashier's evolutionary story is both an exciting and complicated one. And one aspect, which we have only recently discovered, is filled with irony. What I'm about to show you has been buried within the vaults of *Calirah,* on the nearby planet of Darriall, for over eight thousand years. Our ancestors—both recent and old—did not want any of this to become public knowledge. They went to great lengths to bury the data … both figuratively and literally. Surprisingly, this fateful information was locked away by our own kind, and not by the Howsh. But things on Mahli have changed. Our forefathers are no longer. Our planet has been decimated. The *Dirth* plague has taken so many of us that very few now remain, outside those abiding in heritage pods. But soon, as the first officer on board an interstellar spacecraft, I will be part of something truly magnificent—a mission to bring us all home … home to a new life. But we cannot repeat the failures of the past. The secrets of the past must now be revealed. As our fleet of fifteen spacecraft await us above, we leave here not knowing if we will be successful. Our future is unknown. Either way, our contributing *collaboration*, leading to the demise of the Pashier, our wonderful species, must be exposed, for any and all to witness … to learn from. When the time is right … all will be revealed."

"What's he talking about?" Kyle asked.

"I don't know for sure, but it obviously was important to him. He most likely would have been in deep trouble … publicly exposing whatever he's eluding to here."

The homemade movie next revealed a series of ancient-looking, highly detailed illustrations on spread apart scrolls not made of paper or parchment, but more likely on old animal hides. The scenes were beautiful—almost photographic in their depth of color and level of realism.

"That's … that's a Howsh."

Cuddy nodded, studying the image. He certainly looked like a Howsh, and if so, those beings were once magnificent-looking creatures. His fur, appearing more like hair, was both long and lustrous. It cascaded down his elongated torso and down his arms and legs. To Cuddy, the flowing hair was similar to the long manes and tails on impeccably groomed show horses he'd once seen, trotting past crowds in Woodbury's 4th of July parades.

The film image changed to another opened scroll, where six, equally magnificent-looking Howsh were illustrated. Each kneeling down on one knee, they were looking skyward, their arms raised—palms out—as if giving reverent homage to something above. What most was noticeable to Cuddy was the brilliant glow, emanating from each one.

The image changed again, to another open scroll. Tow

was speaking in the background, like a narrator, but Cuddy ignored him, staring at a disturbing-looking image instead. A lone, glowing Howsh figure was seen standing at the water's edge—perhaps a lake or a large river. Again, the arms were raised high. In front of him, suspended above the water, was a giant boulder. Still wet, streams of water flowed down its sides, dripping into the water below. Clearly evident, the Howsh, somehow, had levitated the huge mass out of the watery depths below. But more disturbing about the image was the three savages concealed behind him. Keeping low, their spears raised, their intensions were quite clear: *Kill the lone Howsh.*

"Those are … Pashier," Kyle said, his comment more a statement than a question.

"Yes," Cuddy acknowledged.

Tow was back on film. This time he looked somewhat older; more tired and thinner. Evidently, the entire filming had been one long ongoing work in progress.

"Hundreds of these scrolls have been unearthed from the vaults of *Calirah.* They tell a chilling story," Tow said. "That things are not what they seem. That the Howsh, actually, were once a great and wonderful people … highly spiritual in nature, and also benevolent. Over the centuries, primitive Pashier tribes were instructed in the ancient ways of mind and spirit. The Howsh were kind and asked nothing in return for their guardianship. But as the Pashier evolved over time … becoming more powerful … they turned on their mentors. Hunted them down … eradicating many of them."

The film image changed again—to an illustration of a large heritage pod that was far larger than the one below deck now on the *Evermore.* Male and female Howsh figures were frantically running toward the open pod, while Pashier males, each holding a lit torch, were seen already setting fire to it. Dark smoke billowed into the air. It was a horrific image, one that evoked an immediate emotional response in Cuddy. *How barbaric were the Pashier?*

The image of the burning heritage pod then disappeared and Tow was back on camera. "So, as you can see, there is no evil nemesis here … unless we want to look into a mirror. The Howsh have become what the Pashier made them—hunters upon the weak. Savages. The Howsh and Pashier share a past that neither race is presently aware of. Perhaps the saddest aspect of all is that the Howsh are unaware their short mortal lives were never intended to be thus. That by killing the last of the Pashier, their bleak destiny too may very well be sealed."

Tow's film disappeared from view—replaced with Kyle's earlier selection. Cuddy and Kyle looked up to see Bob hovering nearby.

"Did you know about this, Bob?" Cuddy asked.

"Yes."

"You displayed it here … for us to watch?"

"Yes. And also transmitted it far into open space … out to one and a half billion communication channels."

"So … pretty much to everyone," Tony said.

"Did you do that per Tow's instructions?" Cuddy asked.

"Yes, I was alerted to the movie, with detailed instructions on where and when to transmit it, as soon as I came online. All other intelligent on board systems are tasked with the same directives."

"And those five Howsh warships, now orbiting Primara?"

"They will receive the same film within forty-eight hours."

Chapter 48

The *Evermore* headed out toward open space—leaving the small fleet of damaged Howsh warships behind. According to Bob's most recent sensor scans, there'd been no loss of life on any Howsh ship during their last encounter. With the exception of the command ship, all repairs would take several days, if not a full week. The command ship, on the other hand, undergoing minimal repair, would be ready for travel within a few hours.

Over the following days, life aboard the *Evermore* fell again into a familiar routine. Jackie idled the time away in the galley, concocting even more adventurous meals. Brian now could leave his compartment, if only to eat meals with the others. His swelling, over time, had diminished some, which enabled him to traverse up and down the stairs without assistance. Still a strange looking sight, his appearance was somewhat improving.

Cuddy didn't have a formulated plan yet on how to deal with the Howsh fleet, awaiting them ahead. They certainly wouldn't be able to pull off the same tactics they'd used on those five warships. He found he'd become far more fatalistic about their future—or what was left of it—spending his time on the bridge. Then, less and less time was spent there as they neared their final destination—Primara.

On the final two days, Cuddy hung out with Kyle and Tony in the main cabin, watching movies, playing games, and simply shooting the shit. They laughed a lot. He also spent a significant amount of time sitting in the galley, observing Jackie while she cooked. They spoke of times past, regrets of things not accomplished, and their aspirations for the future. It soon became apparent that there might not be a place for him in Jackie's vision of a perfect life.

Jackie said, "Come on, you must have some idea of what you want to do with your life now that you're … you know, more normal? Hey, and I get it … things are looking pretty bleak for any of us thinking long-term, Cuddy … but humor me."

"I don't know, let me think about it for a while. How about you? What would your plans be?"

She busied herself with completing another casserole and he wondered if they'd ever be able to eat the damn thing. He figured this was how she dealt with stress—always staying busy. She briefly looked up at him. He saw annoyance in her expression and then it was gone.

"Well, I have to finish school. I've always wanted to be a doctor … I can't just let that go. My plan has always been to complete my residency at New York Presbyterian … that's in Manhattan."

"Yeah … I know where that is," Cuddy said flatly. "Where Brian works … lives."

"Yeah … but I would have wanted to be a doctor there anyway."

"Uh huh," Cuddly said, sounding unconvinced.

Cuddy didn't show it, but having a future life with Jackie, if they managed to survive their current predicament, seemed more and more inconceivable.

Watching her now, bending over, sliding the casserole into the oven, he listened to her quietly humming a familiar melody. He didn't know its name, like so many other things he was clueless about. For too many years, he had neither the interest, nor the mental capacity, for learning such things. In many ways, he felt like the same simpleton he'd always been. That would change eventually—though apparently not any time soon enough.

Cuddy stood up and listened.

"What is it … don't like my singing?" Jackie asked, giving him a wry smile.

"The orb just informed me … we're there. We've reached Primara."

"No! Already?" she asked.

Cuddy hesitated for several moments, taking her fully in—the remnants of flour on her nose, the small scratch on her cheek, the odd way she wrapped her long fair hair into a ponytail at the top of her head; and her amazing, highly expressive eyes.

"I need to get to the bridge."

* * *

Cuddy hurried onto the bridge and joined the orb at the forward console. Beyond the observation window, large and brilliant in color, was a world that easily could pass for Earth: Magnificent azure oceans; green continents, containing high-ridged mountains, as well as prairie land that seemed to stretch on and on forever.

He knew Tow would be pleased right now, seeing this world—this new home.

"The Howsh?" Cuddy asked.

"Yes, they are here, Captain," the orb replied.

Cuddy glanced out at the curved horizon—where the planet's blue atmosphere met the blackness of space. No way to spot something as insignificant in size as a few spacecraft, but he looked just the same. "Where?" he asked.

"Like us … in high orbit."

"Have there been any attempts to contact us?"

"No … none."

Cuddy thought about that, though it really didn't mean anything. Whoever was commanding that fleet of warships could take his sweet time. *We are completely at their mercy*, he thought.

"Bob, do you have defined coordinates where we're to go? Where the heritage pod is to be … placed?"

"No, that was not included in my directives. You can make that determination, if you wish, Captain."

"There!"

Cuddy spun around to see Jackie, standing with her arm extended, her finger pointing out. He stepped back and followed the direction of her finger.

"Near that patch of forest. At the base of the mountain ridge," she explained. "Yeah … that's the place," she said with certainty. "Can you take us down there, Bob, so we can take a look?" Her face was animated and her enthusiasm contagious.

Tony and Kyle barged onto the bridge together, their mouths agape as they took in the panorama of beautiful Primara.

"Take us down, Bob … let's bring them home," Cuddy said.

The descent into Primara's lower atmospheres was fairly quick and non-eventful. If anything, Cuddy wished they could slow *time* down—make their moments together last a little longer. With a quick glance over his shoulder, he noticed Brian too had joined them on the bridge, and was now easing his bulk down into a rear seat.

Tony said, "Holy crap … that world is …"

"Incredible!" Kyle exclaimed, finishing his words.

The orb brought the *Evermore* lower—barely skirting the

tops of trees. Cuddy briefly wondered if forests like this one, seeming both endless and undisturbed, still existed back on Earth. He didn't think so.

Out the port window could be seen the ragged mountain ridge they'd spotted from space. Below, the trees were now becoming more and more sparse. Then they were traversing low over long golden grasslands. Something bright sparkled in the distance.

"The lake I saw below us … it's over there," Jackie said.

The orb changed their course slightly. Ahead lay a shimmering body of water—a great lake—that Cuddy could see was rimmed with a wide sandy beach.

Cuddy caught Jackie's eye. "Here okay?"

He watched her eyes take in the landscape beyond, before she nodded, "Yeah … right here."

"Put us down, Bob," Cuddy said.

★ ★ ★

Cuddy was the last one to exit the *Evermore* and walk down the gangway. He breathed in the brisk, fresh air, and held it deep in his lungs for several blissful moments. As he took his first steps onto Primara soil, he acknowledged the good fortune, as well as the sacrifices they'd made to get there. In the distance, he saw Kyle—walking near a stream all by himself. Tony and Jackie were walking together, heading toward the distant lake. Brian, the one nearest him, was slowly waddling toward a nearby stand of Aspen-like trees.

"It is time, Captain."

Cuddy, aware of the orb's close presence, gazed into the sky, wondering if his pledge to Tow was an act in futility. *Would the Howsh begin their attack now*?

"How do I do it? How do I get the heritage pod out of the ship?" Cuddy asked.

"The lower sub-deck of the *Evermore* is a separate construct. It also has a lift mechanism."

A soft whirling sound brought Cuddy's attention to something behind him. The *Evermore* was rising up higher on extended struts. A mid-section of the ship was slowly being lowered downward, beneath the spacecraft's underbelly. He studied the organic shape of the heritage pod as it came into view. In this vast wilderness, it somehow looked small and vulnerable. And then he felt it—a heavy weight on his shoulders, nearly bringing him to his knees. It was the weight of responsibility—the weight of an entire race of people, depending on him.

Cuddy walked back toward the ship and came to a stop, just as the lift settled onto the ground.

The orb, still hovering at Cuddy's side, communicated with him telepathically:

The pod must be moved onto the ground.

Cuddy looked at the orb, then at the heritage pod. It was easily seven or eight feet tall, and twice that size across. "What does it weigh?"

"Ten thousand pounds, Captain."

Cuddy made a face, showing his disbelief. "Well … there's no way I'm lifting that! Even if everyone helps, there's no possible way!"

"The heritage pod will not unfold, unless it is on Primara soil—"

Cuddy cut the orb's words short: "I got it … it needs to be moved." He stared in the direction the others had gone then dismissed their help, again, as a viable solution.

"Sit, Cuddy Perkins, sit upon the ground. I will assist you; you *can* do this."

Cuddy gave the hovering orb a weary look, but eventually did as asked. Although he tried to clear his mind of all thoughts and concern, it quickly became apparent that was not possible. To have come this far—this close—only to be stymied now. He sat there for a long while. The sun lowered into a pink, *orange* sky, as a steady breeze carried the scent of the distant lake. Cuddy's thoughts turned to Tow. He should be here, doing this honored task. He was a true Pashier … with powerful mental abilities—far more powerful than his own.

"Do it! Move the heritage pod, Cuddy!" the orb said.

Jackie, returning, took a seat to his left. He felt her take his hand in hers and hold it tight. "You can do this. Look what you've accomplished so far."

Cuddy felt a hand on his back and knew it was Kyle's. He and Tony seated themselves behind him. Leveling his eyes first on the heritage pod, he then closed them. Exhaling a deep breath, he concentrated—envisioning himself standing next to the pod, far larger than he was in reality. In his mind his arms were huge—like tree trunks. Bending his knees, and lowering his body, he stepped forward and wrapped his arms around the circumference of the pod. He felt the pod's encompassing leaves crinkle and constrict under his tight hold. With all the strength his mind and body could conjure up, he began to straighten out his thick, column-like legs. Immediately, they began to shake and wobble under the immense weight. Cuddy continued lifting, as the joints in shoulders, wrists, elbows, knees and ankles screamed in a torment he could hardly endure. He stepped back with one foot while stepping forward with the other—turning both his body and the pod in the process. Sweat streamed down his forehead, stinging his closed eyes. As moisture crept into his palms, he felt his grip on the heritage pod begin to slip.

Chapter 49

You can do this, Cuddy … I know you can do this … the orb repeated, telepathically.

Cuddy took more hurried steps, to the point he had lost count. He tried to tighten his hold but the enormous pod was slipping even more from his grasp. Another step, then another …

He was helpless as the heritage pod slipped from his grasp. Cuddy opened his eyes. Totally exhausted—spent—he realized he was still seated next to Jackie, who was vigorously shaking out her hand, a pained expression on her face. He glanced over to the *Evermore*—the heritage pod was gone! Looking around the ship's outskirts, no sign of the pod was evident.

A distant voice yelled, "It's over here. Cuddy … it's here!"

Cuddy squinted into the setting sun. No less than fifty yards away, and no longer seated behind him, Kyle and Tony stood by the pod.

But how …?

"You did it, Cuddy! I don't know how … but you did it." Jackie kissed him on the mouth, and he felt her excitement, noting the smile on her lips. She stood and pulled him up to his feet.

The sun slowly dipped behind a distant ridgeline as dusk settled in around them. As they approached the heritage pod, Cuddy detected the slightest movement—at its very top, where all the leaves converged into a single point.

Brian appeared, the last to join them, and they separated out from each other, forming a circle, of sorts, around the heritage pod. The leaves were unfolding now. Like Cuddy had witnessed several times in the past, a spray of glittering lights streamed upward—higher and higher into the air. As the heritage pod continued to unfold, he felt its now-familiar swirling breeze around him.

It took a while for the last few leaves to open, before settling onto the ground. A galaxy of starlight moved above them, but here—on Primara—it spanned out hundreds, if not thousands, of feet, ever ascending higher. The brilliance of light around them made it impossible for Cuddy to concentrate on any one particular thing.

"Look!" Jackie exclaimed. She was now visible to Cuddy, easy to see over the fully opened pod. She was pointing to a moving pinpoint of light above them. The star-like object, approaching fast, was not slowing down. Cuddy wondered if something was wrong. Or was it a new spectacle—one he'd not witnessed before, when within the *Evermore*'s lower subdeck.

The approaching star intensified in both size and brightness. *No,* he thought, *it's not only coming near us, it's going to crash land right into us!* Before he could move—get to his feet—the streaking object struck the middle of the heritage pod in a brilliant flash of blue light. More surprising, the ground didn't shake and no audible sound was heard from its sudden impact. Now standing amidst the flattened leaves of the opened heritage pod stood a lone figure—a Pashier—glowing; standing tall.

Up above, the galaxy of stars swirled brightly. No sooner had the figure stepped away from the center of the pod than a second bright object struck. A bright blue flash erupted forth, and another glowing figure appeared. Soon another and then another. This same awe-inspiring spectacle continued for an additional three hours. Only now, it wasn't a single being arriving—it was ten, or twenty, or even one hundred, at a time.

★ ★ ★

Cuddy and the others retreated back to the *Evermore* to watch from there as the *returning* continued. They sat on the gangway, letting their legs hang over the side. Thousands upon thousands of Pashier had arrived already. Quickly moving away, they hurried off in every direction. It was as if they knew exactly where they were meant to go—where, on this beautiful planet, they were supposed to settle.

Jackie, seated next to Cuddy, continued to watch with rapt fascination. She nestled closer into his shoulder against the cool night air. "You know … what we're witnessing here … no one has ever—*ever ever ever*—seen before." She gazed up at him. "Thank you, Cuddy, for sharing this heavenly experience with me, with us. I'll never forget this time with you." She then leaned up and kissed him tenderly on the forehead.

Cuddy wondered if she was, in some way, telling him goodbye. That they'd come to the end of their long journey together and she would be moving on. He was well aware she had clear-cut plans for her life. With a heavy heart, he stared out at the masses of glowing Pashier, still arriving.

Two glowing figures, hand in hand, approached them from out of the multitude. Whereas all others moved past them—avoiding any contact—these two headed directly for them. By the time Cuddy recognized Tow's unique Pashier features they were almost upon them. Soweng looked as beautiful as ever, and Tow emanated good health, plus a boyish youthfulness that Cuddy hadn't seen in him before.

When he stood to greet his friend, Tow pulled him into a powerful bear hug. Caught off-guard by a sudden onslaught of emotion, Cuddy blinked away the brimming tears.

★ ★ ★

The sun was coming up before the last few Pashier arrived on the beautiful planet. Home again, they too moved off. Tow and Soweng stayed with them for a long while, but soon they were *pulled* away, responding to their own distant callings. Cuddy learned they would be sharing this life together, here, as a couple. That didn't surprise him in the least. Their love for each other was clearly evident. After a heartfelt goodbye, Tow and Soweng headed off.

Cuddy yelled after him, "Will I ever see you again, Tow?"

Tow stopped and turned. "Yes, you and Brian are Pashier. Return here, when you know your *special* time has come." He gave a final wave and walked on.

Cuddy watched until they too merged into the distant landscape.

"Wait! So you get to come back here? Be a part of this … this magic? What about your Earthly girlfriend? What is she supposed to do?"

Cuddy stared back at Jackie uncomprehending. "But I don't have a girlfriend."

She tilted her head sideways, making an exasperated expression.

Then he fully *got* what she was saying, as she slipped her arms around his waist, laying her head on his chest. "I love you, Cuddy … I always have." He then confessed back his deep love for her as well. At that moment, he didn't think he could be any happier.

From out his peripheral vision, he saw one last, brilliant light, streaking down from above. "Somebody's late for the party," Jackie said.

They both looked out to see who had arrived and found the figure was not a two-legged one. Then Cuddly heard a familiar, distant *woof*, and thought, *I'd know that bark anywhere!*

His beloved yellow lab, now running free, snatched up a stick even longer than he was. As his ghostly form appeared near by, Cuddy said, "Bring it here, boy!"

Jackie said, "Maybe one doesn't have to be Pashier … you know … to take part in this?"

Epilogue

The orb, Cuddy, Jackie, Kyle, Tony, Brian, and last but not least Rufus reentered the familiar confines of the *Evermore*.

"I have one question," Kyle said, following after Tony. "What happened to those Howsh ships? I expected them to swoop down on us at any second."

Tony and Kyle, halting in their tracks, stared back at Cuddy. Jackie, already clanging around in the galley, stopped long enough to peer out.

Cuddy said, "I have no idea. I was afraid of the same thing." He looked over to the AI orb. "Bob?"

"The Howsh fleet is gone."

"They just left? When?" Jackie asked.

"Brian transported them away."

"What? Brian did that?" Cuddy asked, total disbelief on his face. "How?"

"That is correct. Using his new Pashier kinetic powers … those ships are now five point eight light years distance away from Primara … away from us."

All eyes turned to Brian. Cuddy realized that the brightly

glowing, half human/half Pashier was levitating nearly a foot off the deck.

Brian smiled, a bit of his former cockiness returning, and said, "All those hours alone in that compartment … well, I've been practicing. Bob, the orb, helped me get started. First by levitating a bread crumb, then a pillow, then a pair of shoes. Eventually, I could levitate myself. My own body above the deck."

"But … five enormous spaceships? Dude, you're a badass!" Tony exclaimed.

Brian shrugged, "Maybe I am."

Cuddy studied Brian's wry crooked smile and wondered if his new, *transcendent,* ability was a good thing or not. *Of course it is,* he thought. *He saved us from certain death, didn't he?*

A part of Cuddy wanted to believe the Howsh wouldn't have attacked anyway. That Tow's home movie—the incredible revelations of their shared past—would have made an impact. Would have given them pause. But how realistic was that? He had little doubt that the information had the capability to alter opinions—but the results could take a long time, perhaps years. It was a start.

"I'm starving!" Tony said, resuming his trek toward the galley.

"So where are we off to now, little brother? Or should I call you Captain Perkins from now on?" Kyle asked.

Cuddy shrugged. "We can head on back to Earth … I guess."

The orb rose several feet higher into the air. "There are twenty-two other Pashier heritage pods within the galaxy. Several survived the decimation back on Mahli, while others are well hidden beneath the surface of another nearby planet. Some are confined within the holds of enemy spacecraft. Those pods must all be brought home … brought here, to Primara."

"What's going to happen to them if that doesn't happen?"

Jackie asked.

"In time, they will break down … turn to dust." The orb continued, "Do not despair. I will pilot the *Evermore,* continuing on with my directives, once I have returned you back to Earth."

"And if I should want to go with you?"

Cuddy was surprised—the question asked was from Tony.

"Me, too …" Kyle said.

Cuddy spotted Jackie, again peering out the galley, and looking at him with a bemused smile. Her brows were raised questioningly.

The End

Thank you for reading The Simpleton.

If you enjoyed this book, PLEASE leave a review on Amazon.com—it really helps!

And yes, there's a lot more books yet to come! To be notified the moment all future books are released—please join my mailing list. I hate spam and will never, ever, share your information. Jump to this link to sign up:

http://eepurl.com/bs7M9r

Acknowledgments

I am ever grateful for the ongoing fan support I receive for all my books. This latest book, my sixteenth—*The Simpleton*—came about through the combined contributions of numerous others. First, I'd like to thank my wonderful wife, Kim, for her never-ending love and support. She helps make this journey rich and so very worthwhile. I'd also like to thank my mother, Lura Genz, for her tireless work as my creative editor and a staunch cheerleader of my writing. I'd like to thank Mia Manns, for her phenomenal line and developmental editing … she is an incredible resource and friend. Others who provided fantastic support include: Lura and James Fischer, Sue Parr, Stuart Church, Eric Sundius, and Chris Derrick.

Other books by MWM

Scrapyard Ship
(Scrapyard Ship series, Book 1)

HAB 12
(Scrapyard Ship series, Book 2)

Space Vengeance
(Scrapyard Ship series, Book 3)

Realms of Time
(Scrapyard Ship series, Book 4)

Craing Dominion
(Scrapyard Ship series, Book 5)

The Great Space
(Scrapyard Ship series, Book 6)

Call To Battle
(Scrapyard Ship series, Book 7)

Mad Powers
(Tapped In series, Book 1)

Lone Star Renegades
(Lone Star Renegades series, Book 1)

Star Watch
(Star Watch series, Book 1)

Ricket
(Star Watch series, Book 2)

Deadly Powers
(Tapped In series, Book 2)

Boomer
(Star Watch series, Book 3)

Glory *for* Sea and Space
(Star Watch series, Book 4)

Space Chase
(Star Watch series, Book 5)

The Simpleton

www.ingramcontent.com/pod-product-compliance
Lightning Source LLC
Chambersburg PA
CBHW062118170626
46813CB00002B/491

* 9 7 8 0 9 9 7 4 5 1 4 7 4 *